PRAISE FOR

HOPE IN THE SHADOWS OF WAR

"In *Hope in the Shadows of War*, Thomas Paul Reilly chronicles the struggles of Tim O'Rourke, a former helicopter pilot and one of many veterans who returned from Vietnam to a society that was at best indifferent and often hostile to him and his comrades. This was particularly hard on those like O'Rourke who, wounded and permanently injured, had to fight his way to an education while supporting himself and his mother as best he could. With grit, a little luck, the support of friends and the love of a good woman, he comes through as his kind invariably will. *Hope in the Shadows of War* is uplifting and well worth reading."

—Neal F. Thompson, Vietnam helicopter pilot, 1st Aviation Brigade, author, *Reckoning: Vietnam and America's Cold War Experience, 1945-1991*

"So I'm in the middle of reading this book, and as a veteran I can identify with Tim, the main character. The characters are real and the issues they grapple with I've seen firsthand with Vietnam veterans while serving in the Corps. Tom does a great job with the settings and references that make you feel like you are back in 1973. Can't wait to finish this book!"

—Scott Morris, Cpl, USMC '77-'81, 1st Floor Manager Central Library St. Louis, MO

"Amazing, awesome, WOW, what a GREAT BOOK! You hit it out of the park, and bases were loaded! Thanks for sharing, what a wonderful story!"

—Jon Alexander, combat engineer, 9th Infantry, Vietnam

"Finally a book written by someone who not only was there, but understands the personal changes wrought by combat from a professional psychological perspective. This is an easy and believable read because Tom Reilly does not embellish any of the real life experiences of a vet. He does not try to make the story one of extreme heroics, dramatic recounts of serious combat aimed at a movie deal, or anything but, 'If you were there, you will understand, and maybe this will help you.' We can remove the word 'Maybe,' because it will."

—Col, USAF (Ret) command pilot, wing vice-commander

"I can identify with many of the situations Timothy was in after Vietnam. I had 7 or 8 jobs my first year back from Nam. Loved the different characters. Spot on and a great read."

—Carl Gordon, Sgt. USMC, Vietnam 1969-70

"This is a for-real book about the Vietnam War and its aftereffects on veterans' struggles to readjust and cope with the emotional toll of war that affect family, friends, and jobs. Well-written, easy to read."

—Charles I. Bess Sr., United States Air Force, sergeant 35th Security Police, air base defense Phan Rang Vietnam 1967-1968

"Having served in Vietnam, what impresses me most is the accuracy with which Tom brings the realism of not only Vietnam, but life after Vietnam to us. Tom is a unique author that brings facts to the forefront in an enjoyable and flowing manner. This is a 'page turner' that will be difficult to put down."

—Doug Harper, SSgt, USMC veteran

"This book should be read by veterans and non veterans of not only the Vietnam era but of all periods of conflict. It should be read by Vietnam vets and Vietnam protesters. I feel this is the best story about young men returning from war since *The best years of our lives*. As a Marine during the Tet Offensive, I felt as if I had just returned home after reading this wonderful book. I came home in 1969. In 45 years, I had about 30 different jobs. I did not get help for my PTSD until I was 62 years old. I read Tim's story and felt like I was there with him. If we really want to continue to send young men to war, we need to consider the consequences. I give this book five very large thumbs up!!"

—**Larry Decker**, former sergeant USMC and Vietnam veteran, February 1968 - March 1969

life after VN

Hope in the Shadows of War

by Thomas Paul Reilly

ISBN 978-1-63393-704-8

Published by

 köehlerbooks™

210 60th Street
Virginia Beach, VA 23451
800-435-4811
www.koehlerbooks.com

HOPE
IN THE
SHADOWS
OF

a novel

THOMAS PAUL REILLY

VIRGINIA BEACH
CAPE CHARLES

To my 58,272 brothers and sisters who
perished in the Vietnam War

Lest we forget

VIETNAM WAR JARGON

This is a partial list of the jargon used by US service members in the Vietnam War and terms used in this book.

Boo-coo: Slang derivation of the French word *beaucoup*, meaning "much" or "many."

Cobras: The Bell AH-1 was a helicopter gunship with rocket pods, 40 mm cannons, and mini-guns (7.62 mm high rate-of-fire machine gun). Cobras were also called "snakes."

Dear John: A letter sent to a serviceman by a girlfriend or wife who was breaking off the relationship. Sometimes used as a verb.

Didi mau: Vietnamese slang meaning "to go quickly"; *didi* is a shortened form that American GIs used.

Dinky dau: Vietnamese slang meaning "crazy."

Doughnut Dollies: Young women who volunteered through the American Red Cross to spend a one-year tour in Vietnam to boost the morale of American troops. They operated recreation centers, visited hospitals, and visited frontline base camps to bring cookies, doughnuts, and Christmas presents to soldiers.

Echo side of LZ: East side of landing zone; *echo* is code for the letter *E*.

Five O'Clock Follies: Daily press briefing given by military personnel in Saigon.

Huey: Bell UH1H helicopters; called slicks or choppers and served as workhorses in Vietnam.

I heard that: An expression of acknowledgement that could mean several things.

Jodie: Term used by GIs to describe men at home who dated servicemen's girlfriends while the servicemen were away.

Lifer: A career military person.

LZ: Landing zone in the field for helicopters.

November: Code for the letter *N*, representing *north*.

One-eight-zero: Due-south heading.

Papa Four: Call sign for ground troops in this story.

Popping smoke: Igniting a smoke grenade to identify one's position.

RLO: "Real live officer"; a commissioned, regular Army officer versus a warrant officer.

RPG: A shoulder-launched, rocket-propelled grenade.

Sierra: Code for the letter *S*, representing *south*.

Slop and slugs: Coffee and doughnuts.

There it is: An expression of acknowledgement that meant whatever the person wanted it to mean.

Tiger Six: Call sign for Timothy in this story.

Tiger Five: Call sign for Bobby in this story.

Viet Cong: AKA Victor Charlies, VC, Chuck, Charlie, Gooks, and Dinks.

Warrant Officer: A highly specialized expert in his or her specialty but different from a commissioned officer.

Whiskey side of LZ: West side of landing zone; *whiskey* is code for the letter *W*.

Xin loi: Vietnamese idiom meaning "sorry" or "too bad."

THE BATTLE OF ADVERSUS

LEGEND HAS IT that at the dawn of time and in the cradle of civilization, opposing forces met on the fields of Adversus in a primeval battle for the minds, bodies, and spirit of humanity. A horrific battle—relentless and fierce—raged for seven suns. Bodies blanketed the blood-soaked soil. Cries of the wounded muffled the thunderous sky. Death welcomed the sweet smell of rotting flesh. A curtain of bitter-tasting air, saturated with the humidity of blood, hung heavy and motionless as the dead slept.

As the eighth sun rose, enemy commanders met at the center of the battlefield. Eados commanded the oppressors—the legions of despair. Dochas commanded the liberators—the warriors of hope. They stood a breath apart. Eados gazed into Dochas's eyes and saw the light of his nemesis—hope. Dochas stared into Eados's eyes and saw the darkness of the great abyss—despair.

Eados stretched his arms over the land and pillars of fire rose to the sky, scorching everything within sight. Dochas reached to the heavens and summoned torrents of rain that smothered the fires, washing the landscape clean of the ashes of despair.

An infuriated Eados said, "This will never end."

"I know," Dochas responded.

They turned and left, knowing they would battle again and forever.

Eados dispatched his legions to the four corners of the world, spreading germs of despair. Dochas commissioned his forces to the four winds, sowing seeds of hope. Each spawned generations of followers to carry out their missions. Eados's followers became the disciples of despair, leaving hopelessness in their dust. Dochas's progeny became the guardians of hope, shepherding the human spirit.

CHAPTER ONE

"WHERE'S THE BODY? Where's the body? Where's the damn body!"

He woke with a jolt, the way a baby startles at loud noises. For Timothy, the line separating nightmares from reality was as thin as an eyelid. Mom stood at the doorway to his bedroom, just as she did when he was a youngster having nightmares, except now he was no youngster.

"Timothy, are you okay? I heard you shouting."

"Huh? Yeah, Mom. I'm fine." But he wasn't fine. He doubted he would ever be fine.

Timothy could feel each heartbeat in every part of his body. Blood raced through his veins. Sweat covered his face, but not from the November night air. Trembling embarrassed him. He viewed it as a form of weakness, and it didn't fit the narrative he had created for himself. Nightmares stripped the bark off his tree, and he felt naked.

"Are you having those dreams again?" Mom asked.

"Yeah." Timothy didn't want this conversation.

"I don't know why those people at the VA can't help you with that. You boys come home and—"

Timothy interrupted. "I'm okay, Mom. Go back to bed."

Timothy stood to get a drink of water from the kitchen. Mom

gave him a hug, burying her head in his chest.

"Try to dream better dreams, Son," Mom said, returning to her bedroom.

"I will. Thanks, Mom."

He sat at the kitchen table and stared at the glass of water, heart thumping and hands trembling. It took a while for this much adrenaline to fade. He returned from the Vietnam War eighteen months earlier, and like tens of thousands of other returning veterans, he learned one of the great paradoxes of war: though he left the war, it never left him. The memories lived a thin layer of skin beneath the surface. The military taught them to fight the war but failed to teach them how to live the peace.

Timothy remembered a story he read about Japanese soldiers returning from World War II. The village elders took the returning soldiers aside and thanked them for their service—for their being brave and loyal soldiers. Then, the elders told them the village needed the soldiers to become good citizens, fathers, and husbands. No one had this conversation with Timothy, though he longed for it. After nearly a decade of fighting, the country was tired of the Vietnam War and felt contempt for its weary warriors.

Timothy rubbed his leg. The long scar was his most visible wound of the war. Pain never slept. At night, the dull ache awakened him, and during the day, sharp pain often reminded him of the day his helicopter was shot down.

A noise on the back porch startled him. He believed Vietnam improved his hearing. He heard every nocturnal sound. He looked out the backdoor window and saw a cat scurry past. He walked around the house to check the windows and doors—perimeter duty. His muscles were still twitching. *Damn adrenaline!*

He finished his water and returned to his bedroom, hoping tonight's nightmare was over. A few hours later, Timothy woke to discover he had overslept. Thankful it was Sunday and not a school day, he dressed quickly, gobbled an egg sandwich his mother made for him, downed a glass of milk, and left for his job at the Christmas tree lot.

The wet November air had turned cold. At thirty-four degrees, things didn't freeze, but they did slow down. The cold breeze stung his face as he walked to his car on the street in front of his house.

The car door squeaked like a tired steel door waking up in the winter. He slid across the cold, cracked vinyl seat and checked his wallet. *Five dollars, that's it? Oh well, it's enough for today. I'll get a half a tank of gas and lunch at McDonald's. Man, I hope my car isn't on empty.*

The car cranked lazily before stalling back asleep. "C'mon, not today, please." The fuel needle sat half a line above empty. *Late, again. Dez is going to be pissed. Too little gas and a dead battery. That's a lousy way to start my day.*

Rob—his neighbor and childhood friend—knocked on the driver's window. Timothy jumped. He startled easily these days.

"Hey, Tim. Sorry to scare you. Trouble gettin' that thing to cooperate this morning?" Rob said.

"Yeah. Hey, Rob. No gas, a dead battery, and I'm trying to get to work."

"Let me help. I'll get some jumper cables, a can of gas, and pull my car around."

"Thanks, man."

Timothy opened the hood of his ten-year-old car. It mimicked the creak of the driver's door. The 1963 Ford Fairlane had a ripped interior, rugged exterior, and retread tires. The silver-moss paint job looked like a spotted, rust overcoat. This sport coupe had become a sport jalopy. Ten years wasn't that old, but it was old before its time. Too many miles and too many bumps in the road for this tired gas-guzzler, already dying a slow death when Timothy bought it a year ago. He'd hoped to restore it at some point. He needed transportation for work and college . . . and church.

Damn, I missed Mass this morning. I've got to quit doing that.

Rob returned with the cables and a gallon gas can, which Timothy poured into the tank while Rob connected the jumper cables. Timothy slid back into the driver's seat, and Rob climbed into his car and started it. Timothy noticed how quickly Rob's car started and thought, *Wouldn't that be nice?*

After a few moments of cranking, Timothy's beast coughed to life, belching a cloud of black smoke.

"Looks like the rings are bad, too, Tim," Rob said.

"Yeah, I'm going to add that to my growing list of things to fix on this thing. Thanks, Rob, I appreciate the help."

"Sure. Happy to do it."

Timothy handed him the empty gas can and promised to replace it.

"It's a gallon of gas. Don't worry about it," Rob said.

"No, I take care of my debts." Timothy wanted to maintain the little self-respect a broke college student could muster.

"Okay, that's fine," said Rob.

"Thanks again."

Rob waved as Timothy pulled away, a Beatles eight-track tape blaring.

"And when the night is cloudy there is still a light that shines on me . . . shine on until tomorrow, let it be . . ."

For Timothy, *dreams* meant *tomorrow*. He never stopped believing in tomorrow, no matter the past. Hope died hard in his DNA. He called it the birthright of the Irish. The weatherman had called for clouds today and sun tomorrow, an appropriate weathercast for Timothy—cloudy with a hope for sunshine.

Let it be, he replayed the song in his head. He pulled into an open space at Schoen's lot, leaving himself enough room for a jump-start if he needed one later. He shut off the engine, but the car spit and stammered as if it didn't want to stay, a fact that didn't escape Timothy. He didn't want to stay either. One last backfire and it quit—Timothy jumped. *Damn backfire. Sounds like a gunshot.*

Dez stood at the edge of the lot waiting for him. Dez cut an unmistakable figure. He stood five-foot-nine wearing a black winter pea jacket and a wool *kartuz* cap. Timothy looked at Dez and dreaded the encounter. Dez was the kind of guy that took pleasure in other people's misfortunes. He grinned at their pain. Most people disliked Dez immediately because it saved a lot of time.

"You're late again, ya mick," Dez said in a gravelly voice. Dez talked out of the side of his mouth and around a cigarette, a permanent fixture. He had thin lips and a heavy jawline. He sized up people by their ancestry and didn't shy away from commenting on it.

"I know. Sorry, Dez. This thing didn't want to start this morning. I think it wanted to sleep a bit longer," Timothy said.

"You talking about you or the car?" Dez said.

"Both, probably. I had to get a jump-start this morning. I'll get a new battery at Sears tomorrow. That's if you decide to pay me for today."

"You oughta get rid of that junk heap." Dez pointed his thumb at the Fairlane. "Besides, you look like a stiff driving that thing. A young man oughta have a young car."

"There it is." Timothy felt like one GI talking to another.

"Get yourself somethin' reliable and cheap to drive, like one of those new Jap cars. You know, the Japs are gettin' their shit together. Cheap cars that don't suck down too much gas. That's pretty important these days the way the ragheads are screwin' the world with their oil," Dez said.

"Those cars cost more money than I have, Dez."

"You could afford it if you got a real job that paid you some decent money," said Dez.

"Are you going to give me a raise?"

"You kiddin'? I'm not the problem, you know."

"What's the problem, then?" Tired of this conversation with Dez, Timothy pushed back.

"You've got a head full of dreams and tuition bills to prove it, but you're working for chump change at that hospital. That's a loser combination. It don't make sense."

"It does when I think about the future. I need an education to do what I want to do," Timothy said.

"See, that's the problem." Dez jabbed his crooked index finger in Timothy's chest. "You got your head soaring in the clouds and your feet stuck in the mud."

"What do you suggest?"

"Take some time off school, get a real job, and save some money. You can buy a new car, take care of your mother, and go back to school once you save enough money. Besides, all learnin' don't just happen in classrooms," Dez said.

"So you're telling me to give up on my dreams and get some dead-end job I have to drink my way through?" Timothy challenged Dez for a better option.

"No, just can the dreams for a while. Get some traction," Dez said.

"What kind of job could I get? No one wants to hire a Vietnam vet these days. They think we're all damaged goods."

"Get a government job. They gotta hire you, right?" Dez said.

"I just left three years with the government, and that's enough."

"I can work you fifty hours a week and pay you more than those nuns pay you at the hospital. What are they payin' now—minimum wage?"

"A little more than that. I get a buck seventy-five an hour. More when I work the night shifts. Thing is, the work at the hospital fits into my plans for the future."

"What plans? Bein' poor?" Dez laughed.

Timothy let it pass.

"Why do you wanna work with a bunch of nuts anyway?" Dez asked.

"I like psychology," Timothy said.

"I like beer but couldn't figure out a way to make a living drinking it." Dez laughed through three days of stubble as he knocked the ash off his cigarette.

"What I lack in pay I make up for with the experience it offers." Timothy got defensive.

"Yeah, that kind of experience is overrated. See, that's how those birds con you into working for them. I'll pay you two bucks an hour—hard money, no tax. That's more than you make now."

"I'll think about it," Timothy said, tired of the banter.

"Yeah, do. Don't be a chump. That's the point. You're workin' for jack shit and drivin' a piece of shit. That clunker ain't taking you nowhere, and neither are those dreams," Dez said.

"I told you. I'll think about it."

"Like I said, those nuns will screw you every time," Dez argued his point. "And they call my people cheap. I'll keep you busy through the holidays, and when spring comes, you can go to fifty hours. I'll work you here and at the other place too. But you gotta have a decent ride to get there. None of this late shit. I gotta business to run. I ain't no charity, you know. And those nuns ain't either. They're tryin' to make some cheddar, just like me."

"All right, thanks, Dez."

"Yeah, no problem. Now, get to work back there and help that simpleton unload the Christmas trees." Dez pointed to the tree lot behind the shop.

"C'mon, Dez. You're pretty tough on Kenny," Timothy said.

"Whatta ya talkin' about? Who else would hire a retard and pay him what I give him? He's lucky to have this job. It's damn near charity. Besides, he's got that creepy side, too. The ol' lady thinks he's a pervert."

"She thinks everyone is a pervert," said Timothy. "Maybe it's because she's lived with one all these years." Timothy liked giving it back to Dez and knew Dez didn't mind an occasional good jab. Dark humor fit him like stink on a dead fish.

Dez showed some teeth, and they weren't a pretty sight. He had a mouthful of chewers with the right amount of vacancies to make his words whistle.

"All I know is he sweats as much as me in the summer and huddles around the fire barrel in the winter when he gets cold." Timothy's nature was to defend the underdog.

"Right, you're always stickin' up for that schlep. Get on back there, and do what I pay you to do. We gotta be ready for the Thanksgiving rush. The suckers always show up that day," Dez said.

"I think it's going to be a good year for us. The weather people say it will be fair by the end of the week. That should help bring out the crowds," Timothy said.

"Hope so. Gotta good deal on trees, so I bought a couple of extra trailers this year. Three different kinds. I'm gonna hire an extra schlub to help you two. Now, get on back there with the mole head. That trailer won't unload itself."

"Alright, I'm going." Timothy walked away shaking his head, wondering how someone became that cynical about life. *I hope I miss that train when it stops for passengers.*

CHAPTER TWO

TIMOTHY WALKED TO the tree lot behind the shop. His wounded leg didn't like the cold weather, so he walked with a slight hitch. His limp seemed out of place for his six-foot, muscular body. In spite of his war experiences, he maintained a boyish quality—cropped, sandy-colored hair and light-blue eyes. But that look of innocence was a façade. He brought home with him a new norm and discovered there was nothing normal about it—another paradox of war.

As he got closer to the barrel, Timothy smelled the smoke and heard the wood crackling in the fire. The breeze made it feel colder than mid-thirties. Kenny stood at the barrel warming his hands.

"Hey, Kenny," Timothy said.

"About time you showed up, GI Joe," Kenny said. He launched a cheek-full of tobacco juice at Timothy. Timothy narrowly dodged the wad attack.

"Watch it, Kenny," Timothy said.

"Almost got ya that time. Pretty good dodge for a gimp." Kenny laughed. "If you woulda dodged like that in Nam, you wouldn't have that screw in your leg."

"Yeah, lucky for me your aim sucks," Timothy said.

Kenny grinned, showing off the rack of brown and yellow

stubs God put in his mouth. Kenny owned the kind of teeth that shouldn't be aired out in public. Like Dez, Kenny didn't make a habit of standing too close to the razor. Spit-and-dodge was everyday play for Kenny. He spit, Timothy dodged. They insulted each other and got to work.

"Why you late?" Kenny asked.

"Car trouble again."

"That's why I walk everywhere. No car problems. My body always works. Besides, I can't get a license—they don't let tards drive," Kenny said.

"Don't call yourself that, Kenny."

Timothy didn't like name-calling, but Dez and Kenny were serial insult slingers. Their target list was comprehensive: Italians, blacks, queers, Irish, Jews, Poles, Arabs, Asians, and the handicapped.

"Why not? Dez calls me that. He says all Polacks are simple," Kenny said.

Timothy shook his head. "He says a lot of things, but that doesn't mean they're all right."

"I don't care if that ol' kike calls me names as long as he pays me hard money. I know how to count what he owes me. I wrote it down and keep it in my wallet," Kenny said.

With that, Kenny opened his wallet and showed Timothy the scrap of paper that kept Dez honest. "See? I told ya," Kenny said.

"You got it all figured out, Kenny," Timothy said.

"Damn straight. You watch Archie last night?" Kenny referred to *All in the Family*, one of his favorite television shows.

"No, I took Cheryl to the show last night," Timothy said.

Cheryl was Timothy's girlfriend, and she was the best part of his life.

"Ya missed a good one. Meathead was really giving Archie shit. Kinda like me and Dez. Sometimes I get ideas on what to say to Dez from the meathead. Pisses 'im off, too, when it's a good one. Wanna smoke?" Kenny said.

Kenny offered Timothy a Parodi cigar, which Timothy considered the worst three-and-a-half-inch stench on the planet.

"Not even. How can you smoke those things? It looks like they swept the floor and rolled it into a shingle." Timothy made a face to show his disgust.

"Dez told me they're *in-ported*, whatever that means. Besides, they're cheap. I get a box of five for fifty cents. Sometimes I get 'em free if I'm sweepin' round the register and the ol' lady ain't lookin'. I pocket a couple of boxes," Kenny said.

"That's stealing, Kenny!"

"Not if the ol' biddy don't catch me." Kenny smiled.

"We better get these trees unloaded or Dez will be after both of us. A lot coming in this year. Three different kinds," Timothy said.

"Why's that?"

"Dez told me he got a deal on them, so he bought two extra truckloads," Timothy said.

"I don't know about all that, but if we got any left after Christmas, Dez ain't gonna be happy."

"He said he may get someone else to help us sell all these trees," said Timothy.

"Don't need nobody else gettin' into our tip money."

"You'll appreciate the help."

"Maybe, so long's he don't take my tip money. How's your momma?" Kenny asked.

"Good. Getting back on her feet. The vein problem in her leg had her down a couple of weeks, but she's comin' around. Thanks for asking."

"I like your momma. Think she'd make me some more of those cookies she made last year?"

"I'll make sure of it. Her oatmeal raisins are the best," Timothy said.

"Bring 'em back on Thursday and I won't spit at ya." Kenny smirked. Timothy knew Kenny was lying.

"Dez wants to sell the trees cheaper than all the other lots this year. He got pissed last year when the Boy Scouts cut their prices. He told me that wouldn't happen again. I think that's part of the reason he bought so many this year—so he could get a better deal on them," Timothy said.

"Yeah, and he don't like the church group selling 'em either. He says, 'I don't sell religion, so why should they sell trees?' Sorta makes sense, don't it?" said Kenny.

"If you're Dez it does." Timothy turned toward the trailer. "Now, let's get to work. It'll take all day to unload this truck."

"Okey, soldier boy." Kenny shot another wad of tobacco juice at Timothy's apron, hitting him center mass.

"You're an asshole, Kenny."

"That's why I stink all the time."

They started to unload the truck.

CHAPTER THREE

AS THE OLD man opened the shop's door, a toxic blend of cheap perfume, stale tobacco smoke, and rotting produce punched him square in the nose. He could taste the garbage in the air. Stomach acid burned his throat as it decided whether to come up all the way. On the radio, Jim Croce sang "Bad, Bad Leroy Brown." The old man looked around at shelves half-stocked with canned goods and other nonperishables and spotted compost bins overflowing with brown oranges, potatoes with barnacles growing on them, and sickly string beans. A sign above the onions read, *10 cents a pound*. The sign over the potatoes read, *99 cents a pound*.

Highway robbery. He took a step toward the register, but his back foot stuck to the floor, and his hand hesitated on the doorknob.

The old woman working behind the counter peered over the register. She stood five-feet-nothing and would have been taller if it weren't for the hump on her back. She had a bulldog face and washed-out hair that hadn't seen a rinse in a while. She was reading *National Enquirer* and spilling cigarette ashes on the counter, blowing them onto the floor. The magazine cover story showed a picture of Richard Nixon with the caption *Nixon blames space aliens for the Watergate break-in*. The only other person in the store was a balding man with muttonchops and a white apron sweeping the floor. The old lady's lips parted enough to spit a few words.

"What do ya need, old-timer?" she said with enough effort to hack up half a lung. The old man thought she sounded like a dog choking on a bone.

"Excuse me, madam. Are you the owner?" the old man said.

"Ha, ya hear that, Kenny? He called me *madam*." She grinned, revealing as many gaps as teeth in her mouth. When she smiled, the mole on her upper lip moved sideways on her leathered skin. Even humor brought little light to her coffee bean eyes.

Kenny laughed.

"You must be sellin' somethin', old-timer," she said.

"Not really, ma'am. I wanted to talk with the owner. Are you the owner?"

"Hear that, Kenny? *Ma'am*. Somebody that polite wants somethin' from ya." She stared piercingly at the old man. Kenny swept and grinned. The old man stood ramrod straight and returned the eye contact. He smiled through his beard like he knew something she didn't know.

"I'm one of 'em. Who wants to know?" she said.

"My name is Hoffen, and I wanted to inquire about some Christmas employment."

"See, I knew ya wanted somethin'," she said. "So, you want a job?"

"Yes, ma'am," Hoffen said.

"Again with the ma'am. You must be desperate. You're as old as Christmas. What can you do around here?"

Hoffen stared at the old lady with his steel-gray eyes. He was one of those people who concealed his mileage well. With a full head of white hair and a barrel chest, he had the look of someone who had worked with his body for decades.

"I can help you sell those Christmas trees I saw out on your back lot."

"Heck, any yutz can sell trees. Even this dimwit can do that. Ain't that right, Kenny?" She brought up more lung laughing at her own joke.

"That's right, Ed. Dez says so," Kenny said. "That's why I got a job."

"Who's Dez? The other owner?" Hoffen asked.

"My ol' man. We own the place. Been owning it for ten years. Bought it when the ol' dago died, and his family needed some quick cash to bury him and pay the bills. Got it cheap." She smiled with pride.

"Congratulations," Hoffen said. He didn't mean it, but he wanted the job.

"If you wanna job, go out back and talk to Dez. He makes decisions about the help. But I'll tell ya, we don't hire nobody on Mondays. Bad luck. Only desperate people lookin' for work on Mondays. Means they ain't got a job. Ain't that right, Kenny?"

"That's right, Ed. Got my job on a Friday. Waited all week to come in on Friday."

"Thank you, ma'am, and your name's Ed?" Hoffen asked.

"Edna, but everyone calls me Ed, like Ed Sullivan." She laughed, and it brought up more lung sap. "Your name is *Huffin*?"

"*Hoffen*."

"First or last?"

"Just Hoffen," he said.

"What kind of name is that? Are you a Kraut?" She scowled.

"Something like that," Hoffen said.

"We don't like krauts much around here. Kenny, take this ol' Kraut out to Dez."

"Okey, Ed," Kenny said.

"Told ya. Jus' like Ed Sullivan," she said.

"Thanks again," Hoffen said.

"Right, get outta here. You're interfering with my readin'." She went back to the *Enquirer*.

"You know those things will kill you," he said.

"What, the *Enquirer*?" She laughed at her own joke. Kenny grunted.

"No, the cigarettes," Hoffen said.

"Now you're a doctor. Get outta here. I wanna finish readin' about the aliens." She dropped more ashes on the counter.

As Hoffen left the store with Kenny, he heard Edna go into a coughing spell that lasted a good twenty paces. The crisp air slapped the old man in the face, and he liked it. He stood there for a few moments sucking it in, trying to cleanse his lungs of the rancid air he breathed in the shop.

"Is she always like that?" Hoffen asked Kenny.

"Nah, most of the time she's pretty nasty. You caught her on a good day."

"Good day?" Hoffen asked, surprised.

"Yeah, she's real bitchy to everyone, except Dez. She's scared of him. He can be a real mean bastard, but I don't care 'cause he leaves me be. I'll take ya to him. C'mon this way."

As they walked to the tree lot behind the confectionary, Hoffen extended his hand to Kenny and said, "I'm Hoffen."

Kenny grabbed it with his fingerless derby glove and said, "Heard. I'm Kenny."

"Nice to meet you, Kenny."

"Yeah, you too." Kenny nodded. "That's why I smoke these things."

"Pardon me?" Hoffen said.

"Parodis." He showed Hoffen the stub he was chewing on. "Cigarettes is bad for ya. These ain't that bad. I don't swallow the smoke. I keep it in my mouth and blow it out. These things last longer than a cig. I only smoke five of 'em a day. If I smoked cigs, I'd go through a pack or two a day. I heard what ya said to Ed. She smokes a couple of packs a day. Might as well—don't cost her nothin'. She owns the place. She can smoke as much as she wants. It ain't like she's stealin' them or nothin'."

"Um-hmm." Hoffen shook his head, trying to make sense of Kenny's comment.

They walked through the lot, which looked like the aftermath of a natural disaster. Some trees were stacked like cordwood while others looked like scattered piles of wood and needles. The leaners rested against each other, and a few lucky trees found their way to wooden tree stands.

"Hey, Dez, Ed told me to bring ya this fella. Name's *Huffin'.* Don't know nothin' 'bout him," Kenney said.

"It's Hoffen." He extended his calloused hand to Dez.

"You gotta a pretty good grip for a creaker," Dez said. Hoffen smiled.

They stared at each other for a few pregnant moments, the way old acquaintances who haven't seen each other in a while size each other up. Hoffen had about four inches on Dez. Dez closed one of his hawkish, brown eyes and cocked his head.

"Hoffen? What kind of name is that—Kraut? You a Kraut? We don't like Krauts much around here. Fought 'em in the war."

"Me too," Hoffen said.

"How'd you fight the Krauts? You look too old to been in the war," Dez said.

"I'm talking about the first war. You know, the one to end all wars," Hoffen said.

"Yeah, well that didn't work out too good, did it? If ya kicked their butts good, we wouldn't have had to fight 'em again in the '40s. We licked 'em good that time," said Dez.

Hoffen nodded. Kenny flashed his yellowed grill.

"What do ya want? You sellin' somethin'?" Dez asked.

"I'd like a job."

"A job! Doin' what? Pushin' up daisies?" Dez said.

Kenny cracked up at the insult. "That's a good one, Dez."

"Selling Christmas trees," Hoffen said.

"Any putz can sell a Christmas tree, even this one here." Dez pointed to Kenny.

Kenny nodded.

"There ain't much to sellin' Christmas trees. The suckers come in here and do all the buying. We take their money and load the trees up on their cars. Ain't that right, Kenny?"

"Yup," Kenny said.

"You've got a lot of trees here. It looks to me you could use some help selling them," Hoffen said.

"Yeah, we got a lot of trees. Too many, maybe. Kenny, go get me a Nehi."

Kenny nodded and left.

"What do you know about selling trees?" Dez asked.

"I know you won't sell all of your trees with your lot looking like this."

"What are ya talkin' about? What's wrong with my lot?"

"First things first. That pile of trees is a mess. People come out here and want to have an experience for the holidays," Hoffen said.

"I don't care what they come out here for as long as the suckers leave with some pine tied to the roof of their cars," Dez said.

"Dez, people want to remember the experience. They want this to be a tradition. It's special for people. That's repeat business," Hoffen said.

"Keep chewing those words, ol' man."

"You've got three types of trees over there." Hoffen pointed to a stack of pine. "You've got Scotch pines, firs, and spruces. They're mixed together like vegetable soup. It's too much work for the customer to find what they want. You have to make it easy for them to buy."

"Keep chirping, ol' man. I like the sound of it," Dez said.

"Once you group them by needle, arrange them by size. Start with the small ones up front and the bigger ones in the back. People can walk down the path and see how the bigger trees compare. Make it easy to choose and buy. Isn't that the point?"

Dez nodded. "What other ideas you got?"

"Play Christmas music. I can see the speakers on the light pole," Hoffen said.

"Yeah, I use the PA system to yell at the mole head when I need him in the shop."

"Use it for Christmas music. Create a holiday atmosphere. Give the children candy canes. It's like the pine smell and smoke from the fire barrel. It reminds people of what Christmas tastes, sounds, and smells like. Make it a holiday experience."

"Yeah, that stuff is pretty cheap. Give it to the kids and the parents feel like they owe ya. Guilt them into buying." Dez nodded like a barnyard chicken. "You got a pretty good head on you, ol' man, and you're dressed for the work You done this before?"

"Yes, a few times," Hoffen said. "I told you I could help. Everyone coming in here wants a Christmas story to go with the tree. What do you say? Do I get the job?"

"Well, you ain't bashful about asking. That can't hurt. And you talk a pretty good story, but you're kinda old to be schlepping around Christmas trees, especially the eight-footers."

"I can handle the trees."

"Well, why not? I got a gimped-up college kid and a retard working for me. Might as well throw an ager into the mix. Maybe the three of you combined add up to one good employee. I pay two bucks an hour cash money and you get paid daily."

"Sounds fine to me. When do I start?" Hoffen said.

"Be back here Thursday morning at nine. And if you can't carry your load, you'll be home early for Thanksgiving dinner," said Dez.

"Fair enough. See you then."

"Hold on a minute, old man." Dez stopped Hoffen before he left. "Have we met before? You look familiar. Seems like I know ya."

"Maybe. I've been around here for a while. Brentwood's a small town. I have kind of a common face."

"Yeah, maybe. All you whitebeards look alike anyway."

"Okay. See you Thursday."

"Hey, on your way out, go in the shop and tell that nitwit to bring me my Nehi."

"Will do."

CHAPTER FOUR

TIMOTHY ARRIVED HOME from Tuesday's day shift at the hospital. The Thanksgiving break freed him up from class so he could work a normal workday. He planned his evening—home after work, a decent dinner, and a date with Cheryl. Between school and work, Timothy and Cheryl didn't get as much time together as they wanted. As he opened the front door, he smelled Mom's afternoon efforts.

Mom peeked around the kitchen doorway and saw Timothy coming through the house. She was wearing her standard dinner attire—house dress, black granny lace-ups, and her favorite apron. She was nearly a foot shorter than Timothy and thick around the middle. She had blue eyes and duller-blue hair.

"I made your favorite tonight, honey," Mom said. "Pot roast, carrots, potatoes, green beans, and lemon meringue pie."

"Thanks, Mom," Timothy said.

"That's the least I can do for you as hard as you work. I don't know how you do it all."

"At twenty-three, people can do a lot," Timothy said.

"With school, work, and studying, I don't see how you manage it all. I don't think it's good to push yourself like that. You've been through a lot."

"Mom, I'm getting a late start. All those other students are at least four years younger than I am. I have a lot of catching up to do."

"That's only because you chose to serve your country. I know. It's the only way poor kids get an education. Those rich kids don't have to worry about that stuff. That's why they can burn draft cards and demonstrate against the war. There are no consequences when you're rich."

"Mom, a lot of poor kids demonstrate, too. I chose to serve. I thought it was important, and I still think what we did was important. I've got plans that require an education. The GI Bill is helping me with that."

"Even at twenty-three you need a break from time to time," Mom said.

"You know what Dad used to say—too many breaks and you end up broke."

"Yes, your father knew a lot about that—being broke that is. Anyway, you're safe now, and that's all a mother can ask for. That's why I went to Mass and communion every morning you were in Vietnam. I prayed you home. No one knows the love a mother has for her son." As she said this her worry lines deepened.

Mom never missed an opportunity to lay it on a little thick. Most of the time it amused Timothy. Sometimes, it made him uneasy, especially when other people were around.

"I know, Mom, and I appreciate that."

She hobbled to the kitchen and returned with the beans and spuds.

"How is your leg? Does it still hurt?" Timothy asked.

"It's better. The doctor said it would be sore still for a couple of weeks. Not like your leg. Mine will get better. You're going to have to live with that leg the rest of your life."

"I'm fine, Mom."

Timothy stared at his salad. Mom had been sick on and off since his father, Frances, died. She turned grief into illness. *Enough amateur psychiatry*, he thought. Cataracts, hernia, blood pressure, skin cancer and, of course, depression. He knew she felt isolated and lonely, something he often experienced. Frances left nothing but unpaid bills and barely enough insurance to bury him—a good man with no head for money. He spent it faster than he made it. Timothy remembered his father mostly as a loving man. Mom loved her husband, but Timothy knew she was still pissed at him for dying too soon.

"I talked to your older brother this morning," she said. "He won't be coming in for Christmas. His job and all requires so much of his time, and Washington's far away."

"You mean he finally called?" Timothy was never that close to his older brother. The ten-year age difference was part of it, and he didn't like the way Frank ignored Mom. She deserved more respect.

"No, I called him. I wanted to be sure about the holidays."

With a sister in town who had a husband and four children, Timothy felt responsible for looking after Mom. He didn't mind the responsibility and wanted to be a good son.

"Doctor Carmel said I should consider the vein-stripping operation. It would repair this leg permanently. No more temporary fixes. I'm not sure what he means, but it would take care of those clots once and for all."

"That sounds like a good idea, Mom."

"I worry about the expense. I'm not sure how much the insurance will pay."

"That should be your last concern, Mom. We'll figure it out."

"You're a good boy, Timmy. Every mother should have such a son."

Tim smiled and Mom changed the conversation.

"I suppose you have to study tonight?"

"Actually, I planned to take Cheryl to the movies. She wants to see that new movie, *The Sting*."

"Oh, I was hoping you could take me to the store so I can get the ingredients to make those rolls you like for Thanksgiving. Maybe your sister can take me. I'll call her after we finish."

"That's okay, Mom. Cheryl and I can go to a later movie."

"Are you sure *sheeee* won't mind?" Mom stretched the word when referring to Cheryl. Tim found it amusing but understood the dynamics of the situation. Mom felt threatened by Cheryl, and maybe even jealous of the attention Cheryl garnered.

The phone rang.

"I'll get it," Timothy said.

Mom began to clear the table to make way for the lemon meringue pie. She went to the kitchen and returned.

"Sure. I'll be there. Thanks." Timothy hung up and returned to the dinner table. "It was the hospital. They want me to work the graveyard shift tonight."

"How can you do that with everything else you've got going on?"

"I'll take you to the store and back, pick up Cheryl for the movie, and I can make it to the hospital by eleven."

"What about studying? Shouldn't you stay home and study or take a nap?"

"Nah, I can take my books with me. Not much happens on the night shift, so I can get some studying done at work."

Mom placed the pie in front of Timothy. "I feel bad you must work this hard. It's not fair."

"Says who? Who said it was going to be easy? I'm fine, Mom. How about we change the subject?"

A few minutes of silence passed as they finished dessert. Mom broke the silence. "I saw in the paper today that Connie's engaged. She looked real pretty."

"Yeah, that's nice." Timothy did not want to talk about Connie.

"She was such a sweet girl. Always nice to me, especially when you were gone at first."

"Mom, that bus left the station a long time ago."

"I know, I thought you would be interested. You know she's marrying that Goodenough boy. He's the one whose father got him a job at the railroad."

"I know who he is."

"Mrs. Bean told me he earns one hundred and fifty a day at that job. That's a lot of money. That's more than you make in a month working at the hospital."

"I know, Mother, but I am part-time, remember?"

"I'm thinking you might want to see if they need any more help at the railroad. That's good money."

Timothy scraped the last bit of pie from the plate.

"I still don't see why she had to send you that letter when you were in Vietnam. It wasn't right. You cared a lot for that girl," Mom said.

"I know, Mom. Like I said, I'm done looking at the taillights of that bus. I don't want to have this conversation anymore, please. Besides, if I hadn't received that letter, I never would have met Cheryl. We're really happy."

"Yes, she's a nice girl, and she does have a good job. That's important to young women today. What does she do again?"

"She's a social worker, Mom."

"Yes, that's right. I don't know why I can't remember that."

I do. It's because you don't want to remember, he thought. "How about we go to the store now, Mom?"

"What about our family dinner on Thanksgiving? You're coming over to Leslie and Ike's house, aren't you? Your sister's cooking a big dinner, and I'm making your favorite rolls."

"Yeah, well, Sis's family has to eat, too. Don't they?"

Mom ignored Tim's sarcasm.

"I suppose you plan to see Cheryl, too?"

"Yes. I'm going by her house after I get off work to see her family and have a small meal. Then she'll come over to Leslie's with me to be with you guys."

"Oh, you're bringing her, too? I guess your brother-in-law can pick me up after his football game. You used to enjoy playing that game with them on Thanksgiving, didn't you? Now, with your leg and all—"

"Let's go, Mom, if you want me to take you to the store."

"Okay, I'll finish clearing the table. Can you go downstairs and check out the furnace? It's been making some funny noises today."

"Sure."

"You're a good son, Timmy. I bet that railroad job sounds pretty good right now?"

Timothy said nothing as he walked to the basement.

CHAPTER FIVE

TIMOTHY THOUGHT ABOUT his date with Cheryl while driving home from his night shift at the hospital. Even a couple of hours with her gave him the lift he needed. She lifted his spirits. Today, he planned to go home, sleep for a while, study for a couple of hours, and meet Scoot for a couple of beers. *Boy, it will be great to see Scoot. Work, school, and life seem to get in the way of our seeing each other.*

Scoot was Timothy's crew chief in Vietnam and one of the few people Timothy trusted. They were closer than two coats of paint. Timothy was grateful they lived in the same hometown and kept the friendship alive.

He arrived home at breakfast time. The smell of bacon, eggs, and coffee greeted him at the front door.

"How was work, honey?" Mom called from the kitchen.

"Good. Not too busy. I got in some good reading."

"I have some breakfast for you here in the kitchen."

"Thanks, Mom. I think I'll go to bed. I'm tired."

"I bet you are. Do you want me to wake you at any special time?"

"No, I'm planning to get about six hours' sleep. Then I'll study a couple of hours before I meet Scoot for a couple of beers."

"That's nice. He's a good friend. I'm glad you two still see each other. I think it helps both of you," Mom said.

"Well, it helps me," he said. "Anyway, night, Mom—or day—or whatever. We'll talk later."

He went to his bedroom and immediately fell asleep, still in his hospital uniform. It didn't take long for Timothy to begin dreaming.

"*Tiger Six, this is Papa Four. Be advised, LZ is hot. Victor Charlie's echo side of LZ*," *the team on the ground tells Timothy.*

"*Roger that, Four. Coming in hot. Tiger Five, you copy?*"

"*Tiger Six, copy that*," *Tiger Five says.* "*Going in one-eight-zero. Hot on the echo side of LZ.*"

"*Popping smoke*," *Papa Four shouts.*

"*I see purple smoke*," *Timothy responds.*

"*Affirmative*," *Papa Four says.*

As they approach the landing zone, tracers streak by the helicopter. Timothy feels the thuds. He yells to his crew chief, "*Scoot, we hit?*"

"*Yeah, couple through the tail, but we're okay. Pretty nasty on this side.*"

"*Tell these guys to jump right, Scoot.*"

"*Got it.*"

The troops jumped off the helicopter at six feet.

"*They're off. Let's get outta here*," *Scoot says.*

"*We're gone*," *Timothy yells.*

As Timothy pulls up on the collective and pushes forward on the cyclic, an RPG strikes the belly of his Huey.

"*Papa Four, Six took an RPG in the gut*," *Tiger Five screams.*

"*We see it, Five. We're on it. Get outta here.*"

Bobby lifts off and performed a quick 360 to see what happened.

"*Tiger Five, get outta here unless you want to join him on the ground. This place is erupting. Get the rest of the troops out here. We need them.*"

"*My friend, Six—*"

"*We got it, go*," *screams Papa Four.*

"*Copy that*," *Tiger Five yells.*

Mom stood at the door to Timothy's room and startled him awake.

"Timothy, you have a phone call. It's Cheryl. I thought you would want to talk to her."

"Thanks, Mom. What time is it?"

"Three-thirty."

"What? I've been asleep for more than seven hours," he said.

"I know. You said you didn't want me to wake you, but I thought for Cheryl you would take the call."

"No, that's fine, Mom. Thanks."

Timothy spotted the coffee percolator light and poured a cup before picking up the phone.

"Hello?" he said.

"Well, hello to you, Mr. Sleepyhead. Your mom said you were still asleep." Cheryl spoke melodically and rhythmically, like someone in the counseling field.

"Yeah, I guess I was more tired than I thought. God, this feels good, though."

"Good, I was worried about you. I noticed you drifted off a couple of times during the movie and wondered how you did at work."

"Oh, it was fine. Things were slow so I caught up on some reading. I'm even better now that I got some sleep. How's your day?"

"Good, we had a couple of new girls come in today, and we're getting them processed and settled."

"Processed? Sounds like the government."

"Oh yeah. You know the drill. Are you still going to meet Scoot later for a few beers?" she said.

"Yeah. I'm going to clean up, read a little, and meet him at Junior's."

"That's the tavern around the block from your house, isn't it?"

"Yep. I figure I'll walk up there just in case," Timothy said.

"Good idea, and Scoot can give you a ride home in case it's, uh, too cold," Cheryl laughed.

"Right, in case it's too cold."

"I'm glad you guys are getting together. You don't do that enough. Women are better than men at that kind of stuff. I see my old friends every month. It's great to stay connected."

"I know. It seems like I'm so busy. Anyway, it'll be fun to see him."

"Be careful and have fun, but not too much fun," she said.

"Always the worrywart, right?"

"Yes, and don't forget about early dinner at my parents' house tomorrow. Be on time so we can go to Leslie's after that."

"I know. Two o'clock, right?" he said.

"Yes, two, or before if Dez lets you off early."

"No chance of that happening, but I'll be there at two. Bye, love you," he said.

"Love you, too, honey. Tomorrow."

"Tomorrow."

Timothy hung up, walked back to his bedroom, and sat on the bed. *God, I love that woman, and she loves me. I don't know why she does, but I'm lucky she does.*

Cheryl was a twenty-five-year-old social worker. She completed her master's degree last May and immediately got a job with the state of Missouri. At a slim five-foot-seven with blond hair, hazel eyes, a perfect smile and a pretty face, she looked more like Miss Missouri than a social worker. She and Timothy met at a concert in Chambers Park about a year ago. Having completed her class work, she still had a practicum to go. Timothy had just returned from the Army and enrolled in school. They called their meeting "fortuitous" and "instant chemistry." She did not know him before the war, and she loved him, warts and all. Timothy often reminded himself of this fact. It made him feel redeemable.

Time to get ready. I can read later, maybe. I'll get to the bar early and save a stool for Scoot.

Timothy walked to Junior's Tavern. The forty-degree weather felt invigorating. Working at the tree lot increased his tolerance for the cold.

When he opened the glass door to Junior's, a cloud of cigarette and cigar smoke poured out. The jukebox played an old country song about a man who lost his wife and dog. It was barely audible above the bar chatter bouncing off the wood-paneled walls like ping-pong balls. Timothy could taste the heavy smoke. He looked around at the collection of businessmen, postal workers, truck drivers, and the local drunks. Two couples huddled in separate booths having romantic moments. *Damn, it's packed today.*

Timothy chose a couple of stools at the bar. He preferred the table next to the wall so he could keep his eye on the exit, but the place was crowded. He nodded at Junior, the owner, whom he knew from the neighborhood. A couple of years earlier, Junior inherited the place from his father after the old man died. People knew Junior as a screw-off. He got in trouble with the local police and the judge gave him a choice—go into the military or go to jail. Junior chose the Air Force for three years. He got out in time to help his father run the bar. Now that he was in business, Junior dropped the troublemaker role. He cleaned up his act. He looked like a bar owner. Neat haircut, dark cotton pants, white shirt, and a towel over his forearm.

Junior walked over to Timothy. "Hey, Tim. Budweiser?"

"Yeah, unless you started serving Pabst," Timothy said.

"Can't do it, man. My beer wholesaler got into a pissing contest with the brewery so he can't buy it anymore. I can get you a Stag or a Schlitz."

"You mean *Schitz*. I can't drink that stuff, and Stag? They might as well call it *Gag*."

"Ah, man. Keep it down. I got a couple of regulars at the end of the bar that love that shit." Junior looked around to see if anyone heard their conversation.

"Bud's fine, and bring two. One for me and Scoot."

"Scoot? Oh man. I told that cycle trash I don't want a bunch of bikers hanging out here too much. It scares the citizens."

"Yeah, he loves you, too." Timothy smiled.

"Alright, two Buds."

Junior pulled a couple of iced longnecks out of the cooler. Even though the cooler was refrigerated, Junior kept the beer in a tub of ice. He did this so he could place wet bottles in front of people. He thought it was good for business to serve ice-cold beer. He brought the beers over to Timothy and placed them on a couple of Falstaff coasters.

"Let me know when you guys need something." Junior walked to the other end of the bar and started talking to some regulars.

Timothy took a long, slow draw from the bottle and swished it around his mouth. He took another pull from the longneck and set it down on the coaster, which already had a sweat ring on it.

"Hey, is that one for me?" Scoot said in a husky voice.

Scoot was a six-foot-three tree trunk. His soft brown eyes were a contrast to his long dark hair and beard. There was no mistaking him for a hippie; Scoot was a die-hard biker. He wore T-shirts in cold weather because he could—and because he had ink on his guns that he liked to show off.

"Damn straight, brother." Timothy stood and offered Scoot the customary grip—not quite a handshake. More like a high five followed by a hand clasp and shoulder bump. Scoot returned the bump.

They sat at the bar and held up the bottles for a toast.

"To the fallen," Timothy said.

"To the fallen." They clinked bottles and took a drink.

"It's good to see you, bro. We don't do this enough," Scoot said.

"I hear you. I feel the same way. School, work, family. It's a lot," said Timothy.

"I know. I got a business to run, remember?"

"Yeah."

Junior pitched a couple of empty bottles in the trash and they jumped.

"Sorry, guys," Junior said. Timothy and Scoot grinned at each other, shaking their heads.

"So, how's your pretty lady doing?" Scoot asked.

"She's great. Just talked to her before coming here. We went to the show last night and saw *The Sting*. Good flick. Did you see it?" Timothy asked.

"Naw, I don't go to the show much. Too busy with the shop and the club."

The club was a group of bikers Scoot rode with but not a gang, or so he said.

"I ain't got a steady squeeze these days, and going to the show by yourself is queer."

"Do you want me to see if Cheryl knows someone you could meet?"

"No, that's okay. Besides, I like my women to be a little less wholesome than Cheryl. You know what I mean." Scoot smiled.

Timothy knew Scoot had good taste in women but preferred a type Cheryl probably didn't know. They sat silently for a couple of minutes, enjoying the beer and the company. Someone dropped a glass, and it shattered on the floor. Timothy nearly jumped off the stool.

"You still doin' that shit?" Scoot laughed. "Me too."

Timothy shook his head, grinned, and took another pull on his beer.

"Do you think they ever found the body?"

"Man, not that shit again. You gotta quit going down that rathole." Scoot took a long draw on his beer.

"I can't, Scoot. I had that fucking dream again today. Like every other week since I left Nam. If I knew how to let go, don't you think I would have done it already?"

"Tim, look. You keep beating yourself up for something that ain't your fault. You gotta let go of that guilt—it's eating you up. There was nothing you could do. You don't walk on water, for Christ's sake."

"I wish I had your ability to let go," Timothy said.

"Look, man, I still hurt too, but I don't like picking scabs. They can't heal then. Sometimes I hurt boo-coo. We left a lot of loose ends over there, man. Too many. I thought we were winning that fuckin' war when we left." Scoot paused. "Look, I don't know if we'll ever get over any of that shit, but I know we have to get past it."

"How? That's my question," Timothy said.

"I don't know. You're the fuckin' psychologist. I figure if you keep movin' forward, sooner or later you'll get tired of draggin' that wagon."

Timothy nodded and drained his beer.

"You boys want another brew?" Junior said.

"Hey, Junior. How's it going?" Scoot said. "Biz good?"

"Could be better," Junior said.

"It would be if you let me and my boys hold our monthly club meeting here. They're a thirsty group, you know."

"Yeah, and they break shit, too," Junior said. "Besides they scare the other customers."

Timothy sat there and watched these two go at it. He had seen this kind of back-and-forth before.

"C'mon, man, it was only a pool stick and a chair, and we paid for both, right?" said Scoot.

"Yeah, but it still caused a ruckus with the citizens. I'll get your beers," said Junior.

"Did your guys really do that, Scoot?" Timothy asked.

"Yeah, but it was no big deal. No one got hurt, and he sold a lot of beer that night. Besides, I like to give him shit. Back to the dream . . ."

"Same dream every time. We do a quick insertion into a hot LZ, take off, and catch an RPG in the gut. The gunner and copilot die.

I shoot a gook with my .45. You and I make it out." He stopped and took a drink of beer.

"Pretty much how I remember it," Scoot said.

"Then, Bobby returned to the LZ, and you know . . ."

"I know. Look, it ain't your fault. You'd done the same for him, right?" Scoot said.

"Yeah," said Timothy.

"Personally, I'm just glad we made it home. You didn't ask for that RPG in the gut, and beatin' yourself up over Bobby ain't gonna bring him home. All it does is keep you stuck in Nam. And if you're stuck in that shithole, how you gonna finish school and marry that girl?"

Timothy nodded.

"You know what I say to the Nam? *Xin loi,* motherfucker. I'm gone."

Timothy laughed.

"Let's drink to making it home." Scoot held up his bottle and Timothy returned the salute. "So tell me about this flick you guys saw last night."

Timothy admired the way Scoot could shift gears. Timothy couldn't; he clenched his memories like a baby gripping a rattle. He couldn't figure out whether the memories had a grip on him or the other way around.

They sat for another hour and a couple more beers.

"Time to *didi mau,*" Scoot said. He had to get back to the shop.

"Yep, I hear you," Timothy said.

Timothy wanted to go home, read a little, and get some sleep. Thanksgiving would be a busy day for him. They said their goodbyes and promised to do this again soon. Timothy walked home and thought about Scoot's comments. *It's not my fault—I wish I believed that. Scoot's right, though. I am tired of draggin' that wagon. I just wish I knew how to let go of the handle.*

CHAPTER SIX

TIMOTHY SLEPT WELL Wednesday night. The beers with Scoot and his irregular work schedule had zapped him. Thursday morning's uneventful drive to Schoen's suited Timothy fine. His car started on the first attempt—a good omen. Light traffic—another good omen. The short line at the service station for gas was unusual because of the Arab oil embargo. *Three good omens on the way to work. This is going to be a good day.*

The Chinese called 1973 the Year of the Ox—a year of hard work, strength, loyalty, dependability, and honesty. This described Timothy's life perfectly. He worked two part-time jobs, attended college full time, wrestled with memories of the war, and felt responsible for his mother. If Timothy were completely honest with himself, he would admit he didn't feel so strong in the year of strength.

As he opened his car door, the smell of pine trees from the lot, smoke from the fire barrel, and the morning chill welcomed him to the workday. Kenny stood at the fire barrel warming his hands. Kenny wore a torn sock cap, fingerless derby gloves, tan Dickies overalls, and an insulated flannel shirt. The Parodi hung from his lips.

"Where you been, GI Joe?" Kenny said.

"Hey, Kenny, how's it going?"

"Good. The ol' kike hired a geezer to help us out."

"Really?"

"Yup."

"Wonder of wonders. I knew he was thinking about it," Timothy said.

"He's over there with Dez. Wanna meet 'im?" Kenny said, pointing to the two men talking.

"Sure."

As they walked from the fire barrel to where Dez and Hoffen stood, Timothy thought about Dez hiring someone else. *This is out of character for Dez.*

"Did your mama send those cookies?" Kenny asked.

"Not yet, but I know she'll be on it soon."

"Okay, but ya gotta remember."

"I will, Kenny. What's his name?"

"Who?"

"The old man," Timothy said.

"Oh, you mean the guy Dez hired? Huffin' or something like that."

"That's an odd name," Timothy said.

"Yeah, don't know nothin' about it. Hey, Huffin', come here."

Hoffen turned from talking to Dez and approached them, limping with age. Timothy favored his bad leg.

"Well, if that ain't a pathetic sight—a gimp and a limp," Dez mocked them.

Dez cackled at his own joke, and Kenny coughed up cigar phlegm. Timothy extended his hand. Hoffen grabbed it.

Bright eyes, a warm smile, and a strong grip made Hoffen look to be in good shape in spite of his limp. Hoffen stood eye-to-eye with Timothy. The piercing depth of Hoffen's eye contact caught Timothy's attention, showing confidence without being competitive the way some men liked to stare each other down. Timothy sensed these eyes had seen a lot of life. Hoffen had a good spirit about him. Timothy instantly liked this man.

"Hi, I'm Tim."

"Nice to meet you, Tim. I'm Hoffen."

"Hoffen. First or last?" Timothy said.

"Neither. Just Hoffen."

Timothy nodded. "Okay."

"Hoffen, tell him your ideas to sell more trees," Dez said. "This old goat may not be dead in the head yet."

Hoffen grinned, and Timothy noticed it. *He's got a sense of humor, and that helps if he's going to work for Dez.*

"Sure. Thanks for the vote of confidence, Dez."

Hoffen impressed Timothy with the way he handled Dez's insults.

"I told Dez if we separated the trees by type and size, it would make it easier for the customers to choose their tree," Hoffen said.

"Good idea, Hoffen," Timothy said.

"Tell 'im what else . . . the rest of your ideas," Dez said excitedly.

"I also suggested we play Christmas music over the PA system and give the children peppermint canes."

"Hey, I like those things. They take away the taste of my Parodis," Kenny said.

"Kenny, I told you a million times. The only thing that gets rid of the taste of those shit sticks is if you brush your teeth with Borax after you smoke 'em," Dez said.

"Hah, that's a good one, Dez," Kenny said.

Timothy and Hoffen laughed.

"Those are great ideas, Dez. Are you going to do it?" Timothy said.

"If it helps me sell trees, I'll do it."

"Why not have a Santa Claus here for the kids to visit?" Timothy joked, but Dez jumped on it.

"Good idea. If it brings in the suckers and makes 'em buy trees, I'll dress up in the suit myself," Dez said.

"Hah, Dez. You can't be Santa Claus. You're an old kike," Kenny said.

"Shut up, Kenny. What do you know? You ain't no smarter than those pine trees," Dez said.

Timothy shook his head. Though accustomed to this banter, Timothy tired of it. Hoffen didn't react either way—laugh or frown.

"They're always like this. I think they actually like each other, and that's how they show it," Timothy said to Hoffen.

"Could be. That's a great idea, Dez, dressing up like Santa Claus. I bet you've done this before," Hoffen said.

"I don't know, maybe. I've been at this a long time. I got to get inside. The ol' lady needs her ten o'clock bathroom break. Hoffen, tell these guys about the different trees we got so they have a story for the suckers when they come in." Dez turned and walked to the shop.

"Okay, Dez," Hoffen said.

"What's he mean about a story? I don't know no stories about Christmas trees. The only story I know is about a three-legged chicken," Kenny said.

"I'd like to hear that sometime," Hoffen said.

"There was a farmer who raised three-legged chickens—" Kenny started.

"Later, Kenny," Timothy interrupted.

"I suggested to Dez we give customers some background on the trees they're looking at. Each has a different story. The right tree with the right story can make a family happy. It adds to the holiday spirit and makes it special. You're giving them a Christmas experience," Hoffen said.

Timothy nodded, and Kenny scratched his head.

"For example, we have three types of trees on this lot. Some come from Ohio, some from Wisconsin, and some from Colorado," Hoffen said.

"Why do people care where trees come from?" Kenny asked.

"When you can explain to people the tree they're looking at came a long distance just for them, they feel special, and that's what this season is all about," Hoffen said.

Kenny nodded. Timothy smiled.

Hoffen had an easy spirit, and Timothy liked it. For the next few minutes, Hoffen explained the difference between Douglas firs, blue spruces, and Scotch pines. Hoffen shared with Timothy and Kenny the legends of the different trees and how to care for them. Kenny sat on a stack of pallets, listening as a child listens to a bedtime story. Timothy smiled and nodded. He enjoyed the lesson and the stories.

"Makes sense to me. I like it. It sounds like you're no stranger to Christmas trees," Timothy said.

Hoffen nodded. "I have been around them for a while. Might as well learn something about them."

"I like the idea of some cheer for the customers. A festive

atmosphere puts everyone in a better mood. It's good psychology," Timothy said.

"Yeah, maybe we'll get bigger tips, too," Kenny said.

"Tis the season," Hoffen said.

In the background, they heard Elvis singing about a blue Christmas. Dez already figured out a way to get Christmas music on the PA system.

"I guess Dez is serious about this?" Timothy said.

Hoffen nodded. "I hope so."

Around eleven, a rush of customers showed up, and for the next three hours, the whole crew—Timothy, Kenny, Hoffen, and Dez—sold trees as fast as they could. With good tips and lots of pine moving out, everyone seemed happy. About two o'clock, Dez told Timothy he could take off.

"Like I promised, O'Rourke. You get the rest of the day off. The old man and the mole head can finish up here," Dez said.

"Thanks, Dez. See you tomorrow." He turned to Hoffen and Kenny. "Have a good Thanksgiving, guys."

"You too, Timothy," Hoffen said.

"Plan to, soldier boy," Kenny said.

Timothy walked to the car feeling good about his day. *Good tips, home to shower and clean up for Cheryl's family dinner, then to Leslie's for dinner with my family. A lot to be thankful for.* His car started on the first twist of the key.

Timothy celebrated an early Thanksgiving meal with Cheryl and her family. He ate enough to be polite but not enough to prevent him from eating again with his family later. After dessert, Timothy and Cheryl said goodbye to her family and headed out to his car. He opened the door for Cheryl, and it squeaked itself awake. He never locked the doors because even car thieves had some pride.

Cheryl sat quietly as he tried to start it. As usual, the Fairlane woke lazily. He shook his head as the car coughed its way to life.

"Maybe I ought to rename this heap Lazarus, as many times as I've brought it back to life," he said.

Cheryl smiled. She knew this embarrassed and frustrated him. As usual, Timothy's default was to grin and bear it. She thought, *I wonder how long he can go on like this, dealing with all these frustrations.*

Timothy looked at her and said, "I replaced the battery this week, and it's still hard to start."

"We could take my car," Cheryl said.

"No, it's fine once we get going."

The car belched a black cloud and coughed before settling into an irregular rhythm.

"See, I told you this beast still had some life in it," Timothy said.

Cheryl smiled sympathetically. "Thanks for coming today. My family wanted to see you. They like you, Tim."

"I know. It worked out fine. I appreciated the invitation."

"You work hard," she said. She could tell Timothy didn't want to go there. With most people, he appeared stoic, but Cheryl saw through his façade.

"Your family is nice. In fact, they are so nice they're dysfunctionally normal," Timothy said and laughed. "I thought Norman Rockwell holidays happened only in picture frames."

"That's sweet."

"I don't know if I'm ready for my family," he said.

"Oh, Tim, your family is fine. They've had to deal with a lot, and that affects people. They're trying to get through life."

"Always the social worker, eh?" he said.

Cheryl smiled. Even though he wanted to become a psychologist, Cheryl was his therapist. She enjoyed this nugget of delicious irony.

"We'll have a good time tonight. It'll be good to see all of them. I don't get to see Leslie and her family as often as I would like. Everyone is so busy these days. And your mom, I want to see how she's feeling," Cheryl said.

"Leslie likes you, too. You know, she's your champion with Mom. She's on your side."

"Tim, there are no sides here. Your mother has dealt with a lot. Your father's death, you in Vietnam, her health; that's a lot for anyone to process."

Timothy sat silently as Cheryl's words took root. Then he changed the conversation.

"Professor Leibert is giving me grief again," Timothy said. "He thinks he's a political science genius, and he's never been outside of this country. I bet he would have gone to Canada if he hadn't had that 2-S deferment as a student," he said.

"Yeah, I remember him. He's pretty opinionated," Cheryl said.

"That's about the nicest thing you can say about this guy. He has this whole thing about the military-industrial complex. He probably loves Uncle Ho and Mao's *Little Red Book*. He's got it in for me and the other vets. He goes out of his way to antagonize us. We're all pretty fed up."

"Guys who served make it difficult for people like that to look in the mirror. They're not happy with what stares back at them. So they take it out on you," she said.

"Are you apologizing for him?" Timothy said.

"No, I'm not excusing anything. I'm explaining what I suspect is really going on."

"You're way more understanding than I am. All I want is my B in this class and to be done with him."

"Good strategy. No sense trying to win an argument with him," she said.

The monotony of road noise comforted them. Cheryl thought, *He will grin and bear it, but warriors are wired to fight, not to yield to someone like Professor Leibert.*

"Are you thinking about Bobby today?" she asked.

"Whoa, where did that come from?"

"It's Thanksgiving, and the holidays make people think. It's natural for you to think of him."

"Yeah, he's been on my mind the last couple of days. I wonder what he's doing today. Scoot and I talked about it last night."

"Scoot's a good friend," Cheryl said.

"Yep, he's the best. He's always had my back."

"We've been studying gross stress disorders at the clinic. It used to be called combat fatigue, but new theories are beginning to emerge. I know you're not fond of the VA, but have you considered talking to them again? They have experience with this, you know. Unfortunately, too much," she said.

"I told you. I went there one time, and the shrink laughed at me. I'll never go back. Besides, I've got you. You're my therapist, right?"

The road noise absorbed the silence until the car did its second act. At a stoplight it stalled again. Timothy coached it back to life.

"See, I told you. Still some life in this old heap," he said.

Cheryl liked to hear him talk like this. She hoped this optimism would spill over into other areas of his life. As they pulled up to the curb in front of Mom's house, the car jerked to a stop. He looked at her.

"Are you ready for this?" he said.

"Let's go, big fella. I want some of those rolls you're always talkin' about," she said.

They walked arm in arm up the front steps of Leslie's house.

CHAPTER SEVEN

TIMOTHY KNOCKED BEFORE he opened the front door to Leslie and Ike's home, a habit he developed a long time ago—knock and enter. Thanksgiving rushed to greet Cheryl and him. The smell of turkey, dressing, and Mom's rolls baking in the oven filled the house. Two of Leslie and Ike's children, Amy and Jeannie, played games in the background. The other two children, Peter and Albert, parked themselves in front of the television set with Ike, watching football. Leslie set the dining room table for this special occasion. Mom stood at the table arranging silverware. She looked up when she heard them come in.

"I was beginning to worry you weren't going to make it," Mom said.

"We made it, Mom," Timothy said. "A little car trouble."

"Again?" Mom said.

"Hey, man, get rid of that clunker and get a real car. That new Camaro's boss," Ike said. He rose to shake hands with his brother-in-law.

"Hi, Ike. Wouldn't that be nice?" Timothy said. "Sometime—maybe next year."

"Well, look who finally made it," Leslie said.

She hugged Timothy and Cheryl. Leslie played the consummate big sister—part advocate, part voice of reason when family situations demanded a measured approach. Mom listened to her, too.

"Cheryl, it's good to see you. Come on in, guys. We're still getting ready. Peter, take their coats and hang them up," said Leslie.

"Okay, Mom. Hi, Uncle Tim. Hi, Cheryl. Can I take your coats?" Peter said.

"Sure," Tim said. He helped Cheryl take off her coat.

"Ike, make yourself useful and get them a drink," Leslie said.

"On it," Ike said. "Beer, wine, hard stuff?"

"White wine for me," Cheryl said.

"I'll take a brew," Timothy said.

Leslie, Cheryl, and Mom went to the kitchen while Timothy joined the boys in front of the television. After giving Cheryl her glass of wine, Ike returned to the living room with a beer for Timothy.

"What do you think, Ike? Can the Dolphins do it again this year?" Timothy said.

"They're not going undefeated if that's what you mean, but yeah, they could make it back to the big game," said Ike.

Timothy took a sip of beer. "What's going on in this game?"

"They've sacked Staubach three times, and if Miami holds onto the lead, they will be ten and one."

"On their way," Timothy said. "Did you guys play your game this morning?"

"Yeah, muddy as hell," Ike said.

"Mud and cold are a lousy combination, aren't they?"

"I heard that," Ike said.

The four of them sat watching a Cardinals game, chatting idly about the NFL, the weather, almost any neutral topic.

"Soup's on, guys. TV off," Leslie called.

"C'mon, Mom, the game's almost over," Peter said.

"Let's go. Food's ready," she said.

They moved to the dining table. Mom sat closest to the kitchen. She motioned Timothy to the head of the table, which made him feel uncomfortable. Cheryl sat at his right with Ike and Leslie next to her. The children sat across from them.

"Albert, please say grace," Ike said.

"Okay, Dad."

They blessed the meal and filled their plates. Turkey, "smashed potatoes," as Albert called them, bread stuffing, cranberry sauce, green bean casserole, and Mom's homemade rolls. The plates seemed small by comparison, and one helping never sufficed.

"Cheryl, I understand your family had a little gathering today," Mom said. The way Mom said "little" made the meal at Cheryl's home seem small and insignificant.

"Yes, we did, thank you. Everyone was thrilled Timothy could make it. They know he's busy, and it meant a lot to them that he came over. They really like him," Cheryl said. She smiled at Mom.

"He's so likable," Ike said. He coughed as he laughed.

Leslie gave Ike a sharp elbow, and Timothy tipped his beer bottle in response.

"Yes, his plate is full with work and school. Not much time for anything else in his life," Mom said.

"I know. That's one of the things I'm most proud of—how hard he works," Chery said. "He somehow manages to get it all done."

"Really? I can tell you he didn't get that from his father."

"He must have gotten it from you, Mrs. O," Cheryl said.

Timothy smiled at Leslie.

"Could be." Mom took a bite of turkey.

Ike opened his mouth to say something when Timothy chimed in. "Ike, how's it going at the post office?"

"Good. Far as I know, we're doing okay. First-class is going up to seven cents next year, and we're all hoping to see some of that in a raise."

"Yes, Tim. Ike's got a good government job. Secure and steady. Do they need help down there, Ike?" Mom said.

"They do hire a lot of vets. After that fiasco last year, I think it's the law."

"What was that, Ike?" Mom said.

"Someone blew the whistle on an internal memo that advised against hiring Vietnam vets."

"Why on earth would they say that?"

Timothy jumped in. "Because they think we're all nuts."

"That's terrible," Cheryl said.

"Agreed," said Leslie.

"So after that got out, the postmaster went on the record and said we would hire Vietnam vets. A lot of the guys drive the nightshift around town. If you're interested, Tim, I could check into it for you. You might be able to get some part-time work."

"Thanks, Ike. I've got my hospital job, and even though it's not the best money, I get a lot of real-world experience working with the patients."

"Timothy has his eyes on becoming a psychologist. He's really focused on this," Cheryl said.

"You're some kind of counselor, aren't you?" Mom said.

"I'm a social worker. I work mostly with single moms and children that have learning disabilities."

"Well, I always thought those women should think about the consequences of their actions before having a child," Mom said.

"Hold on a minute, Mom. Most of these unwed mothers had husbands that left them," Timothy said. "They've had a tough go of it. A lot of them are not at fault for their situation." He paused to let a few moments of silence emphasize his point.

"Yes, Mrs. O, once you get to know these women and understand how tough their lives have been, it's pretty hard to judge them," Cheryl said.

Timothy decided to let the awkward silence hang.

"Hey, Tim. I drove by the tree lot the other day. Man, that thing is full. You guys have your work cut out for you this year," Ike said.

"Yeah, Dez ordered a couple of extra truckloads. He got a deal on them. We may need some extra help to move all of those trees this year."

"I wish you didn't work for that vile man. He's crude," Mom said.

"Dez? He thinks a lot of you too, Mom," Timothy said.

Leslie laughed.

"Besides, you know how those people are," Mom said.

"Those people?" Leslie said.

"Timothy knows what I mean, dear," Mom said.

"Mom, you remember what Pope Paul said, don't you? We Catholics don't have a lock on heaven," said Timothy.

Any conversation in which Timothy invoked Paul VI's name caused Mom to cross herself and measure her words. As a faithful, old-school Catholic, she did not violate anything the pope said. She didn't want to be banished from heaven on a technicality.

"Mother, little pitchers have big ears," Leslie said.

"What does that mean, anyway?" Peter said.

"Never mind, Peter, Grandma understands," Leslie said.

"Timothy, would you like another roll?" Mom said. "You know, Cheryl, it takes me twelve hours to make them. I make them from scratch."

"That's real love, Mrs. O. Timothy talks about these all the time. He's a real salesman for your rolls. They're every bit as good as he promised."

"Do you cook, Cheryl?" Mom said.

"Not as well as Leslie or you, but I do know the difference between a pot and a pan."

Timothy liked that Cheryl could bob and weave with Mom.

"Grandma, what does it mean when pitchers have ears?" Peter asked.

"It means, Peter, that your mother wants me to change the topic."

"I'll second that," Timothy said.

"Here, here," Ike said. He held up his beer.

"Mrs. O, I would love to learn how to make these rolls. Do you suppose you could teach me?" Cheryl said.

Timothy liked the way Cheryl called Mom "Mrs. O." He thought this endearing term disarmed much of Mom's sarcasm. *How could anyone not like Cheryl?*

"Well, uh, yes, I could. But you must understand, I put more love than dough in these," Mom said.

Mom looked at Timothy and smiled. Timothy squirmed and Ike grinned. Leslie shook her head.

"I can see that, and it works fine for me," Cheryl said.

Peter snagged a roll from Albert's plate. Albert slapped at Peter and the girls giggled.

They finished their meal with typical family small talk. The children talked about school, Ike talked about work, and Leslie detailed her busy schedule of work and home life. Mom didn't say much more.

"Who wants pumpkin pie?" Leslie said.

"We're in, Sis. Right, Cheryl?" Timothy said. Cheryl nodded.

"Whipped cream?" Leslie asked.

"You bet," said Timothy.

"I'll have a sliver, honey," Mom said.

"I'll help you," Ike said.

After pie, coffee and more small talk, the evening wound down. Timothy yawned.

"You look tired, honey," Mom said.

"Yeah, I think it's the turkey and the drinks. We better go. I have to be at the tree lot early tomorrow, and Cheryl has an early morning, too."

"Thanks for coming tonight, guys. It's fun to get together. We're all so busy these days. We have to make time to do more of this," Leslie said.

Ike nodded. Timothy and Cheryl rose, he gave the kids high fives, kissed Mom on the forehead, gave Sis a hug, and said to Ike, "Bro, it's always good to break bread with you."

"Back at ya, man," Ike said.

Cheryl looked at Leslie and Ike. "Thanks for inviting me."

"Anytime. You're always welcome here," Leslie said.

Leslie hugged Cheryl, which pleased Timothy. Mom noticed, too.

"Mrs. O, thank you, too. And I'm going to hold you to teaching me how to make the rolls. May I give you a hug?" Cheryl said.

"Uh, okay, Cheryl," Mom said. Cheryl walked over and hugged Mom. Timothy watched and thought, *This woman is a master of human relations.*

As they walked to the car, Timothy thought about the evening.

"Sorry about that," he said.

"About what?"

"My mom," he said.

"Timothy, she loves you. You're her baby boy. She's glad you're home. And she's still trying to figure out how I fit into all of this. That's all. She's being a mother—a loving one, at that."

"Yeah, maybe a little too much loving mother at times, but you're right."

"And I love you, too," Cheryl said.

They hugged and kissed on the curb before climbing in the Fairlane.

Timothy twisted the key, and it fired up on the second request. He drove Cheryl home.

CHAPTER EIGHT

TIMOTHY ARRIVED AT the tree lot a few minutes before nine. Dez wanted everyone in place for the rush of customers. The first couple of hours passed quickly as the crew arranged trees, cleaned up the aisles, and made small talk. Kenny excelled at small talk, especially when it went nowhere. Kenny claimed Dez told him, "Simple people make simple talk." Hoffen joined in some of the good-natured banter between Timothy and Kenny. Groups of customers began to arrive. Dez stood around to ensure the crew took care of the suckers. He barked orders like a field commander in combat.

"It's your up, Hoffen," Timothy said.

Hoffen looked up to see a family admiring a tree. "Go ahead, Tim, they're looking at the big ones."

"You sure?"

"Yep," Hoffen said.

"Okay then." Timothy turned toward the family.

Timothy had a hitch in his step this morning. *It must be the cold weather today,* Hoffen thought. It was Hoffen's turn to sell, but he knew Timothy should handle this one.

"Merry Christmas," Timothy said.

The family of four smiled—father, mother, son, and daughter, well dressed and polite. Standing there, they looked like the all-American family. Timothy handed the children a peppermint stick. Bing Crosby crooned in the background, and smoke from the fire barrel eased over them. Hoffen painted this picture yesterday for the crew. Hoffen expected Dez to show up in a Santa outfit.

"Thank you," the children said.

Mom smiled and Dad said, "Merry Christmas to you, sir."

"Thanks. So you like spruces?" Timothy said.

"Oh, yeah, bluish green. We've been getting them ever since I was a kid. I grew up in Colorado, and we got one every year," the father said.

"Good news, kids; this tree grew up in Colorado, too. Come over here, and smell the mountains," Timothy said.

"Be careful, children. Those needles get stiff and may stick you in the eye," the mother said.

"Listen to your mother, guys," the father said.

"Is this going in your living room?" Timothy said.

"Yes. We have nine-foot ceilings," the mother said.

"In that case, the biggest tree you want is a seven-footer. Figure room on top for a star or angel and about a foot on the bottom for the stand. This is a nice, full one." Timothy lifted the tree from the wooden rack, pounded the trunk on the ground to release the branches, and placed it in the aisle for the family to see.

"It's a beauty," the father said.

"Kids, let me tell you about the trip this tree made to get here," Timothy began his tale.

Hoffen stood next to the spruce rack, leaning in to hear the story. He enjoyed each twist and turn of the tree's journey. He admired Timothy's storytelling. The children listened wide-eyed as if it were a bedtime story. Mom moved closer and Dad put his arm around her.

Hoffen thought, *This family's getting its money's worth.*

"Can we take this one home, Dad?" The boy said.

"Can we, Daddy, please?" The girl said.

"Sure, we'll take it," Dad said.

"Great. You've had spruces before, so you know about room temperature and how often you must water it?" Timothy said.

"Sure. It's a thirsty tree. Otherwise, the needles get hard," said Dad.

"You got it. I'll carry this to the cutting area and prep the trunk for you," Timothy said.

The father followed and watched Timothy sculpt the base.

"Boy, you know your trees," the father said.

"I had a pretty good teacher," Timothy said and glanced at Hoffen. Hoffen nodded.

"This is the first time my children have ever heard a Christmas tree story. They—we—enjoyed it," the father said.

"I'm thrilled to tell it. You know, I took some artistic license with it," Timothy said.

"I know you did, but the kids really enjoyed it. You made it magical, and that's what this season is all about."

The father watched as Timothy finished his trimming. He stared at the patches on Timothy's Army fatigue jacket. He handed Timothy thirty-five dollars.

"Sir, this it too much. The tree is only fifteen."

"I know. The rest is for you."

"Oh no, that's way too much, sir. It's generous, but I can't take it."

"Actually, it's not close to being enough, Warrant Officer O'Rourke," the father said.

Timothy paused his trimming and stared at the man. Hoffen leaned into the conversation.

"I see you know these insignias," Timothy said.

"I've seen plenty, maybe too many, though I don't recognize your unit patch," the father said.

"It's the 68th Assault Helicopter Company, sir. UH1H Hueys. Part of the First Aviation Brigade. We flew out of Bien Hoa airbase."

"Yes, Bien Hoa, of course," the father said.

Hoffen moved closer.

"I never flew into Bien Hoa. I landed at Tan Son Nhut when I flew to Vietnam," the father said.

"Yeah, Saigon. Pilot, huh?"

"Yes, civilian. I flew for Flying Tigers Airline. We ferried a lot of you men there and home. Most of the time, we flew from Travis Air Force Base outside of San Francisco with a stop in Japan at Yokota Air Base. Sometimes Guam, too."

"Right. Been there and done that," Timothy said.

"The flights home were better. They called us Freedom Birds when we brought you guys back. I remember clearly the cheers from the cabin when we went wheels up. It sounded like a year's worth of anticipation. It was too many flights and too many young men," the father said.

"There were a lot of us for sure," Timothy said and went back to trimming the trunk of the tree.

After a few moments of awkward silence, Hoffen watched and sensed that the man wanted to say something else to Timothy.

"I noticed you're favoring one leg."

"A little something I brought home with me."

Timothy paused and rubbed his head just as "I'll Be Home for Christmas" began playing over the PA speakers.

"We took an RPG in the belly of our Huey. Spent some time in the Saigon hospital and a few weeks in Frankfurt. Not exactly the way I planned to see Germany. Anyway, I made it home, and I'm doing okay now."

"I can see that. We appreciate your service. I know you guys don't hear that often these days, but many of us respect your service," the father said.

"It was an honor to serve, sir," Timothy said.

The children started climbing on the tree stands and throwing the pine trimmings at each other. The crowd of customers grew. Kenny spun a yarn about a fir tree in the background. Hoffen didn't recall telling him this particular story, but he enjoyed Kenny's imagination.

"I guess we better get going," the father said. "Bobby, come over here and help me carry this tree. It's time to get home."

Timothy froze momentarily and said, "Sir, let me do it. I'll get some rope to secure it to your car top."

"No, thank you. You've done enough already," the father said.

"Are you sure?"

"Absolutely."

The two shook hands, their eyes locked like survivors of some terrible experience. Hoffen liked what he witnessed. *A little appreciation goes a long way toward healing. And this young man needs some healing.* Timothy smiled at the family and waved as they drove off.

"Nice tip?" Hoffen said.

"You bet, Hoffen. I feel like I should share it with you," Timothy said.

"Nah, you earned it. An RPG in the gut? That's a tough way to land," Hoffen said.

"Real tough. I wish it had been more of a landing," Timothy said.

"You made it out, though," Hoffen said.

"Yes, two of us did."

"And you were the pilot?"

"Yep. The left seat," Timothy said.

"Left seat?" Hoffen asked.

"Sorry, the AC, aircraft commander," Timothy said.

Timothy began to pick at his fingernails and shuffle his feet. His left eye twitched. Hoffen watched and listened.

"My crew chief and I made it back. My assistant pilot and the gunner died in the crash."

"Tough thing to carry around with you," Hoffen said.

"You can't imagine," Timothy said.

"Oh, I think I can," Hoffen said. "Grief dies a slow death."

Timothy paused and stared at Hoffen, whose eyes and tone said, "I know exactly how it feels." Timothy saw that look a hundred times. Vets called it the thousand-yard stare, a penetrating gaze into nothingness, the great abyss. Hoffen displayed the look and confidence of a survivor, unflappable yet full of pain. They nodded and said nothing else. Hoffen knew not to push harder today.

"O'Rourke. Go inside. The ol' lady's got a phone call for you," Dez yelled across the lot.

"Okay, Dez," Timothy shouted. He turned and walked toward the shop.

Hoffen followed Timothy into the shop. The stale air assaulted them like the bad breath of evil incarnate. Hoffen stood close enough to hear but remained far enough to stay out of the conversation.

"For you, soldier boy," Edna said as she handed him the phone.

"Thanks, Ed. Hello?"

Timothy's cold, red cheeks turned pale. Hoffen knew it must be serious. He felt glad he followed Timothy into the shop.

Timothy's voice quivered. "What's going on? Is she okay? Is she in the emergency room still?"

The urgency in Timothy's voice sounded serious. Edna stopped counting money in the cash drawer and looked up at Timothy.

"Failure or what?" Timothy said.

Hoffen didn't like to hear failure in a conversation about health issues. Edna blew the ash from her cigarette.

"Has she seen a doctor? What did he say? How serious is this?"

Kenny walked in, and Hoffen motioned to him to keep it down. Dez stayed with the customers. Someone had to pay the bills.

"I know, but that's not my concern right now. She's going to be okay, right?"

Timothy nodded slightly and Hoffen saw relief creep into his face. Timothy's tone changed, too.

"I'll go to Cheryl's. I can sleep in her brother's room. That's not important right now. Mom is the concern."

Hoffen had witnessed selflessness like this in the past from people who placed the welfare of others above their own. He suspected Timothy demonstrated self-sacrifice in the war but never talked about it. Bragging didn't fit him.

"Of course, I'm on my way. I'll be there in a few minutes," Timothy said.

He hung up the phone and stared at space. His gaze hung frozen in the air for a few moments. Hoffen saw the thousand-yard stare. From Timothy's face and round shoulders, Hoffen knew this was serious. Even Kenny remained silent. Edna went back to scratching around her cash drawer.

"My mom's in the hospital. It's a respiratory problem, a reaction to toxic furnace fumes at home. They backed up in the house, and she choked on them. She called my brother-in-law to come and get her. He took her straight to the emergency room. I have to meet them up here. Ed, I've got to go to the hospital, now."

"All right. How serious?" Edna asked.

"Serious but not critical. She'll be there for a few days until her lungs clear out."

Timothy's response surprised Hoffen. It sounded too clinical and almost dispassionate. Hoffen wondered what strength Timothy mustered from those few moments of silence. Hoffen knew war did not allow time to mourn. That happened later, in dreams and nightmares.

"Okay, but Dez won't be happy you're leaving. How long you gonna be gone? We can't pay you if you're not here," Edna said.

"Edna, I'll stay late tonight to help close up," Hoffen said.

"Me too," Kenny said. "Buy me a sandwich?"

Timothy smiled. Kenny's request brought some needed relief to the moment.

"All right, I guess Dez will be okay with that," Edna said.

"Thanks, Ed. Thanks, you guys. I appreciate it," Timothy said. "I'll be back in the morning on time."

"That's fine, Timothy. We're glad to help," Hoffen said.

"Yeah, no problem," said Kenny.

"What about the furnace?" Edna asked. She went back to business.

"I'll call someone in the morning and have them look at it so we can see what we're dealing with."

"Where will you stay tonight? You can stay at my place if you want."

"Thanks, Hoffen. I'll stay at my girlfriend's house."

Kenny raised his eyebrows.

"In her brother's room," Timothy said, and Kenny nodded. "Look, guys, I've got to go."

Timothy left the shop, and the three of them said nothing. Hoffen figured none of them knew what to say. He knew he could help Timothy when the time came. They heard Timothy attempting to start his car. On the third crank it coughed its way to life.

Kenny looked at Edna. "How 'bout that sandwich?"

CHAPTER NINE

TIMOTHY RUSHED TO the hospital and a receptionist gave him a room number on the Med-Surg floor. As usual, he took the stairs. Hospital elevators moved too slow for concerned family members. Though he worked there, things smelled different to Timothy as the relative of a patient—the combination of disinfectant and sick people. Things sounded different, too—patients calling from their beds, doctor pages on the intercom system, and dinner trays clanking in the hallway. And things looked different—patients sitting in wheelchairs and lying on gurneys in the hallway. *How long have they been sitting there? Are they being ignored?*

"Mom, how are you?" Timothy leaned over the bed and kissed Mom on the forehead. She felt clammy and looked pale.

"Okay, I guess. My chest hurts a little," she said, massaging it.

"She's going to be okay, but it was touch and go when she got here," Leslie said.

"You didn't tell me that on the phone," Timothy said.

"I didn't want to worry you unnecessarily. I figured it could wait until you got here," she said.

"Mom, what happened?"

"I laid down for a nap because I felt sick to my stomach, and then I had trouble breathing, so I called your sister, and Ike came right over. He's such a fine son-in-law."

"When I got there, the house smelled terrible from the furnace fumes," Ike said. "It choked me and burned my eyes. I couldn't believe Mom had been breathing that stuff. When I saw her, I knew we had to get her to the hospital. Her color was bad, so I brought her to the ER."

"He got me here just in time," Mom said.

"I'm sorry, Mom," Timothy said.

"It's not your fault. You were at work," Mom said.

"No, I'm sorry the furnace got so bad. I should've taken care of that earlier in the week."

"You didn't know this would happen," Mom said.

Timothy glanced at Leslie and noticed her wet eyes. Ike looked solemn. Mom asked for a sip of water and for someone to adjust the head of her bed so she could sit up a little. She also wanted another blanket. She looked about as pitiful as Timothy had ever seen her.

Doctor Hanson came in.

"Evening, Tim," the doctor said.

"Hi, Doc. Thanks for taking care of my mom."

"She was one sick cookie when they brought her in here. The fact she has only one lung didn't help. She told me she had it removed about twenty years ago because of a tumor."

"Yes, that's true," Leslie said.

"That didn't help with this," Doctor Hanson said. "She got here just in time, thanks to your brother-in-law."

"Yes, he's a sweet man," Mom said.

"I know. Ike knows how much we appreciate his swift action." Timothy nodded to Ike, the reluctant hero.

"You know you can't stay in that house? It's toxic for anyone, especially your mother," Doctor Hanson said.

"I know, Doc. I'll deal with it first thing in the morning," Timothy said.

"Okay. We want to keep your mother for a couple of days to watch for any complications. Where will she go when I discharge her?"

"She'll come home with us for a few days," Leslie said.

"Thank you, dear. You're so good to me. I don't want to impose."

"I shut down the furnace when I was there and opened a few windows. You may want to go by and close the windows tonight, Tim. It should have cleared enough by now to go in there to do that."

"Thanks, Ike," Timothy said.

"Aren't I lucky to have a family like this, Doctor Hanson?"

"Yes, ma'am, you are. Now, just think about getting better, and I'll be in tomorrow to check on you."

Timothy felt responsible for this. Mom had asked him to look at the furnace a few days earlier, but he didn't see any problems. He thought, *Thank God she had her wits about her to call Leslie, or who knows what could have happened?*

"Timothy, I don't know how we're going to pay for this."

"For what, Mom?" he asked.

"The hospital, the furnace—"

"You let me take care of that, Mom," Timothy said.

Timothy knew she did not have the money to pay for a new furnace, so he mentally reviewed his finances to figure out where to get it.

"You're a good boy too, Timmy. Where will you stay tonight?" Mom said.

"I'll call Cheryl. I'm sure I can stay in her brother's room. He went back to school today."

"Oh, you don't want to impose on her family. I imagine your sister could make some room for you."

"I'm fine, Mom."

"He'll be okay, Mom," Leslie said.

"All right, do what you think is best. I'm sure your friend's family won't mind too much. Her parents will be there, right?"

Even in her condition, Mom still had enough strength to comment on Cheryl, the other woman. Timothy shook his head and grinned at Ike.

"What will you do about the furnace?" Mom said.

"In the morning, I'll call the repair service and see when they can come out. I'm sure they will understand it's an emergency."

"Do they offer financing? I only have a few hundred dollars in my savings account and fifty dollars in my checking account."

"Mom, I told you not to worry about this. I'll take care of it," Timothy said.

"Okay, but if you get over to your friend's house and there's no room for you, go to Leslie's house, and she'll make room for you. Family takes care of blood."

"Like Ike took care of you, right Mom?" Leslie said.

"Yes, dear. Ike knows what I mean."

Timothy released a deep breath full of anxiety and leaned over and kissed Mom on the forehead.

She grabbed his hand tightly. "Timmy, I feel bad you have to work so hard. I don't know what I would do without you. I don't want you to feel guilty about the furnace."

"Okay, Mom. I'll see you guys tomorrow. Bye."

In the hallway, Timothy paused to collect his thoughts. *It's just life. Things like this happen all the time to everyone; just one more thing. Cheryl is always reminding me bad things happen, then good things happen, to everyone, not just me.*

Self-talk helped him bounce back, especially during his recovery from his injuries.

He stopped at the first-floor telephone bank and dropped a dime to call Cheryl. He told her what happened and asked if he could spend the night. She had a lot of questions, and he told her he would answer them when he got to her house. First, he had to go by his house, close the windows, and lock up.

Timothy felt the cold air on his face and hands. The temperature dropped below freezing after dark. *Gotta get home and close those windows.* His car started on the third attempt, but the heater did not cooperate on the ride home. *Probably the damn thermostat.*

CHAPTER TEN

AFTER SPENDING THE night at Cheryl's, Timothy called the furnace company first thing on Saturday. The owner of the company promised to meet him at his mom's house in a few minutes. Timothy told Cheryl his plans and thanked her parents for letting him spend the night.

The thirty-degree morning made the house feel more like a refrigerator. Even with the heat shut off overnight, he still smelled pungent fumes. He wondered how Mom could have stayed there with the fumes. *Maybe she got confused. Maybe the fumes were so insidious she couldn't tell what was happening.* It reminded him of an article he read in biology class by William Sedgwick, educator and scientist. Sedgwick experimented with frogs in boiling water. The temperature of the water changed so gradually the frog never noticed. The frogs boiled to death.

The doorbell broke his train of thought. Timothy opened the front door.

"Morning, sir. I'm Fred, the furnace guy."

"Hi, come on in," Timothy said.

"Man, this place stinks."

"You can smell it, huh?" Timothy said.

"You bet. This beak can sniff sulfur a mile away."

"It's been off since yesterday afternoon," Timothy said.

"The hang time on sulfur fumes is high. This stuff sticks around for a while. That's one reason people hate coal furnaces. The stink gets on the walls, in the upholstery, and on the carpet. It sticks around longer than a pesky relative. The other reason is . . . uh, coal. It's messy. Where's the stoker?"

"Follow me." Timothy limped down the steps to the basement where the moribund furnace waited for them.

"Man, this is an old beast. Haven't seen one of these in a while. They don't make them like this anymore. Thank God. You can't believe how many of these old things we've replaced in the past five years. Be glad it went bad, otherwise you'd end up with black lung disease," Fred said.

"Really?"

"No, you'd croak long before that happened because of carbon monoxide and sulfur fumes."

"That's why you're here. The fumes put my mom in the hospital."

"Sorry to hear that, but I'm not surprised. Happens all the time."

"So what are we talking about?" Timothy said.

"Replacement, not repair. You can't get parts for these old coal burners anymore. The manufacturer doesn't make parts, and you can't scavenge any because when they break the whole damn thing craps out. I don't even need to look any further to tell you what's wrong or what to do. See all that soot buildup? That means you replace it."

"What are we looking at for replacement?"

"You want gas. It burns cheap, clean, and hot. Ever had trouble getting this place warm?"

"Only in the morning before I could stoke it. I would see my mom standing in front by the dining room register to get warm."

"Closest to the furnace, I bet," Fred said.

"Yeah, the warmest place in the house."

"You won't have that problem with the new unit. The whole house will be warm."

"Man, that sounds good," Timothy said. "What size unit?"

"How big is the house?"

"About sixteen hundred square feet," Timothy said.

"Sixty thousand BTUs will do it."

"Is that a common size?"

"Common as a sedan. For this size house, it's perfect."

"Okay. How much and how soon?"

"We can be back Monday morning first thing. It's a two-day job. On the first day, we will tear out the old system, inspect, and clean the ductwork. Then, we do the make-ready for the new unit. It'll take the gas company until Monday to get out here and hook up a line. They move pretty quick on a job like this. I'll call them this afternoon on their emergency line, and they will be here early on Monday. Tuesday, we install the new unit. You'll have heat by dinnertime."

"That sounds good. Okay, how much?"

"For the tear down, haul away, new furnace and install, we're talking somewhere in the neighborhood of twelve hundred."

Timothy took a long breath and let it out slowly, delaying the decision as long as possible.

"That's a pretty ritzy neighborhood. Do you guys offer financing?"

"Nope. We gotta deal going with the banks. We don't lend money, and they don't sell furnaces."

Timothy wanted to laugh but didn't have it in him. Fred didn't laugh either.

"Okay, how do you want to be paid?" Timothy asked.

"Full amount due when you have heat. Check's fine because I know where you live. We leave Tuesday with the money and leave you with the heat."

"Is that your best deal?"

"We always give our best deal. Is the money going to be a problem for you?" Fred asked.

"No, I can move some funds around on Monday."

Fred stuck out his hand. Timothy liked a handshake to seal a deal. It meant the other person made a personal commitment.

"I need to take some measurements and fill out some paperwork for you to sign. It'll take a few minutes," Fred said.

"All right, I'll be upstairs in the dining room. Come up when you're done."

"Okay, boss," said Fred.

Timothy labored up the stairs one at a time. His leg hurt, and Fred watched him struggle. Timothy sat at the dining room table and spread out his financial reality—a passbook for his modest savings account, an anemic checking account statement, and a tax bill for the house due in four weeks. He had a little more than 1,300 in his savings, 122 bucks in his checking, and a tax bill for almost 600. The tax bill plus the cost of replacing a furnace left him short and without money for next semester's tuition.

I can pay for the furnace out of my savings. That gives us heat. But I still have a tax bill and a thousand-dollar tuition payment due next month. I wonder if I could get an extension on the tax bill. Maybe I could work out something with tuition. His VA check and disability barely covered tuition, books, and fees. They still had a small mortgage payment, groceries, insurance, and Mom's hospital bills. This depended on his car lasting for a while. He had to forget about getting Cheryl the engagement ring he wanted to give her for Christmas. *How can someone with so little money have so many financial problems? Being broke should be simple. No money. No options.*

Fred entered the room. "Here's the paperwork. I need your signature here."

Timothy read the contract and played with the pen. He didn't want to make this decision.

"A check on Tuesday, right?" Fred said.

"Right, I pay when we have heat."

"We'll be here early on Monday morning to get rid of that old oven. The new one is in stock at the warehouse, so there will be no delay getting it. The only hitch may be the old ductwork. We won't know until we can look inside them and see how bad the soot is caked on there. Since it just happened, I don't see any issues there."

"Would that cost extra? I'm already tapped out."

"Don't worry about that. Let's get some heat turned on in here."

"Deal. Where do I sign?"

Fred pointed to a blank line on the contract. "Here."

They shook hands again and walked to the door. The cold in the house stiffened Timothy's leg. He limped until it loosened up.

"So where'd you get that?" Fred said, pointing to Timothy's bad leg.

"A crash."

"Motorcycle?"

"Not the kind of chopper you're thinking about," Timothy said.

"Nam?" Fred asked. Timothy nodded.

Fred paused.

"Tell you what, pay me in cash instead of a check, and I'll knock off a hundred bucks."

"I can do that, thanks."

"See you Monday." Fred left and Timothy retreated to the kitchen.

Timothy sat at the kitchen table, which had been the scene of a lot of living over the years. On the wall next to him hung the blackboard he drew on as a child. Mom used it these days to keep her A&P grocery shopping list—coffee, milk, corn, flour, and Ajax. As he sat there thinking about his financial situation, he found himself banging his head softly against the wall.

His father did the same thing years ago when he came home for lunch to tell Mom he lost his job and they might lose the car. Timothy remembered how the old man looked doing this. Defeated. Frustrated. Lost. Old before his time. Timothy understood this fully. Timothy channeled the old man's angst. The metaphor of his banging his head against the wall did not escape Timothy either. *School? Work? Car? Engagement ring? Taxes? Furnace? I am banging my head against the same damn wall.*

An idea occurred to him. Mom kept her address book on the shelf next to the kitchen table. Timothy opened it and looked for Uncle Bill's phone number. He and Timothy had a good relationship, though Bill lived in Tennessee.

On the fourth ring, Uncle Bill answered.

"Uncle Bill?" Timothy said.

"Hey, Tim. How are you, son?"

"I've had better days." Timothy told him about the recent events. He held back nothing.

After a long pause, Bill said, "Tim, I'd like to help you out. Heck, she's my sister, and you're my nephew, but things are not good for us this year. Business is way down. It's that oil embargo thing. The Arabs are screwing us, and Nixon's letting it happen. It's killing small business. I haven't taken a paycheck in six months. Everything I have is tied up in cash flow to keep the business afloat. I wish I could do something, son, but I can't."

"I understand, Uncle Bill. Things are tight everywhere these days. Things are tight for Sis and Ike, too. They're making ends meet. I'll figure out something. You know what they say—what doesn't kill you makes you stronger."

"That's my boy. You always were a positive young fella. How's school going?"

"Going well. Finals in a couple of weeks."

"You know the advice I gave your cousins. Study an hour longer than you think you need to and drink one less beer than you want to," Bill laughed.

"Not much time for beer drinking now, Uncle Bill. Well, I better get going. Thanks for listening."

"Anytime, son. My ears are always open. Tell your mom I'm thinking about her."

"Will do."

Why don't you call her yourself and tell her you're thinking about her if you're that concerned? Timothy felt like Sisyphus pushing that bolder up the hill. *Man, this is familiar ground. On my own. Again. No safety net. It'll probably be like this my whole life. What now? Frank.*

Timothy had not talked to his older brother, Frank, since last Christmas. They never got closer than the ten years that separated them. As the oldest, Frank thought too much had been heaped on him. He received a 4-F medical exemption for poor eyesight and never had to serve in the military. Timothy's service and Frank's exemption widened the gap between them.

Frank disconnected from his family after divorcing his first wife after just one year. He moved to Seattle, remarried, and had twins with his new wife. Frank called it a new life with a new wife. Frank hadn't seen the family in five years. He didn't even attend his father's funeral.

Frank worked in a dead-end management position for a banking company. Expecting Frank to help financially was a fool's folly, but Timothy needed to ask.

Frank answered the phone on the first ring. "Yeah?"

"Frank?"

"Tim, is that you?"

"Yes, how are you?" Timothy asked.

"Fine. Is she dead?"

"Who?"

"Mom. Isn't that why you're calling?"

Timothy told him what happened. He laid it all out there—the furnace, taxes, hospital bills, everything. He held back on his tuition bills, car situation and Cheryl's ring because he knew Frank didn't care anyway.

"Yeah, sounds tough. Wish I could help, but things are not good here. Mary has been laid up for the past six months. She got hurt at work, and they put her on pain pills, which she got hooked on, so now we're dealing with that while we're waiting for a settlement from her company. We enrolled the twins in public school because we couldn't afford to send them to a private school. Mary is real upset over that. Yeah, things are tough here, too. Did you call Uncle Bill?"

"Yes, and he can't do anything. It seems there's a whole lot of tough going around," Timothy said.

"Isn't that like the old goat? He never was much of an uncle to us, was he?" Frank continued with his tirade on Bill. Timothy recognized the tactic. Anytime he asked Frank for something, Frank redirected the conversation to some other obscure topic. In military terms, Frank used a diversionary tactic.

"Like I told ya, I'd like to help out, but we're already way into our emergency funds to pay the bills. The lawyer told us it might be another year before the company settles. Just can't do it. It's up to you, little brother. You've got to pull that wagon yourself. I know Leslie and Ike can't help. Too many kids and all. It's tough when you have a family depending on you."

"All right, Frank, but why don't you call her in the hospital?"

"Too much going on right now. By the way, how's your leg?"

"It depends on the day," Timothy said.

"You never had a problem with those painkillers, did you?" Frank said.

Just like Frank. He faked an interest in me to talk about Mary's addiction. "No, Frank. I did not have a problem with painkillers, just the pain."

"See, that's the way Mary got hooked. The pain wouldn't go away. Now, all she can do is sit in her chair and watch TV. It's tough, Brother."

"Sorry to hear it, Frank. I've got to go. Take care."

Pull that wagon yourself. What else is new, Frank?

Timothy knew the only place to find help was in the mirror. He returned to the dining room table and reviewed his scratch pad with the numbers on it. He wanted to sit there longer, hoping the numbers would change, but he was already late for work. He changed into his work clothes and left for the tree lot.

CHAPTER ELEVEN

TIMOTHY'S CAR STARTED immediately in spite of the temperature. This and light traffic made the drive to Schoen's easier. He thought, *Thank God for small blessings. Maybe the powers that be are conspiring to give me a break.* He pulled into the lot and saw Dez waiting.

"Is your clock broken, O'Rourke?"

"Sorry, Dez, I had to wait for the furnace guy to come by and give me an estimate."

"Yeah, that's right. Ed told me. What's that gonna cost you?"

"About twelve hundred."

"Man, those guys are thieves. They stick it to you when you need them the most. I should have gone into that business. You know, if you didn't have bad luck, you wouldn't have any luck at all."

"Yeah, thanks, Dez. Is that supposed to make me feel better?"

"Just statin' the obvious," Dez taunted.

Hoffen showed up. "Hey, Tim, how's your mother?"

"Hi, Hoffen. She's going to be okay. She'll have to stay in the hospital for a few days. The doctor said it was a lung inflammation from the furnace fumes. He called it respiratory failure. My brother-in-law got there in the nick of time and took her to the emergency room."

"It's good news she'll recover. What about your furnace? Can it be fixed?" Hoffen asked.

"Didn't you hear, old man? They're trying to stick it to him for twelve hundred bucks. That's the way those vultures operate. They go after the people who are desperate. It's a real racket, but what are ya gonna do? You need heat. It's a license to steal, I'm telling you."

"You know, Dez, you're not helping. The guy said he'd knock off one hundred if I paid cash."

"They do that so they don't have to report the income. Smart."

"I don't think so, Dez. The guy seemed like a pretty straight shooter," Timothy said.

"That's their shtick. They fake sincerity when you need them and then stick it to you. I'll tell you, O'Rourke, I don't plan on standing next to you in the next lightning storm."

"Come on, Dez. You're making the young man feel worse," Hoffen said.

"Just saying—"

Hoffen cut him off. "Tim didn't cause any of this. It happens. Mechanical stuff breaks down. It's just life."

"Yeah, like his car." Dez looked at Timothy. "I'm telling you, soldier boy, you need to get yourself a full-time job to get some scratch together so you can straighten out your life." Dez walked away.

"Man, talk about piling on."

"Oh, don't pay attention to any of that. Guys like Dez only see the cracks in the plaster."

"What do you mean?"

"When I was in Paris, I visited the Louvre. I stood in front of the Mona Lisa, admiring da Vinci's masterpiece. The man standing next to me said, 'Look at the wall around that painting. You'd think they would repair those cracks.' He was so obsessed with the cracks in the plaster surrounding the painting he couldn't see the beauty of the art. That's the kind of guy Dez is. He only sees the cracks and misses the beautiful things in life. Some people are like that."

"I understand what you're saying, Hoffen, but what if he's right? I reached out to my uncle and my brother to ask for help and they both turned me down. Tough times, they said."

"Okay, so?"

"So maybe I should listen to Dez and take some time off from school. I could get a full-time job, and once I straighten out my finances I can go back to school."

"You want to give up on your education?" Hoffen said.

"Not give up, just delay," Timothy said.

"Do you know how many people walk away from their dreams when things get a little tough, thinking they'll return to the dream when the timing is better? Too many. And the time never gets any better for them. Then, when it's almost too late, they discover that they have walked away from the one thing that gives them hope—their dreams."

Timothy looked confused. "I don't know, Hoffen."

"Look, Tim, the only question you should be asking yourself at this point is how you can make all of this work. You've been in a lot tougher spots than this, haven't you?"

"Yeah, I guess so."

"Then concentrate on what you can do right now to make this work. Never lose sight of your options. Don't listen to Dez. He's a distraction, even if he thinks he's doing you a favor. If you give up on your dreams, will that make your life better or worse?"

"Worse, I suppose."

"See, you're already beginning to think clearer. Stay with it. Keep moving forward. You can't move past something unless you keep moving."

Where have I heard that before?

"Come on ladies, let's get back to work," Dez yelled as he returned. "I ain't payin' you to stand around and jaw. Sell some pine."

Customers tended to take trees out of the racks and looked at them without putting them back where they got them. Straightening out the trees was cheap therapy for Timothy. Arranging the trees in some type of order relaxed him, and he reflected on his options. *How can I make my finances work? I have the early shift tomorrow at the hospital. I'll talk to the folks in the accounting department to see if there is a payment plan for Mom's hospital bills. That would take care of one of my problems. It's a start.*

"Sorry to hear about your mom, Tim. Furnace, too. Dez was in the shop tellin' Ed, and I heard 'em. I feel bad for ya. Tell ya what, I won't spit no tobacco on you for a few days. Ain't no fun teasin' ya when you're down," Kenny said.

"Thanks, Kenny, that's a relief. One less thing to worry about." Timothy grinned.

"Don't get used to it. Spittin' at ya and getting ya upset is one of the best parts of working here," Kenny said and flashed his pencil-lead teeth at Timothy.

Timothy finished his shift at the lot and drove home with a pocketful of tip money, which would come in handy for his date with Cheryl that night. They planned to go to Rossino's for some St. Louis–style pizza, but first he had to go home for a change of clothes.

CHAPTER TWELVE

AFTER WORK, A shower, and a change of clothes, Timothy picked up Cheryl. At Rossino's Timothy asked for a table where he could sit with his back to the wall.

"Man, I love this place," Timothy said.

"Me too. You remember our first date here?" Cheryl said.

"I do. The place was really crowded. I was awkward, nervous, and made lots of small talk."

"I thought it was cute. I had this vision of you as this war hero who faced danger, and you were struggling to hold eye contact with a girl," she said.

"I didn't feel like a hero—more like an awkward kid. It was high school all over again."

"See? Cute." Cheryl smiled.

Rossino's sat six short blocks from the university. The location and ambience appealed to the students. This basement of a large, 1930s apartment building had low ceilings, exposed pipes, too many tables, and a hodgepodge of chairs that did not match. Customers sat so close to other tables that they could hear each other's conversations. Most of the lighting came from candles on the tables. A few bare bulbs hung overhead. The smell of good food filled the air. People joked that they gained weight in there by taking a deep breath. This family-run Italian restaurant had the best pizza—thin crust and loaded with meat and vegetables. With five-star service, the owners treated guests more like family than customers. The prices attracted the poor college students, which made Timothy feel like he belonged.

"The usual?" Timothy asked Cheryl.

"Of course."

The waitress brought menus to their table. "Welcome to Rossino's. What can I get you guys?"

"Two Buds and a large Rossino's special without anchovies, and how about a couple of house salads to get us started?" Timothy said.

"I guess you don't need these." The waitress picked up the menus she'd laid on the table. "You got it, hon."

They talked about nothing in particular. With the crowd at this time of the evening, the noise bounced off the stone walls and wooden ceilings. Timothy found it difficult to hear Cheryl's voice. It was one of the few crowded places he could tolerate without feeling anxious.

The waitress returned with the beers. Cheryl fidgeted with her bottle, drawing sweat tracks on the table and picking at the label. Timothy sensed she wanted an opening for a conversation he didn't want to have. He didn't need any special training to recognize her signals. The time he spent with her took care of that.

He became more tight-lipped. *Better to keep it to myself,* he thought.

"To a crazy year." Timothy held up his beer for a toast, and Cheryl clinked his bottle.

She toasted with her left hand, and Timothy focused on the naked ring finger. It made him more self-conscious of his situation. *Why would she stay with a guy like me?*

"Timothy, I can see your mind is somewhere else tonight. What's bothering you?"

"You playing therapist?"

"No, I'm a concerned girlfriend. I can see the worry in your face. You're not that good at hiding your feelings, though I know you try."

He laughed and it took some steam out of his response.

"Hiding, huh? I'm trying to, but apparently I'm no good at it," he said.

"Timothy, when people get overwhelmed, it shows. It's tough to mask."

"Overwhelmed. That word makes me uncomfortable. It sounds like I'm out of control." He took a long pull on the beer, trying to wash the words out of his mouth.

"And that doesn't suit you?"

"No. Guys like me aren't supposed to get overwhelmed."

"Right, and doctors aren't supposed to get sick," she said. "It's okay to feel those things. You've got a lot going on right now. If you talked about them, you would feel better."

"What do you want to hear? That I feel guilty my mom went to the hospital because I didn't do more to fix the furnace?"

"That's a start," she said.

"Do you want to hear about next semester's tuition, or that I have to empty my savings to pay for the furnace? Do you want to hear I haven't figured out what to do about the real estate taxes and home insurance this year or Mom's hospital bills?"

"That's a lot to carry around with you," Cheryl said.

"Yeah, well, I've got big shoulders." Timothy said dismissively.

"They're not that big, and they don't have to be."

"I called my Uncle Bill and Frank, and they can't help. I'll figure it out." He drained the bottle on this draw and scanned the room for the waitress.

"Tim, I have some money put aside. I would be thrilled to help," Cheryl said.

Her words pierced his armor like a lightning bolt. His girlfriend, for whom he could not afford to buy a ring, wanted to help him financially. He teetered between hurt and insulted.

"I don't think so," he said sharply and then tried to be more gracious. "Thank you, no. I'll figure something out."

The salads arrived, and they ate in silence. After a few minutes, Cheryl broke the silence. "Those bills are not your fault. You may feel responsible to pay them, but you're not responsible for your mother's hospital bills, the furnace, or the taxes and insurance. Those things happen. You didn't cause any of it," she said.

"Yeah, well, they happened at a lousy time."

"There's never a good time to replace a furnace or to get sick," she said.

"Leslie and Ike can't help. They have too much going on with their kids. It's up to me."

"That's one of the things I love about you. You want to make things right. A lot of people would run from that responsibility." She had tears in her eyes.

"I guess." His tone softened with her words and tears. "I've been thinking about how I could make this work. Just because I want to go to school doesn't make it the right decision at this moment. Dez said he could keep me busy full time for a while. I could set aside enough to pay off what we owe and start back to school in the fall."

"Do you really want to walk away from your dream?" she asked.

He saw the disappointment in her eyes. "No."

The pizza arrived on a thin aluminum platter that had served thousands of pizzas before this and bore the scars to prove it. The waitress set it on the wire rack on the table. It hovered there, waiting to land on the empty plates in front of them.

"Another beer, hon?" she said to Cheryl.

"Sure, that would be great," Cheryl said.

"Me too," Timothy said.

"Got it. *Buon appetite.*"

Timothy looked at Cheryl and held up his bottle. "You know me; if one is good, two is better."

"And three's not enough," Cheryl added.

They ate in awkward silence for the next few minutes.

Timothy wiped his mouth and washed down the pizza with a swallow of beer. "There is another option. I've been giving this some thought. The hospital has a tuition program that if an employee works thirty-two hours a week and keeps his grades up, the hospital reimburses the tuition."

"That's a lot of hours with your school schedule," Cheryl said.

"Here's what I figure I can do. I will work Saturday, Sunday, Tuesday, and Thursday. Most of my classes are on Monday, Wednesday, and Friday. If I have a lab or something on Tuesday or Thursday, I can work the evening shift if needed."

"That's a heavy load, Timothy. It doesn't leave much wiggle room."

"I don't have to start until the Christmas season is over. Also, when I go in to work tomorrow at the hospital, I'm going to ask the folks in accounting if they can work out a payment plan for me so I can pay a little each pay period for Mom's bills."

Cheryl listened patiently to his plan. "That would be nice if they'll work with you."

"Yeah, I think so. That gets tuition and the hospital bills off the table. I can still take care of the furnace with my savings. The GI Bill and VA disability will be enough for Mom and me to live on. It's tight, but this could work. Mom gets a little Social Security, which could take care of some incidentals."

"It's good to see you focused on a solution. You have given this some thought. That's good. What about Dez's offer?"

"I'll talk to him and explain I don't want to do that yet."

"Good. You're staying in school and making it work," she said.

"Yep."

They sat for a while, Timothy loosening up. Cheryl smiled. He thought about how much she meant to him, but he still had some unfinished business to take care of. Tonight, he stepped forward on a new path. They sat for another round and left for Cheryl's house where he planned to stay in her brother's room for a few more days.

CHAPTER THIRTEEN

TIMOTHY LEFT CHERYL'S house on Sunday morning before anyone else had woken. He stopped on the way to work for a doughnut and coffee and arrived at Saint Elizabeth's for the 7:00 to 3:30 day shift. The psychiatry department at the hospital had two units. Timothy worked on an open unit next to the medical-surgical unit, Med-Surg for short. The other was locked and housed severely disturbed patients. Timothy preferred his shifts with the patients who had less severe problems. They came and went as they pleased throughout the hospital.

Sunday mornings had no scheduled procedures and this meant lighter duty. A few of the patients went to the chapel for Mass in the morning, and Timothy took those patients who needed help. That way he went to Mass, too. Timothy liked his coworkers. He saw them as hardworking and dedicated. He especially liked Walter, a Korean War veteran. Walter worked two jobs—one at Saint Elizabeth's and the other at the VA hospital. Though it was tough to raise a family on an orderly's pay, Walter and his wife made it work. Timothy respected that.

Timothy walked into the patient dayroom. "Hey, Walter. How's it going?"

"Oh, it's going, Tim," Walter said.

"How's Mr. Marconi?"

"He's stable, but the meds ain't doing much for his depression. Doctor Faro plans to start ECT tomorrow morning," Walter said.

During electro-convulsive therapy, the doctor sedated the patient and sent an electrical charge through the patient's brain to interrupt faulty thinking. Sometimes it worked. Other times, it didn't. Timothy had seen both outcomes. Either way, the brain was altered, and that bothered Timothy.

"Um, that's tough. Boy, Faro is pretty quick to use the button, isn't he?" Timothy said.

Walter looked around, leaned forward, and said, "Yeah, but don't say that too loud. He's got plenty of juice around here."

"I know. It's a bummer the drugs aren't helping Mr. Marconi. He's a nice guy. I hate to see him lose part of his memory."

"Well, that's what they do sometimes to make 'em better. Some stuff is better forgotten," Walter said.

"Maybe." *I've got a few things I would like to forget.*

"Timothy, Sister Mary Margaret would like to see you," said Katie, the charge nurse. Katie recently graduated from the nursing school at Timothy's university. They often talked about school topics. She was a cute and enthusiastic young nurse, and he enjoyed working with her. He even took some ribbing from Walter about Katie. Walter kidded him that Katie lit up when Timothy worked. This unwanted attention embarrassed him.

"It sounds mysterious," Timothy joked. He looked at Walter and winked. Walter grinned.

"I don't know. They called and asked for you to come down to Sister's office right now," Katie said.

"Okay, I'll go down there and be back in a few minutes," Timothy said.

He left the patients' dayroom and took the stairs down to the main floor. He preferred the stairs to the elevator and climbed them multiple times every day he worked. The stairs and his work at Schoen's made up his entire fitness program these days. His leg disliked the climbing, but it cooperated.

While walking to Sister's office, he thought, *This might be serendipity.* He told Cheryl last night he wanted to work out a payment schedule and pursue the hospital's tuition reimbursement option. Not knowing what Sister wanted, he thought he might have a chance to discuss this with her and gain her support.

Things are looking up. I still may have a way out of this.

The door to Sister Mary Margaret's office was open.

"Mr. O'Rourke, come in please," Sister Mary Margaret said. Her tone sounded icier than he remembered from previous conversations. When he entered the office, he saw Monica Kleinschmidt, director of nursing, sitting there.

That's odd. I didn't think Monica worked weekends. He nodded to her.

"Good morning, Tim, please take a seat," Monica said.

"Morning, Monica, Sister. If this is about my mother's hospital bill, I was hoping to work out a payment schedule—"

Sister Mary Margaret cut him off. "I was sorry to hear about your mother. No, this is not about her hospital bill. The accounting department can talk to you about that on Monday if you like. I'll get to the point. We know there's an effort to organize our employees and encourage them to vote on representation by the Service Workers' Union. The union has been vocal about their plans. We have seen them collecting signatures on the sidewalks outside of the hospital. It's public property, so we cannot do anything about that. We also know they are planning a demonstration and rally during the week between Christmas and New Year's. Union members and workers will be protesting wages and hours."

"Okay, what does this have to do with me?" Timothy said.

"One of our staff members saw you talking to a union representative in their picket line. It appeared you had taken some literature and wrote something on a clipboard."

"Okay, so?" Timothy tried to hide his irritation.

"Tim, the hospital is opposed to any move that attempts to unionize our employees. It would deal a devastating blow to us financially. Besides, this is not who we are. We are not a chemical plant or automobile factory that must worry about workers' safety issues. We are a hospital. We take care of people," Monica said in a softer tone than Sister's.

This must be the good-cop, bad-cop routine. "I still don't see why I'm here."

"Let me be direct, Mr. O'Rourke. Any employee found to be

supporting this effort will be terminated immediately," Sister Mary Margaret said with piercing eye contact.

"Sister, I have so many things running through my mind right now I don't even know where to begin. First, do you honestly believe I'm a union organizer?"

"Mr. O'Rourke, we're not sure what to believe," Sister said.

"Sister, you give me more credit than I deserve. That came out wrong. Look, I'm a full-time student and part-time employee. The only thing I'm trying to organize is my week so I can work more hours and maximize my study time."

Monica jumped in. "Tim, you must look at this from our position. We are trying to nip in the bud anything that would have a negative financial impact on our hospital. We are in the business of helping patients get better. It's unseemly that a hospital should have to deal with this sort of thing."

"I hear you, Monica. I don't know how to respond."

"Mr. O'Rourke, all you need to say is you have no intention of supporting this effort," Sister Mary Margaret said.

"Sister, with all due respect, is this even legal?" Timothy's blood began to boil. He spent the past few years fighting authoritarian powers and now he had to deal with this from a nun.

Sister smiled for the first time since he walked in the door. "We are a non-profit organization. We are exempt from many of the rules and regulations that define the limits of commerce in this country. We will be putting out communications to employees explaining our position. We want to be sure everyone understands the consequences of this unfortunate turn of events."

"You mean you will fire anyone who supports this?"

"Tim, those who support this initiative will probably find Saint Elizabeth's an uncomfortable place to work. Are we clear?" Monica smiled.

"Perfectly. No union," Timothy said.

"No union. We are a charitable institution and want to keep it that way," Sister Mary Margaret said.

Charitable? You're shitting me, right? Timothy wanted to laugh at the nun's words.

"One other thing, Tim. We are making some scheduling changes on hours. We will be moving you to nights on Tuesday and Thursday.

We will only need you sixteen hours a week for a while," Monica said. "It will begin on the next pay period."

"What? You're cutting my hours and putting me on nights because someone saw me talking to a union rep?"

"No, Mr. O'Rourke, we are changing your schedule because Doctor Faro complained you spend too much time counseling his patients," Sister Mary Margaret said.

"Sister, I don't counsel anyone. I listen. That's all. They want to talk, and I give them a sympathetic ear. Isn't that what we are supposed to do?"

"Mr. O'Rourke, you're an orderly. You serve meals, change linens, empty bedpans, and escort patients if they need help. Am I being clear?" Sister Mary Margaret said.

"Crystal. That goes to show you have nothing to fear union-wise from such a low-level employee."

"Okay, Tim, thanks for coming in to discuss this. It's good to see you." Monica continued to play the good cop, not good enough, though.

Timothy walked slowly to the elevator. *Why would they care if a low-level employee talked to some union people on the street? What a difference a few minutes made.* He went in there hoping to strike a deal for tuition and hospital bills and now felt lucky to get sixteen hours of work every week. *There's no future in this place. At least I have Dez's offer.* He climbed the stairs back to the unit and told Walter what happened.

Walter shook his head. "The man's at it again."

"Yeah, the man in a habit," Timothy said.

Sunday's shift dragged. Timothy wanted out of there fast, but the clock moved slowly. This happened when people felt unwanted somewhere. Timothy learned that time tortured the vulnerable. A hospital was supposed to be a place of hope, where people come to get well, not a place where dreams came to die. Hope was on life support that day.

Timothy finished his shift, changed clothes in the men's locker room, and headed to the employee's parking lot at the hospital. He saw a couple of union organizers hanging out but skirted around them, leaving plenty of daylight between him and them.

CHAPTER FOURTEEN

TIMOTHY PULLED UP to the Christmas tree lot thinking of it as an unlikely refuge from the hospital. Cars packed the lot, wedged in like books on a library shelf. *I bet Dez loves this.* He shut off the car's engine, but it sputtered for twenty seconds as if clinging to life.

He looked around and saw Kenny and Hoffen but no Dez. *Must be Ed's naptime. Dez is in the shop.*

Timothy walked through the lot, past Kenny, who was delivering a fabricated story about a tree to a customer. Timothy walked past Hoffen without saying a word and went directly to the shop to talk to Dez.

He opened the door and saw Dez and the register. "Hey, can we talk?"

"Sure, soldier boy. You're early. Did your car decide to cooperate today?"

"Not today, Dez. I've had a pretty tough day."

"What's on your mind?"

"Is the deal to work here full time still on the table?"

"Sure. Why the change of heart?"

Timothy told Dez what happened at the hospital, and how he had planned to pay his mother's hospital bills and get tuition reimbursement. He told him how the nun and administrator ganged up on him. He spilled everything. The union talk, the threats, and the cuts in hours. Timothy hadn't noticed that Hoffen followed him into the shop. The old man stood at a distance but close enough to hear the conversation.

"What did I tell you about those nuns? You can't trust nobody, ya schmo. Especially those birds. They'll screw ya every time. What do they call themselves, Sisters of Charity? Ha! The only charity they care about is how they line their pockets. What a racket. Are you willing to listen to me now?" Dez was smiling. He won.

"That's why I'm here. What did you say you would offer me full time?"

"After Christmas, you can start full time. I'll work you sixty hours a week between here and the other place. Tell you what I'll do. I'll raise your pay to two-fifty an hour and no taxes. That's a hundred and fifty a week, cash money. That's good money for a guy like you. It'll help you start digging out of that pit you're in," Dez said.

"What about the other guys?"

"You mean the mole head and the old man?"

"Yeah."

"The old man is gone anyway. He's temporary. I'll cut Kenny's hours. He's pretty much useless. Besides, he can't drive out to the nursery, and that's where I'm gonna need some help."

"So you're going to cut Kenny's hours to work me full time?"

"Yeah, I told you. This place ain't a home for the handicapped. Heck, him working part-time is charity for the most part anyway."

"I don't know. I have to think about this."

"Don't take too long. I'm gonna get someone else if you don't take it."

"All right, thanks, Dez. I'll let you know."

"Remember, I gotta make plans. Get out there, and help those morons sell some pine."

Timothy didn't notice Hoffen standing in the next aisle. He walked out with his head down, thinking about what he just heard. It disturbed him that Kenny would be cut back to part time. He believed this was the only place Kenny could work. He went directly to the fire barrel. The heat felt good on this cold afternoon. In the background, Kenny spun a yarn about a California tree. Timothy smiled for the first time since he left the hospital. He tried to laugh but didn't have it in him. Hoffen followed him out to the lot.

"Hey, Tim, I see you made it in," Hoffen said.

"Yeah, with time to spare. How's that grab you?"

"Everything okay?"

"No, not really," Timothy said.

"What's wrong?"

For the next few minutes, Timothy spilled his guts to Hoffen. The furnace bill, hospital bill, taxes and insurance, tuition, a car on life support, the hospital's threats of firing him, and reduced hours. He even disclosed his abandoned plans for Cheryl's ring.

As he stared into the fire, he said to Hoffen, "See this smoke? These are my dreams. Here and gone in the same moment. I'm beginning to think dreams are the poor man's religion."

"You sound like a political science professor paraphrasing Karl Marx," Hoffen joked.

"That's a scary thought," Timothy grinned.

"What are your plans?"

"Dez offered me a full-time job paying about a hundred and fifty a week. If I take it and work it through the end of summer, I will have enough to start back to school next fall."

"It would be difficult to work sixty hours a week and go to school," Hoffen said.

"The way I see it, a dream delayed is not necessarily a dream denied," Timothy said.

"That's poetic but not entirely true. What are the chances you won't go back to school in the fall?" Hoffen said.

"Probably fifty-fifty," Timothy said.

"So you're saying it's an even chance of abandoning your dreams and pursuing them?"

"Probably."

"How can you change those odds?"

"I don't know. Do you know what really hurts? Last night, before I even had to deal with the hospital, I told Cheryl about my money problems, and she offered me some of her savings. Can you believe that? Do you know how that makes me feel?"

"Loved?" Hoffen asked.

"No, embarrassed. I can't afford to buy her a ring for Christmas, and she wants me to take her money? She can do a lot better than me."

"She's trying to help."

"I don't want that kind of help. It makes me feel small. I'm too embarrassed to go back to her house tonight and tell her what happened to me today. I'll sleep at Leslie's on the sofa," Timothy said.

"So you think avoiding Cheryl is the best way to deal with this now?"

"For the time being."

"Timothy, one of the great benefits of living a long life is people get smarter by studying life's lessons. Right now, you're feeling low. Things look dark, I understand that. The problem with staring into the darkness is that it stares back at you. Some people let that darkness enter their souls. Sooner or later, they forget what the light looks like," Hoffen said.

"That sounds a lot like denial to me," Timothy said.

Hoffen smiled. "The only denial going on here is your denying yourself the hope that things will get better. Hey, I've got a customer to help."

Timothy finished his shift and called Cheryl to tell her he planned to spend the night at Leslie's home because it was closer to Mom's house and he had to be there early the next morning for the furnace repairmen. She bought the excuse, and he immediately regretted it.

CHAPTER FIFTEEN

MONDAY MORNING ROLLED in and Timothy had a hankering for caffeine. Coffee from this old percolator tasted bitter. Not strong, just bitter. Timothy grew up on the smell and taste. He remembered his father making morning coffee with this pot when Timothy was in grade school. The only thing that changed in the past twenty years was that Mom bought bags of coffee versus cans. She said it was fresher. That didn't matter, because the moment it hit that basket it tasted like the same old bitter syrup it had brewed for years.

He made a full pot of mud today in case the furnace guys wanted some. Timothy drank from a mug he purchased on his trip home from the war. It was heavy ceramic and wore the Ernest Hemingway quote, *Courage is grace under pressure.* He wondered how much grace he could show under the pressure he was feeling.

He liked drinking coffee at the dining room table. It reminded him of better days, family celebrations and big meals filled with adult chatter and cigarette smoke. They were good days—safe and innocent. While he was downing his first cup of the thick brown syrup, reminiscing, the doorbell rang.

"Morning, Tim."

"Morning, Fred. You guys are here bright and early."

"Like I said, we'll take care of you." Fred had the matter-of-fact conviction of a simple, working man.

"I've got some coffee in here if you guys want some."

"Might take some later. I wanna get these guys working. I don't pay 'em to drink coffee."

"Good enough," Timothy said. "Did you call that emergency line at the gas company?"

"Yeah, they said they would be here sometime this morning," Fred said.

"I plan to be here all day. I'm taking a day off classes to study."

"That sounds funny. Taking off school to study. Isn't that what you do in school?"

"Yeah, I guess it does sound funny, but on some level, it makes sense," Timothy said.

"Got it. You got the cash we talked about?"

"Yep. I will have it in hand tomorrow when you finish."

"Good enough for me." Fred turned to the crew. "C'mon, guys, let's get started on this."

"I'll be in the dining room if you need me," Timothy said.

"All right," Fred said.

The dining room was the heart of the house. People had to pass through it to get from one room to another. It was a comfortable place for Timothy to study when Mom wasn't around. He could spread out all of his books and materials on the table. Coffee, a comfortable chair, and a big table. As he sat he heard rolling thunder. It was the roar of Scoot's Harley-Davidson, announcing his arrival from a block away. Timothy smiled and went to the front door.

"Hey, Pete," Scoot hollered. Pete was short for Peter Pilot, the name given to all new helicopter pilots in Vietnam. Rank didn't mean much in a chopper. The pilots, who were warrant officers, knew that the gunners and crew chiefs, who were enlisted, had their backs; that was all that mattered. The crews joined in the good-natured hazing of new pilots. They were all Peter Pilots. New enlisted men were called FNGs, shorthand for *fuckin' new guys*.

"Hey, Scoot, that thing is louder than 519." That was the tail number of their chopper. Anyone who had ever heard the *whomp-whomp-whomp-whomp* of a UH-1H "Huey" helicopter would never forget it. It was as distinctive as the crack of an AK-47.

"I saw Fred at the doughnut shop this morning and he told me they were coming over here to replace your furnace," Scoot said.

"Yeah." Timothy filled in Scoot on the happenings of the past few days.

"Sorry to hear all this, man. How's Mom doing?" Scoot called her Mom too.

"She'll be okay. She's at the hospital still. She's going to Leslie's tonight. I spent the night there last night."

"I figured you didn't sleep here last night. Hey, when is she gonna make her oatmeal raisins?"

"God, Scoot, you sound like Kenny."

"Hey, don't compare me to that genius."

They laughed. This was the first time in a few days Timothy let loose.

"How do you know Fred?" Timothy said.

"I work on his bike. Good guy, Nam vet, Air Force. He was in maintenance or something. He told me he was giving you a cash discount."

"That's right."

"You gotta know that's a pretty big deal for him. He doesn't cut his price for anyone. Says it insults his craftsmanship."

"Really."

"Yep, he gave you the vet's discount. You know how it is, brother taking care of brother."

Timothy nodded.

"Speaking of that, did you hear the latest on the POWs?" Scoot asked.

"No, what?"

"Good news and bad news. Good news is Laos is releasing some pilots. Bad news is Bobby ain't on the list," Scoot said.

Timothy stared off into space. For him, this conversation was a time machine transporting him back to the day he and Bobby were shot down.

"C'mon, man, we all lost something that day."

"I don't know, Scoot. Bobby was supposed to transition to Cobras but stuck around to fly with me until the end of my tour."

"Listen, man, the snakes got shot down too. He could have as easily been shot down flying a gunship as he did flying slicks."

"True," Timothy said.

"You keep this shit up and you will be *dinky dau.*"

Timothy nodded.

"So how's your woman?" Scoot asked.

"She's good. Too good for me."

"Man, you're really feeling sorry for yourself today. You keep saying that kind of shit often enough, and she might agree with you someday."

"Maybe she should, Scoot."

"Hey, knock it off. She'd be lucky to get you. And you'd be lucky to have her. Look, I gotta go—this pity party is getting too crowded for me," Scoot fired back.

Scoot's straight talk put a different spin on things for Timothy. He nodded slowly.

"Thanks, Scoot. I appreciate you stopping by. Want some coffee?"

"No way. That sludge looks worse than the oil I drain from my bike. Look, Tim, I want you to do me a solid."

"What's that?"

"Lose the attitude. It doesn't wear good on a guy like you. You've always been a guy from the light side. Don't let the darkness blind you."

"You're right, Scoot. Thanks."

They exchanged fist bumps. Scoot kick-started his motorcycle and the windows shook. He cracked the throttle and left some rubber on the street as he rode away.

Timothy sat at the table. *What can I do to make this work?* He sipped the sludge and a name popped into his head: *Father Schmitt,* the dean of students and a former Army chaplain. When Tim started back to school, Father Schmitt had a meeting for all the veterans who were attending that semester. He told them if they ever needed anything, they should reach out to him. *Maybe he can help me with tuition assistance.*

Timothy went down to the basement.

"Fred, how long do you guys think you'll be here today?"

"Probably four o'clock, at least," Fred said.

"All right, I have to go out for a while. I should be back in a couple of hours."

"No sweat," Fred said. "If the gas company guy comes by, I'll sign the papers for you. I know those guys and they cut me some slack."

CHAPTER SIXTEEN

TIMOTHY WALKED TO Father Schmitt's office, rehearsing what he wanted to say. A secretary greeted him and said to wait while she checked with the priest. Timothy thumbed through some magazines.

After a few minutes, the secretary directed him into the inner office.

"Come on in, Tim. Good to see you." Father Schmitt extended his hand. It looked more like a fielder's mitt. He had a strong grip for a priest. It probably came from his chaplain days. "Have a seat, son."

"Thanks, Father."

"So how are things? Are you adjusting to civilian life?"

"I'm getting there, sir."

"*Sir*?" Both smiled. "Yeah, me too. It takes a while," Father Schmitt said.

"It's weird, Father. When I pass a professor in the hall or in the quadrangle, I catch myself thinking about saluting." After he said this, Timothy felt embarrassed to admit it. The priest's demeanor encouraged Timothy to open up.

"Tim, a lot of guys have trouble adjusting. At the end of their tours, most guys got on an airplane and were home within twenty-four hours. Did you know the World War II vets spent weeks getting home?"

"No."

"The government called it Operation Magic Carpet. They boarded transports that took a week or two to get home. They processed through repatriation centers on the West Coast. Then, because of the sheer numbers of veterans trying to get home, they faced delays crossing the country. They were welcomed home by the kindness and hospitality of grateful strangers. These strangers fed and housed the returning vets. That extra time made a difference for them. It gave them time to let things settle in. Your generation didn't have that luxury. You were greeted with jeers instead of cheers."

"Sounds nice for them. There was no magic carpet for us. I can see how that would help, Father."

"So why did you come in today?"

Timothy looked at the floor. "I didn't know where else to go."

"Is this a priest visit or a dean visit, Tim?"

"Both, I think."

"What's going on?" Father asked.

Father Schmitt listened as patiently as a therapist as Timothy told all.

"When you bring your girlfriend into it, it makes me feel like I'm back on duty, listening to lovesick and forlorn GIs." He smiled warmly. "What are you looking to do?"

"I don't know, Father. That's why I'm here. I need financial help and some hope. I already have student loans and don't want to dig that hole any deeper. Is there any type of help for a guy like me?"

"You mean like grants or scholarships?"

"Yes, any type of help."

"Candidly, no. Your grades are up there but not scholarship material," Father Schmitt said. He had lost none of his military bluntness. "You're already working, so it's not like you lack income, plus you get the GI Bill tuition assistance. I do understand your debt load is heavier than most students; I don't think more loans are the answer either."

They sat in silence until Father Schmitt piped, "One option is to talk to Colonel Flagger in the ROTC department to see what he could do."

"You mean go into ROTC and give the Army four more years?"

"It's an option, Tim. A lot of folks do this. It may not be ideal, but it is a solution."

"With all due respect, Father, it's not for me. Besides, my leg would be an issue."

"That's right. I forgot, sorry. The only other thing I can think of is a teaching assistant position next semester. It will give you some tuition relief. The problem is those usually go to graduate students."

"I would be willing to do that. It's mostly grunt work, right?" asked Timothy.

"Generally. There may be some class work or lab work. We've awarded these to undergrads in the past. Give me a couple of days, and let me see what I can do. Come back later in the week, and we can talk some more."

"Thanks, Father. I appreciate your help."

"Anything for our boys, Tim. By the way, speaking of the boys, tomorrow morning I'm taking a group of vets to sandbag at the River Des Peres. The Mississippi is pushing its banks, spilling onto the Des Peres, and the folks down there need some help. Who better to fill sandbags than a bunch of ex-GIs?" Father Schmitt said.

"I have to work the three-to-seven shift at the hospital tomorrow night, but I could be there in the morning. I don't have any classes scheduled for the morning."

"Great. We'll meet at nine at the Steak 'n Shake on the corner of Watson and River Des Peres. You know where that is?"

"Sure. I'll be there. Thanks, Father."

"My pleasure, son."

Timothy went over to the Student Union and called Cheryl at work with the news.

Smiling, he said, "Hey, guess what?"

"What?"

"I may have a way out. I talked to Father Schmitt today, and he's looking into a TA position for me next semester. It would help with tuition."

"That's great, honey. You work so hard it's nice to see some things go your way."

"Yeah, and get this. He asked me if I would join a group of vets tomorrow morning filling sandbags for the River Des Peres."

"How are you going to have time for that? Don't you have to work at the hospital?"

"Yeah, but that's tomorrow evening. Look, I'm trying to get some financial help, and it doesn't hurt to do a favor for the guy who can help me."

"I understand," she said.

"I'll swing by later, and we'll get a beer to celebrate."

"Sure. That would be fine. See you then. Tim, I love you."

"Yeah, me too." He smiled at this private joke between them. He had no difficulty with the words, but the way he said this made fun of guys in general.

"You goof, see you later," she said.

Timothy stopped at the bank on the way home from school. When Fred and his crew prepared to leave, Timothy told him about his plans for Tuesday. He said he would be there in the morning to open the house, but would leave for a few hours to help the other vets sandbag.

"Seems like you got a lot on your plate, brother," Fred said.

"Yeah, trying to keep it all together."

"Gotta respect that," Fred said.

"We should finish sandbagging by lunch, and I'll be right home. We can square up then if that works for you," Timothy said.

"Works for me. We'll be finishing up by then. It's going pretty fast down there. Not a lot to do with the ductwork. The new system will go in easy."

"That's good news," Timothy said.

CHAPTER SEVENTEEN

TIMOTHY HAD DECIDED to spend the night at Cheryl's after they went out for drinks. He only drank a couple of beers because he knew hangovers and sandbags didn't mix well. Morning suited Timothy's sober personality. He was an early riser. The Army made it a permanent habit for him.

Fred and his crew arrived on time at Mom's house and Timothy left for sandbagging. Even though he'd already driven it this morning, Timothy's car fell into a deep sleep. He cranked it dead. His neighbor Rob heard the grinding of the starter and offered to help.

"Again?" Rob said.

"Yep. This thing is dying a slow death, I think," Timothy said.

"I'll get my cables and we'll get this thing going," Rob said.

On the third crank the old Fairlane finally churned. Timothy thanked Rob and got to the rally point just in time. He saw the rugged-looking crew of vets standing around.

"You gotta be kidding me," a vet named Stubs yelled. "I can't believe my lying eyes. An officer is out here to help sandbag. What do you think boys?"

"A warrant officer, Stubs," Timothy said.

"I heard that," Stubs said. "No RLOs here except for the padre. Ain't that right, sir?"

"What's that, Stubs?" Father Schmitt shouted.

"Nothing, padre. Talking about real-live officers," Stubs said.

Stubs's real name was Leonard Stubble. He picked up the nickname Stubs in Vietnam. Everyone thought it was a shortened version of his name, but his buddies called him that because he rarely shaved.

"I see you're still not standing too close to the razor these days, Stubs," Timothy said.

"Got that right, Tim," Stubs said.

Green Beret Sergeant First-Class Stubble served two tours of duty in Vietnam as a member of the 5th Special Forces Group out of Nha Trang. Discharged from the Army in 1972, he started back to school and met Timothy there. They became fast friends.

"Padre Schmitt got you down here too?" Stubs asked Timothy.

"Yeah, I've been thinking about doing this, and he told me about it yesterday, so I thought I would come down and show a bunch of grunts how to do this job right. Besides, it keeps me on Father Schmitt's good side."

"Hear that, boys? This officer is going to show us how to fill sandbags," Stubs said. The group hissed.

"It's good to see you, Tim," Stubs said.

"Back at ya, Stubs. It seems like our schedules don't overlap much this semester, except for political science," Timothy said.

"Speaking of that, is Professor Leibert giving you any more grief?"

"No more than usual or anyone else, I guess."

"Well, he's leaning hard on the rest of us. You know that low-life burned his draft card in '68 when he was a graduate student," Stubs said.

"I heard that too. And it was all bullshit anyway, since he had a 2-S deferment for school. Just shows what a hypocritical asshole he is. He burned the card to make himself look good in front of those other assholes," Timothy said.

"I wouldn't be surprised if he was one of those hippie pricks that burned down the ROTC building at Washington U back in '70," Stubs said.

"Could be. I don't know where he was in those days," Timothy said.

The vets in his class nicknamed the freshly minted PhD David Leibert "Comrade" Leibert. Like much of the country, he hated the Vietnam War and anything associated with it, especially the warriors. He made no secret in the classroom about his feelings. Most had to sit quietly and bear it to salvage a grade.

"A group of us were thinking of complaining or boycotting or something. Want to join us?" Stubs asked.

"Not me. I'm not interested in his view on anything. All I need is my B in political science this semester, and I'm finished with him."

"Do you honestly think he will give you a B?" Stubs said.

"If I answer the questions correctly on the multiple-choice exam, he'll have to," Timothy said.

"You've got more faith in the system than I do, brother," Stubs said.

"What are you two men talking about?" Father Schmitt walked in on the tail end of the conversation.

"Nothing, sir. A couple of GIs griping about the system," Timothy said. "You know how it is."

"Yeah, nothing changes." Father Schmitt walked away.

Timothy looked back at Stubs. "I heard a rumor about you. Are you thinking about quitting school and going back in the Army?"

"Yes, that's mostly true. I'm thinking about it. Why?" Stubs asked.

"Why?"

"Man, I don't fit in here. I'm six or seven years older than the other students. I look at them and see boys and girls, not men and women. It's like we're a generation apart," Stubs said.

"Shit, Stubs, none of us fit in. People think we're all crazy, don't you know? Just watch the news." Timothy grinned and Stubs laughed. "When was the last time you felt you fit in somewhere?"

"When I was still in the military," Stubs said.

"That's my point. Nobody out here wants to hear about what we saw or did. They don't want to talk about that shit. It scares the hell out of them. Look, you've been around the world and seen things these kids can't even imagine. You've lived through stuff that wouldn't make it into their nightmares. Hell, most of them have probably never left Saint Louis. You're here for an education, not a fraternity party," Timothy said.

"Copy that. But there's more. When I was in Special Forces, it seemed like what we did mattered. We had a mission, a purpose. This stuff out here doesn't seem to matter. When I got back from Nam, I was stationed at Fort Bragg for eight months until I was discharged. Everything was fine there. I fit in. Here, back in the world, I don't. It's different here and now," Stubs said.

"Yes, it is, and thank God it's different. You're getting an education. You can do something with that," Timothy said.

"I hear you. The problem is that I look around and try to figure out stuff. In Nam, life was simple—kill or get killed. Being that close to death made me feel more alive. I miss the action. I miss jumping out of airplanes. Fuck, I even miss being shot at. Don't you ever miss that shit?"

"Yeah, I miss some of it. I miss flying. I miss my brothers. Sometimes, I miss the rush. You can't tell people that, though. They'll think you're nuts," Timothy said.

"Maybe we are. Here, nothing makes sense. There are times I want to start running and never stop. I see people protesting, and a lot the of times they don't even know what they're protesting. They have no respect for anything. No discipline. No sacrifice. All I see is the 'Me Generation,' a bunch of spoiled brats complaining about everything. It pisses me off. I don't want to be a part of that," Stubs said.

"So don't. It pisses me off too. It's like they're getting a free ride on all of us. Get your education, and do something meaningful with it."

"You're right, dude. Sorry to puke on you," Stubs said.

"I get it, bro. No problem. Did you talk to Father Schmitt about this?"

"Yeah, he said most of us go through this stuff. He even asked me if I was depressed. What the fuck? Like I'm gonna say *yes* to that. I told him that guys like me don't get depressed. He encouraged me to stay another semester and make my decision next summer. He told me I didn't have to make that decision today."

"That sounds like a good idea. Heck, if you could survive jungle school and Nam, you can last five more months around here," Timothy said.

"Good way to look at it."

"Right on," Timothy said and gave Stubs a high five.

For the next two and a half hours, they filled enough sandbags to protect a gasoline station in the path of floodwaters. The owner showed his appreciation by offering each of the guys a free tank of gas. Timothy rarely had the money to fill his tank to full. As crazy as it sounded to most people, Timothy thought his car ran better with a full tank.

When Timothy arrived home, Fred's crew was just finishing up. Fred demonstrated the new furnace to him, and Timothy paid Fred eleven hundred-dollar bills. Feeling broke, Timothy cleaned up for his Tuesday evening at the hospital. *Time to fill the coffers again.*

CHAPTER EIGHTEEN

HOFFEN STOOD AT the fire barrel warming his hands as the temperature hung just above freezing. Close by, Kenny fabricated a Christmas tree story. Dez and Edna worked the shop. Rush hour didn't apply to the tree business, but it picked up after dinnertime. Hoffen heard Timothy's car pull into the lot. He couldn't miss the sound. The engine gagged like a sick patient.

"Hey, Tim, how goes it?" Hoffen said.

"Oh, it's goin," Timothy said.

"Pardon?" Hoffen said.

"My life these days."

"You do keep busy."

"Got to. It's easier that way. Otherwise, I have too much time to sit around and think."

"I understand," Hoffen said. "Is your home warm again?"

"Yeah, we got the new furnace yesterday, and Mom came home last night."

"Glad to hear it. How's everything else?"

Timothy told him about the meeting with Father Schmitt and sandbagging.

"Yeah, life gets messy sometimes," Hoffen said.

"Some days are messier than others."

"You know, Tim, lots of things in life end messy."

"True."

"And some things never end."

"What do you mean, Hoffen?"

"War is unfinished business; lots of loose ends," Hoffen said.

"*Okaaay.* Where's this coming from?"

"I asked you about your week. You told me things were fine at home, next you told me about meeting with a priest who is a former Army chaplain, and then sandbagging with a group of vets. Last Friday, you told me about being shot down and two of your crewmembers died. I saw your face when that customer last week called his son Bobby. And you walk around in an Army jacket. Do you see a pattern here, Tim? You never mentioned your girlfriend."

"And so?"

"Tim, you've got unfinished business. You must realize you left the war, but it did not leave you. It traveled all the way home with you. You carry it around with you everywhere you go. Some men understand this. Others don't want to think about it. It's not going to leave. It's part of your life experience. For the lucky ones, it finds a space, somewhere to fit in. Until then, it's unfinished business, and that affects your life."

Timothy stood silently for a few moments. Hoffen didn't rush him.

"You sound like you know this firsthand," Timothy said.

"Yes, I was a medical assistant in World War I. My job was to help put people back together. I learned something valuable from that experience."

"What's that?"

"We're all broken in some fashion—that's the nature of the human condition. But that's not the issue. What counts is how we put ourselves back together," Hoffen said.

"That's pretty deep, but I get it."

"I'd like to take credit for that profundity, but I'm not the first to see it. I learned it from a friend I met in Italy, Ernie. I was attached to a field hospital in Milan. Ernie was one of my patients. We hit it off immediately, both Americans. He was wounded on a Good Samaritan mission to the front. He took shrapnel to the leg, a lot of it. It nearly took off his leg."

"I know what that feels like. What happened to him?" Timothy said.

"I left before he recovered. I wondered that myself. I was reassigned to the front in France."

"That's the way it is, isn't it?" Timothy spoke from experience.

"Yes, unfinished. After the war, I stayed in France for a while. In the summer of '21, I was walking down the Champs-Elysees and heard someone call my name. Strange hearing that in a foreign country. I looked over to the small café and saw Ernie sipping a glass of wine. We finished that bottle and another. Imagine that, all the years that passed, and I found him in Paris."

"What was he doing there?" Timothy asked.

"He was working for a newspaper. I left him sitting there that day and never saw him again. Just one of life's loose ends, unfinished business. There's a lot of that in life."

"That's how I feel. When I came home, I left friends behind. I left one in particular on the battlefield. For the first three months I was home, I sat in front of the television watching Walter Cronkite deliver the latest war news. I went through a lot of beer in those months. I kept thinking about those we left behind and feeling guilty I was home and they were still there. You can't leave those guys that quickly when you've gone through a lot together," Timothy said. "You're too invested in each other."

"Good point. Feel sad—that's okay. Be remorseful over the loss, but don't feel guilty because you made it home. Guilt is one of the most useless emotions. Once it takes root, it spreads like weeds into other areas of your life. When a person has seen what you've seen, feeling sad at times is about one of the most human things you can do for yourself. What would it say about you if you didn't feel sad about those experiences?"

"That's a pretty good point. Guilt and loose ends pretty much describe where I'm at."

"See? You brought home unfinished business. Once you begin finishing what you're supposed to finish, you'll feel better. I know," Hoffen said.

"What do you mean what I am supposed to finish?"

"You have something you must do in this world. That's why you're here. That's why you must stay true to your dreams. They are the path to your destiny."

"You're still patching people together, aren't you?" Timothy said.

Hoffen smiled. "We all do something. Remember, Tim, it's as easy to listen to the voices of hope as it is to stare into the darkness of the abyss. You've got a choice."

"Speaking of darkness, I've got to go inside and talk to Dez. He wants an answer on his offer. I keep trying to dodge it. I'll tell him I've got to wait to talk with Father Schmitt again. Dez should be okay with that," Timothy said.

"You know how to listen to Dez? Listen with your ears, not your heart. Don't let him in. Hear him, don't believe him," Hoffen said.

"Good advice. Thanks. Hey, do you want to come to dinner on Saturday after work? You can meet my mom and Cheryl."

"Wouldn't miss it," Hoffen said.

"Great, we'll go straight to my house after work."

"Perfect," Hoffen said.

CHAPTER NINETEEN

CHERYL INVITED TIMOTHY over for dinner on Thursday evening to show off her culinary talents. Her parents went to Chicago to visit her younger sister, so they had the house to themselves, a luxury they rarely enjoyed. Timothy loved how she made life simple. He arrived at her house.

They smiled, kissed, and hugged in the doorway.

"I'm excited. It's not every day I get to show off my domestic talents," Cheryl said.

"Me too. Can't wait," Timothy said. "So, your parents are in Chicago to visit your sister?"

"Yeah, but I think Mom wanted an excuse to go Christmas shopping on Michigan Avenue."

"So we're all alone?" he said.

"Yes, Mister O'Rourke, and we're going to enjoy this wonderful dinner I prepared." Cheryl called him *Mister* when she wanted to change the tone of a conversation.

"Wow, it smells good in here. What's for chow?"

"Fried chicken. My own recipe. Peas, carrots, and rolls. I don't know how the rolls will turn out. I followed your mom's recipe, hoping I got it right. I'm sure I added the right amount of love." Cheryl smiled.

"I'm sure they will be fine," Timothy said. "How about a beer?" He held up a bag with the beer.

"The red-white-and-blue cans?" Cheryl said.

"Yep, PBR," he said.

"You're predictable if anything."

"I told you. I got a taste for this stuff in Nam. We used to drink this stuff warm when it came in on pallets."

"Well, I don't like my beer warm, so put it in the refrigerator," she said.

Cheryl walked to the dining room, and Timothy went to the kitchen. She thought, *That conversation is always just below the surface. He never passes on an opportunity to say something. It's trying to work its way out. He's struggling to get this into words.*

"Come on in here after you put that beer away," she said.

They talked while sitting at a perfectly set dining room table. China. Crystal goblets. The right amount of silverware in the right places. Cloth napkins.

"Is this your stuff?" Timothy said.

"Yes."

"It's beautiful. Looks expensive," he said.

"Thanks. I reached deep into my hope chest and pulled it out." The moment she said this Cheryl regretted it. Timothy didn't respond. She didn't want to appear to be pressuring him. She knew he already had enough on his mind. She shifted topics quickly.

"So, I bet Mom is thrilled with the new furnace," she said.

"Oh yeah. She loves the heat but is worried about how I paid for it. She feels guilty that I emptied my savings account."

"I can understand that," Cheryl said. "When do you see Father Schmitt again?"

"I'm going by his office tomorrow to see if he was able to do anything for me."

"That's good news. TA positions go mostly to grad students," she said.

"They do, but he said he would look into it. I don't know if there's anything there, but I know he's a man of his word. If it's there, he'll find it."

Cheryl didn't want to discourage Timothy, but she knew TA positions did not go to undergrads. "Tim, I worry about you. You work hard to keep everything together. I worry about you breaking."

"I work as hard as I need to. Besides, as Hoffen says, we're all broken in some way. It's how we put ourselves together that matters," he said.

"Good advice. Even though I haven't met him, I think I like that man," she said.

"Then you can meet him Saturday night at dinner. I asked him to join us. Mom said she would make a pot roast."

"I would like that." She got up from the table. "I'm going to check on things."

Cheryl left Timothy sitting at the table, picking at the beer can. He downed the Pabst and went for another. They returned to the table with the food and sat in silence until it became awkward. Cheryl used silence in her job and at times found it helpful to draw out other people.

"Man, this is great chicken," said Timothy.

"Thank you, Mister O'Rourke. I'm pleased it meets your palette's approval."

Timothy pushed the food around on his plate. Cheryl sensed that Timothy was struggling with the small talk.

"You know what's really bugging me? You could do a lot better than me," he said.

"*What*? What do you mean better than you?"

"Look at me. Not just broke—in debt. I'm in a hole, and I keep digging. You deserve more than this."

"More than what?" she said.

"Look, I'm damaged goods. Why waste your time waiting for me to get out of this hole?"

"First, you're not damaged goods. Second, I'm not wasting my time. This is how relationships work. You go through stuff together. And as far as your debt goes, who cares? I don't care about the money."

"It's easy to not care about the money when you have some," Timothy said.

"I'm sorry, that came out wrong," Cheryl said. "I didn't set out to find a rich man. I set out to find a good man, and you're a good man."

"It's just when we talk about the future, I have nothing to offer you. People need more than hope in their hope chests," Timothy said.

His sarcasm about the hope chest did not escape Cheryl, but she let it slide.

"Are you talking about material things?" she said.

"Yes, and debt. How can I take care of you when I can't even take care of myself?"

"So there it is. The male ego?"

"Yeah, so?"

"So you don't have to do this all by yourself. This is what couples do. They are there for each other. I am here for you. Besides, I don't need you to take care of me. I can take care of myself."

"I didn't mean it that way. I don't want your money," he said.

"I'm not offering you money. I'm talking emotional support. We'll figure out the other stuff. Timothy, you have this thing about carrying the world's problems on your shoulders. They're not that big, and it's not your job. Others have to help, too."

"I didn't mean to be flip," he said.

"I know. Look, you're loyal, generous to a fault, and loving. You're a good person. That's the man I love."

"Even if I'm broke?"

"Even when you're broken," Cheryl said.

They sat quietly for a few moments.

"I'm defensive tonight. Hoffen said something that is chewing on me. He talked about unfinished business. It describes my life perfectly. Too many loose ends. No security. No stability. When will I ever feel safe again?"

"Safe?" Cheryl zeroed in on this word.

"Stable—you know, financially," Timothy said.

"Things are a little unsteady in your life right now. It's natural for you to react this way. You want to tie up your loose ends or, in Hoffen's words, finish your business," she said.

Timothy rubbed his leg.

"Does it hurt tonight?" Cheryl asked.

"Yeah, a bit. I think sandbagging got to it, but I couldn't let a bunch of grunts see it."

"Guy thing?"

"Yes, a guy thing."

"Timothy, look at me. I want you. I want the war hero, the scared little boy, and the in-debt you. All of you. And yes, the broken you."

"But you could do much better."

"Stop saying that. It's insulting to me. Settling with you is not settling in life. Look at me. I love you, warts and all. Can you say the same about me?"

"Yes, of course. I don't want to disappoint you."

"You won't, unless you give up. Hang on a minute, I have something for you."

Cheryl left the room and returned with a coffee mug.

"I found this in a gift shop the other day and thought of you. What do you think of the inscription?"

Timothy read aloud the inscription on the mug. "Don't die wondering!" He smiled. "You know, it could read *Don't die wandering.*"

"Yes, that too. Timothy, the only time I feel disappointed is when you stare so deeply into the darkness that you cannot see light."

"Boy, you sound like Hoffen."

"I told you. I like him already."

"Like I said, you'll get a chance to meet him Saturday."

"I look forward to it."

"So, how long are your parents going to be gone?"

They both smiled.

CHAPTER TWENTY

TIMOTHY ARRIVED AT Father Schmitt's office at about two on Friday, after his final class of the day. He had a small window of time before he needed to be at the hospital for his evening shift. *No sense being late and giving the old penguin a reason to fire me.*

Waiting rooms had the broadest selection of yesterday's magazines. Old news. Timothy rummaged through the stack and one cover grabbed his attention—a February 1973 *Time* issue. The cover pictured a family holding a sign that said, *Welcome home Daddy!* The headline below the *Time* emblem read, *The Prisoners Return.* Timothy began reading the cover story about the repatriation of POWs from North Vietnam. His thoughts drifted to Bobby.

What's happened to him? Where is he? Dead or alive? Captured? Will he come home? What has his family heard? These questions fired in his mind faster than a minigun burst.

A growing restlessness made him want to get up and run out of the office. He'd learned about anxiety and panic attacks in psychology class and recognized the symptoms. In real life, anxiety made his bones itch. He experienced distress in small, confined spaces. The walls closed in. He developed tunnel vision. He wanted to run, break loose, and scream.

"Father will see you now," the secretary said.

Her words startled him back into the moment. *Thank God. I was ready to crawl out of my skin.*

"Thanks, Mrs. Ford."

"Timothy, come on in and please sit," Father Schmitt said.

"Thanks for seeing me again, Father."

"Happy to do it, but I wish I had better news."

Timothy saw the military background in this priest. Though a man of God, Father Schmitt had the directness of a military officer.

"Are you still sore from sandbagging?"

"Not really, but I'd be lying if I said I didn't feel it on Wednesday." *Come on, Father, enough foreplay. Let's get to the point. Are you going to help me or not?*

"Like I said, I wish I had something positive to tell you," Father Schmitt said. "As I suspected, the TA positions are already filled for next semester except for the one in the Political Science Department. And they—"

"I know. They're not looking for someone with my background," Timothy said, irritated. *Let's add insult to injury.*

"I was going to say they want a political science major, preferably a grad student," Father Schmitt said.

"Okay." He was embarrassed by his defensiveness.

"As far as scholarship money, your grades aren't there yet. If you get a 4.0 this semester and next, there may be something we can do," the priest said.

"That's all?" Timothy said sarcastically. "At this point, Father, that's a pipe dream."

Father Schmitt ignored the comment. "The other thing—because of your GI Bill benefits, I can't get you any hardship money because the awards committee feels you receive enough to cover tuition. They don't take into account other living expenses."

Timothy sighed and looked to the ground.

"Also, on a whim, I talked to Colonel Flagler about ROTC help. He said because of—"

"My leg?" Timothy said.

"Er, yes," Father Schmitt said.

"That's okay, Father, I get it. Damaged goods."

"Timothy, look. A lot of the guys who came back have similar financial challenges, and for the married ones, it's worse. You can't lose hope. That's what will keep you going."

"Father, it's not losing hope that's the issue. It's the obstacles I deal with."

"Tim, I feel more like a chaplain now than a dean. I'll tell you what I tell all the other vets who come through here. What you're dealing with now is nothing compared to what you've been through. You're stronger than your problems. You have stared into darker places than this and prevailed."

"Thanks for the pep talk, Father, but I don't feel stronger at this moment. I've got to go. Work and studies. Two papers to write and exams coming up. I'll be fine, Father. I'll figure out something."

"Okay, Tim. I'm here whenever. You know that, right?"

"Yes, I do. Thanks, Father. Bye."

Timothy left the office and crossed the quadrangle to the parking lot. He felt like the damaged goods that he was. *Everyone keeps telling me not to give up hope. A lack of hope isn't the problem. It's the lack of options that is getting to me.*

On his drive to the hospital, Timothy thought more about his conversation with Father Schmitt. *What else is there but hope for a guy like me? Hope dies a slow death for the desperate.*

Timothy had not yet begun his new work schedule. Nights were tough on sleep patterns and relationships, but he would earn a thirty-five-cent-an-hour premium for working these hours. If he timed it right, he could get some sleep before work on Tuesdays and Thursdays and nap after school the next day. It could work if nothing else got in the way. He held out hope for the thirty-two-hour schedule and tuition reimbursement. Today, he had picked up an additional shift in the evening.

The pickets stood by the front door this afternoon. When Timothy saw one approaching, he held out his arm like a fullback stiff-arming a tackler. He didn't want anyone in the administration to see him talking to an organizer. He dodged the organizer but not Sister Mary Margaret's watchful eye. As he entered that main door, he saw her talking to a member of the medical staff. She gave Timothy a perfunctory nod as he passed her.

Did she see the picket approach me? "Good evening, Sister."

She responded coolly, "Timothy."

This is a woman of God? A "sister of charity"? The world is strange.

Maybe Dez is right. Maybe it's all a racket. Stop! I can't start thinking like Dez. That's like giving up on life.

Timothy took the stairs to the second floor. Every step sent a sharp pain up his leg. He sucked up the pain and climbed. As he approached the nurses' station, he saw Walter charting his notes for the evening shift.

"Hey, Walter," Timothy said.

"Hey, Tim. Where you been?"

"School. Work. You know. They're moving me to nights."

"Yeah, I heard. Some nights are better than no nights."

"What do you mean by that?" Timothy asked.

"Word's out that layoffs are coming."

"What?" Timothy said.

"Yeah. Man, these nuns are serious about this union mess. They say they're gonna cut off the head of the snake," Walter said.

"Great, I'm probably on the short list," said Timothy.

"Don't know, man."

"Timothy, I need to see you," Loretta said.

"Here it comes, man," Timothy said to Walter.

Walter raised his eyebrows and shook his head like a man who had seen plenty of trouble.

Loretta, the head nurse for the Psych unit, ushered Timothy into the breakroom behind the nurses' station. "Timothy, as you know, the administration is concerned about the organizing activity outside the hospital."

Here we go again.

"Yeah, I heard firsthand from Sister and the director of nursing." *So you're doing their dirty work, right?* Timothy took a deep breath. *Take it easy, big boy.*

"And because of that, they're letting some people go—"

Timothy didn't wait for Loretta to finish the sentence. He had his fill. "Do I finish this shift or should I leave?"

"Oh, heaven's no. You're not being terminated. We're transferring you to a different floor. They need a night orderly because of the folks leaving that floor."

"Oh. Where to?"

"You'll be working nights on Three-Main," she said.

"The Med-Surg unit?"

"Yes. They work a different pace than the psych unit. They do treatments and vitals all night. There's no studying on nights there," Loretta said.

"Oh, I know. I've worked it before when they needed help. At least it makes the time pass faster. I guess the good news is I'm still working."

"Timothy, I know what's going on and I don't like it, but I'm just the messenger."

"Thanks, Loretta. I'm wondering how a religious organization can treat people like this?"

"On the record, I cannot respond to that. Off the record, you're not alone in your feelings. You start next week—enjoy this evening's shift," the head nurse said.

"Okay, thanks. I guess," he said.

He left the breakroom. Walter looked up when he heard Timothy approach.

"Still here, Walter," Timothy said.

"That's good to hear, man."

"At least for this evening."

"Say what?"

"Beginning next week, I'm moving to Three-Main on nights," Timothy said.

"Oh man, you know what they doing?" Walter said.

"I know, but at least I still have a job."

"Now you know how the brothers feel. The man's always messin' with ya," Walter said.

"I hear that," Timothy said.

"VA may still have openings if you want me to check it out for ya," Walter said.

"Thanks, Walter, but I can't work there. I've got the wrong kind of history with that place."

"Well, there's always room for a good man who wants to work. Good luck, my brother."

"Thanks, Walter. And if you get bored here, we'll probably need some help on Three-Main."

"Oh, hell no," Walter said.

CHAPTER TWENTY-ONE

TIMOTHY GOT A good night's sleep Friday after working the evening shift at the hospital. Time passed quickly on Saturday at Schoen's. They moved a lot of pine, which made Dez happy, and the tips made Timothy, Hoffen, and Kenny cheerful, too.

Hoffen and Timothy finished their shift at four o'clock. Kenny worked a little later to help Dez get ready for Sunday. Hoffen told Timothy he wanted to go home and change for dinner and would meet him back at the store at six. Timothy agreed and went home to clean up for dinner. At six, Timothy picked up Hoffen in the parking lot at Dez's.

Hoffen dressed for the occasion. He wore a blue sport coat with gray trousers and a tie.

"I'm glad you're joining us tonight for dinner, Hoffen. The house smells great. Mom has been working on this most of the day. But you didn't have to get so dressed up for tonight."

"It's a generous offer, Timothy. I don't often get a home-cooked meal made by someone else. I wanted to show my respect for the invitation."

Timothy nodded.

"I was surprised at how busy we were today," Hoffen said.

Timothy nodded again, looking straight ahead. "Yeah, I think people are beginning to feel the urgency of the holidays. Cold weather does that. Did you notice Dez's mood? Money makes him smile."

"Yes, I did notice. Unusual, for sure," Hoffen said. "The smile, that is."

"I don't know how to take him. Probably, the simplest explanation works best. His psychology doesn't seem to run deep. He's miserable most of the time. He seems mad at the world."

"Timothy, people like Dez never get over the anger of being born," Hoffen said.

"Wow, I never thought in those terms. I have to chew on that," Timothy said.

They rode in silence for a while. Hoffen wanted Timothy to digest his observation.

"What do you mean angry over being born?" Timothy asked.

"Some people enjoy being miserable and enjoy watching other people's misery, too. I know that sounds odd, but it's true. For one reason or another, they have learned not to expect much from life. No expectations mean no disappointments. In turn, they don't expect to give much back, either," Hoffen said.

Timothy looked pensive. Hoffen let the silence simmer. Five minutes later, they arrived at Timothy's home.

"Well, we're here." Timothy slowed to a stop in front of the 1940s Cape Cod–style home—stained-glass window in the front door, faded green shingles, chipped white trim, and a roof that needed some work. Timothy shut off the engine and, like most days, the car sputtered and gasped.

"Have you lived here your whole life?" Hoffen asked.

"Yes, except for the years I worked for Uncle Sam."

"Of course. It has a comfortable feel to it. Do you know who Edgar Guest is?"

"No, I can't say that I do."

"He was a newspaper columnist, and he wrote a piece called 'It takes a heap of livin' to make a house a home,'" Hoffen said.

"We've done a heap of livin' here. Don't ask Mom, or she'll give you more than an earful," Timothy said.

"That's fine," Hoffen said.

Timothy opened the heavy wooden front door. It squeaked, announcing their arrival. The smell of pot roast enveloped them the way clouds surround an airplane. Hoffen inhaled the aroma like a drowning man gasping for air. Every breath fed him.

"Mom, we're here," Timothy said.

Mom came out of the kitchen to greet them. They didn't often have company for dinner, and Mom loved to polish the apple. She wore her best apron and wiped her hands with a fresh dishtowel. She'd fixed her hair and colored her face with some makeup. She called this "company-ready."

"Mr. Hoffen, it's nice to meet you," Mom said.

"Mrs. O'Rourke, the pleasure is all mine." Hoffen extended his hand. "It's kind of you to invite me to dinner. It smells wonderful. I've been looking forward to this all day."

"It's nice to meet Timothy's friends and coworkers," Mom said.

"Thank you," Hoffen said.

"Yes, Timothy was the kind of child who brought home the stray dogs."

"Mom," Timothy said.

"Oh, Mr. Hoffen knows what I mean. One time, Timothy even brought home that other man he works with. I think his name is Kenny. Deplorable table manners, but he tried to be polite. He must have been hungry since he ate a whole plate of my oatmeal raisin cookies."

"Mom, Hoffen doesn't want to hear this," Timothy said.

"Oh, dear, I'm sure it's fine, isn't that right Mr. Hoffen?" Mom said.

"Yes ma'am, it is. And please, call me Hoffen."

"Mom, I saw Cheryl's car out there. Where is she?"

"In the kitchen. I gave her a job to do. Honestly, I don't think that girl has ever mashed potatoes before. I don't know what these younger women are coming to."

"Well, Mrs. O'Rourke, if ladies like yourself show them the way, I'm sure they will be fine."

"Why thank you, Mr. Hoffen." Mom touched her hair.

Timothy smiled at Hoffen.

"Come on, Hoffen, let me introduce you to Cheryl," Timothy said.

They walked past the dining room table. Mom used her best place settings, china and crystal from better times. Thanksgiving and Christmas were big family gatherings when his father was still here. That all passed away with his father.

"Mrs. O'Rourke, you have set an elegant table," Hoffen said.

"I can tell you're a man who enjoys the finer things," Mom said. She beamed whenever someone noticed her preparations.

"Cheryl, I want you to meet someone," Timothy said.

"Hi, sweetie." She gave him a peck on the lips.

"This is Hoffen. Hoffen, this is the best part of my life, Cheryl."

"I can see she is. And Timothy, I know you're pretty good with words, but your words did not do her justice. Cheryl, you are breathtaking," Hoffen said.

"Oh my. Timothy told me a lot about you, but he didn't tell me what a charmer you are," Cheryl said.

"All right, you two, get something to drink and quit distracting the help," Mom said.

Timothy grabbed a couple of beers from the fridge, and he and Hoffen retreated to the living room to wait for dinner. In the kitchen, Mom and Cheryl continued to work on dinner.

"He seems nice, Mrs. O, doesn't he?" Cheryl said.

"Yes, Cheryl, he does. He's certainly not like those other dreadful people that work at Schoen's. Okay, put the potatoes and rolls on the table, and I'll get the meat."

"Yes, ma'am," Cheryl said.

In the living room, Timothy and Hoffen drank their beers and talked. Hoffen said, "How long has your father been gone?"

"Ten years," Timothy said. "Don't raise his name to Mom or we'll be here all night."

"Timothy, your mother seems like a delightful woman—a little lonely maybe, and I suspect she's trying to get used to the idea there's another woman in your life. Mothers get kind of funny that way," Hoffen said.

"Yep. That's Mom. She's funny that way." Timothy gulped his beer.

Walking into the living room, Mom said, "Okay, soup's on. Who's funny?"

"You, Mom. You're a scream," Timothy said.

They sat to a meal of pot roast, green beans smothered in mushroom soup, mashed potatoes, gravy, fruit salad, and Mom's homemade rolls. Apple pie waited for them in the kitchen. They said grace, followed by the necessary small talk to move food around the table. They took their first bites and Mom broke the silence.

"Mr. Hoffen, are you from around these parts?"

"It's just Hoffen, ma'am."

"Okay, I'll call you Hoffen if you call me Dorothy," Mom said.

"Fair enough, and no. I'm not from here, but I've been in the area for the past few years," he said.

"Yes, I wondered why I haven't seen you around here. You know this is a small community," Mom said.

"It is, Dorothy. I'm not from any one place. I've moved around most of my life."

"So you're a traveling man?" Mom said.

"You could say that. That's a nice way to describe it. Cheryl, these mashed potatoes are excellent. You did a great job. Dorothy, you taught her well," Hoffen said, deflecting the conversation away from him.

"Thank you, Hoffen," Cheryl said.

"So, Mr. Hoffen . . ." Mom began between bites, "don't you think Timothy works too hard?"

"*I* do," Cheryl said.

"Yes, dear." Mom shot Cheryl a dismissive look. Hoffen noticed the look and nodded at Timothy.

"Yes, ma'am, he works hard. Too hard? I don't know. Timothy is an ambitious young man. He has dreams and a lot of drive. And the world needs a lot of people like him."

"That's true. But I feel he pushes himself too hard. With schoolwork, two jobs, and trying to keep things together around here for me, I think it's too much," Mom said.

"He's a good man," Hoffen said.

"Yes he is," Cheryl added.

"Cheryl, I understand you're a social worker, is that right?" Hoffen asked.

"Yes, that's true. I mostly work with single moms."

"That's wonderful, a real calling," he said.

"Mr. Hoffen, did you know Timothy was a war hero, too?" Mom said.

Timothy turned red. "Mom, Hoffen didn't come over to hear my life story."

"What? Well, it's true, dear. You were a war hero," Mom said.

"We've talked about it a little," Hoffen said.

"He earned two Bronze Stars in that dreadful war. He's a brave man. He doesn't run when things get tough. I don't know where he gets that from. Certainly not his father."

"Dorothy, he probably gets that from you," Hoffen said.

Mom started to put a bite of roast beef in her mouth but stopped at Hoffen's compliment. She smiled. Timothy shook his head in disbelief. Cheryl smiled, and he returned it.

"Why, thank you, Mr. Hoffen. That's kind of you to see that," Mom said.

"Hoffen, do you think the Cardiac Cardinals will make the playoffs this year?" Timothy said, trying to change the conversation.

"They might. They certainly have earned that name this season, haven't they?" Hoffen said.

"They sure have—"

Mom cut him off.

"Do you have a family, Mr. Hoffen?"

"No, Dorothy, I do not."

"Have you ever had one?" she pressed.

"Yes ma'am, but they're gone."

"That's a shame; what happened to them?"

Mom would not let up. Hoffen noticed Timothy frown. Cheryl said nothing and stared at the pot roast.

"I lost my son in the war, and my wife died about a year later of a broken heart."

"Oh my, that is so sad," Cheryl said.

"Was it the Vietnam War?" Mom said.

"Oh, no. It was a long time ago—Word War II," Hoffen said.

"I didn't know that, Hoffen," Timothy said.

"I guess it never came up," Hoffen said.

"That was a different type of war, wasn't it, Mr. Hoffen? People knew how to treat the boys when they came home. Not like today. The boys today get no respect," Mom said.

"Different times for sure, Dorothy," Hoffen said.

They spent the next few minutes finishing dinner. Hoffen relaxed when the conversation ended. Mom went to the kitchen for the apple pie and coffee. They finished with customary small talk about the meal.

"You put on a feast here this evening, Dorothy. Cheryl, I think you have a great teacher here," Hoffen said.

"Thank you, Mr. Hoffen. Please come any time," Mom said. "Would you like to take a plate of leftovers with you?"

"That's generous, Dorothy, but I will spend the next week working off this wonderful meal."

"Are you ready to head back?" Timothy said to Hoffen.

"Sure. Dorothy, thanks again for your hospitality. Cheryl, it was nice to meet you," Hoffen said.

"Good night," Mom said.

"Cheryl, will you be here when I get back?" Timothy asked.

"Probably not. I want to help clean up and I'll head home. I'll walk with you to the car," she said.

Hoffen got in first to give them a couple of minutes to say goodbye. They hugged and kissed.

"What a night," Timothy said.

"It was fun. Nice to meet Hoffen. I see why you like him. We'll talk tomorrow," Cheryl said.

"Okay, night," Timothy said.

Timothy cranked the engine twice to get it started. "Second try. That's a good sign," Timothy said. "I bet you didn't expect that floor show to go with the dinner, did you?"

"It was fine. The food was exceptional, and Cheryl is everything you described and then some. And your mother is like every other mother. I understand completely," Hoffen said.

They drove in silence to Hoffen's house. It wasn't much of a house—more like a shack on the edge of the Brentwood junkyard.

"Is this it?"

"Yes."

"Wow. I have seen that shack—uh, house—for years but never knew anyone lived there," Timothy said.

"Oh, sure. And it's okay. It is a shack but perfect for me. I'll see you tomorrow," Hoffen said.

"Good night, Hoffen."

Hoffen opened the door to his shack, turned on the light, and waved. *Boy, do I have some work to do.*

CHAPTER TWENTY-TWO

"TIGER SIX, THIS is Papa Four. Be advised, LZ is hot. Victor Charlie's echo side of LZ," the team on the ground tells Timothy.

"Roger that, Four. Coming in hot. Tiger Five, you copy?"

"Tiger Six, copy that," Tiger Five says. "Going in one-eight-zero. Hot on the echo side of LZ." Tiger Five is Bobby.

"Popping smoke," Papa Four shouts.

"I see purple smoke," Timothy responds.

"Affirmative," Papa Four says.

As they approach the landing zone, tracers streak by the helicopter. Timothy feels the thuds. He yells to his crew chief, "Scoot, we hit?"

"Yeah, couple through the tail, but we're okay. Pretty nasty on this side."

"Tell these guys to jump right, Scoot."

"Got it."

The troops jump off the helicopter at six feet.

"They're off. Let's get outta here," Scoot says.

"We're gone—" Timothy yells.

As Timothy pulls up on the collective and pushes forward on the cyclic, an RPG strikes the belly of his Huey.

"Papa Four, Six took an RPG in the gut," Tiger Five screams.

"We see it, Five. We're on it. Get outta here."

Bobby lifts off and performs a quick 360.

"Tiger Five, get outta here unless you want to join him on the ground. This place is erupting. Get the rest of the troops out here. We need them."

Papa Four is at the crash site.

"My friend, Six—"

"Copy, Five. We're on it. Stay safe."

"Roger that—" The radio goes silent.

"Tiger Five. Tiger Five. Do you read? Tiger Five, this is Papa Four."

Radio silence.

"Tiger Five, hold tight. We're on the way."

Timothy listens on Papa Four's radio. The impact tosses the gunner and crew chief away from the wreckage. The copilot, a Vietnamese trainee, dies on impact. The gunner dies from shrapnel. Scoot, cut and bleeding, gets to Timothy first, who fades in and out of consciousness. His leg has a gaping wound from the impact of the RPG.

"Tim, can you hear me? You okay?" Scoot says.

"I can't feel my leg, Scoot."

Scoot rips open Timothy's pant leg to see the wound. "Yeah, it's pretty beat up, but it's still there. That chicken plate you sat on saved your ass."

"Get down, Scoot."

Timothy draws his .45 caliber pistol and shoots a charging VC.

"Shit, that was close," Scoot says.

"Bobby—" Timothy says.

"Dust-Off Two, this is Papa Four, popping smoke."

"Roger, Four, I see red smoke," Dust-Off Two says.

"Confirmed. This place is fucking hot. Be quick," Papa Four says.

"What are we picking up?" Dust-Off Two says.

"Two KIAs and two wounded. Again, be quick."

"What happened to Bobby?" Timothy asks.

"They're going for them, man. I'm going to stay and make sure we find them," Scoot assures.

Dust-Off Two touches down to pick up two KIAs and Timothy. Scoot refuses to go. Timothy falls unconscious on the way to the field hospital in Saigon.

Timothy startled awake, sweating, shaking, and screaming. He knew this dream too well. He lived the nightmare. As he lay in his sweat-soaked bed, in the safety of his home in Saint Louis, he tried to calm himself.

Mom stood at the door to his room. "Timmy, are you okay?"

"Yeah, Mom. I'm okay."

"I heard you screaming. Are you having those dreams again?"

"Yes," he said.

"Are you sure you're okay, Son?"

"I'll be okay, Mom. I just want to lie here a few minutes before I go back to sleep."

"Okay then, I'll leave you alone," she said along with other unintelligible utterances as she walked away.

Okay? How can I be okay? I'll never be okay. I will always be broken. This thing never ends. I always wake before finding out what happened to Bobby. Maybe if I go back to sleep, I'll find out what happened.

From the dozens of times he dreamed this sequence, he knew going back to sleep did not help him figure out what happened. He rolled over and closed his eyes anyway. He wanted to get up and walk around the house—one more perimeter check—but resisted the impulse. Eventually, he found sleep.

The sun in his eyes jarred him awake. Timothy looked at the clock radio, which read 9 AM. He slept longer than he planned. He had to be at Schoen's at ten. He shook his head as if to shake off his nightmare. He rubbed his injured leg to see if all of this was real or one big nasty dream. The twelve-inch scar answered his question.

Damn, I'm going to miss Mass again.

CHAPTER TWENTY-THREE

TIMOTHY TOOK AN extra cup of Mom's coffee with him to drink on his way to work. It was a security blanket of sorts. The bitter taste reminded him he was home. Sundays were busy days at the tree lot. Classes were over and Timothy welcomed the change of pace.

"Hey, Tim. How's it going?" Hoffen said.

"I've been better."

"Looks like you had a rough night."

"That's one way to look at it."

"Anything you want to talk about?"

"Christmas trees," Timothy grinned.

"Hey, soldier boy, the ol' kike put up a sale sign. Wants us to work our butts off today," Kenny taunted.

"Hi, Kenny," Timothy said.

"Boy, you look worse than a wad of Red Man," Kenny said.

"Feel like it, too."

"Hey, I can help with that," Kenny said as he rolled around a wad in his mouth.

"Not today, Kenny," Timothy said.

"All right. Hey mister! That's a real deal on that tree." Kenny walked away.

"What's new at the hospital?" Hoffen asked.

"They moved me to another floor. Med-Surg. You work from the moment you get there until you leave. Most of the time you eat on the run. A lot to do."

"Why did they move you there?" Hoffen said.

"I call it hospital Siberia. The head nun is suspicious of me and the union."

"What do you mean about the union?"

"The Service Workers Union is trying to organize at the hospital, and the administration saw me talking to them one day. They assume I'm a rabble rouser."

"Are you involved in that?"

"No, of course not. With all I have going on, I have no time for any of that."

"Then why give it a second thought?"

"I'm not. They are."

"That's tough." Hoffen paused for a moment. "Hey, that was a great dinner last night. Your mom is a great cook and gracious hostess. And Cheryl, you hit the jackpot there."

"Thanks, Hoffen. I'm not sure she could say the same about me. I don't feel like a grand prize. More like a booby prize."

"What are you saying? You're a good man. An honorable man. You're ambitious and want to make a good life for you two. Those are good things."

Timothy grunted agreement.

"How did it go with Father Schmitt last week?"

"Not well. There's nothing they can do until I get my grades up. Maybe down the road."

"That's something to shoot for."

"If I can hang on that long."

"O'Rourke, it's about time you got here," Dez said.

"Hi, Dez. Nice suit," Timothy said.

"Yeah, picked it out myself."

The irony of Dez as Santa was not lost on Timothy. In Timothy's crazy world, all of this somehow made sense—or at least wasn't that bizarre.

"Hey, Dez, come here a minute. This guy has a question," Kenny yelled.

"On the way," he yelled back. "Simpleton. Can't even answer a question about a tree. I told him to make up something if he didn't know the answer." He stared at Timothy and Hoffen. "You two, get to work."

For the next couple of hours, the lot buzzed. It was getting close to Christmas and last-minute shoppers were out. The sale sign worked the way Dez wanted. Fathers held trees for mothers to evaluate. Children ran from one aisle to another, playing hide-and-seek. Kenny spun endless yarns about trees. He never let the facts get in the way of telling the customer what they wanted to hear. Timothy stood at the fire barrel warming his hands.

"O'Rourke, come over here," Dez said.

"Coming, Dez."

"So what have you decided? Are you gonna take me up on my offer or not? I need an answer." Dez pushed like a siding salesman trying to close a deal.

"Dez, I'd like to give you an answer, but the problem is I'm busy with school, exams and all, I haven't thought much about it." *That's a load of crap. That's all I've been thinking about. Shit, I'm obsessed.*

"Look, stiff-leg, you're going down the wrong path in life and I'm tryin' to help you. You got your head filled with wild dreams that ain't for guys like you and me. We ain't cut out for that kind of life. We're supposed to scratch out a livin' any way we can. Me and the ol' lady ain't done bad by it either. You're smart enough, but you ain't got the resources to make it work. That's the way it is for some folks, and you might as well get with the program. You is one of those folks and don't never forget it."

"A person has to have dreams, Dez."

"Yeah, and some people's dreams are nightmares."

An offhand comment like this would normally pass Timothy easily, but not today. Not after last night.

"Some days, dreams seem like both," Timothy said.

"That's my point, boy. When dreams turn into nightmares, it's time to wake up. That's what you need to do. Wake up."

"Maybe you're right. My dreams seem more like bubbles, floating away and ready to burst."

"Damn straight I'm right. You gotta deal with the realities in front of you. I'm givin' it to you plain. You got bills and no money and no prospects other than the chance I'm giving you."

"Maybe I should take the deal."

"I know you should."

"Can I wait until after exams? That's the only thing I want to think about right now."

"How long's that?"

"I'm off this week to study and exams are the following week."

"That's it. I ain't waitin' no longer than that."

"You're right, Dez. I owe you that. I better get back to work."

"Yeah, get over there and make sure the mole head doesn't give away the lot."

For the next couple of hours, Timothy mulled over Dez's words. *Maybe Dez is right. One man's dream is another man's nightmare.*

Timothy lost himself in the pine scent, the smoke from the barrel, and the Christmas music playing over the PA system. He was beginning to feel like having an imagination and dreaming was more a curse than a blessing.

"Hey, stranger." Cheryl's words caught him off guard. "I thought you might come by last night after you dropped off Hoffen," she said.

"Sorry, hon." Timothy kissed and hugged her. "I was exhausted and had to get up early for today."

"I understand. I was kidding you," she said.

"And I'll tell ya somethin' else about these trees. Santa Claus delivered them himself. Don't ya want your kids to have a real Santa tree?"

Cheryl and Timothy grinned as Kenny told another whopper to a family. The father winked at the mother, and the children lit up when they heard this.

"Maybe Kenny's not as simple as Dez thinks he is," Cheryl said.

"Maybe. So why did you stop by today?"

"I wanted to see my boyfriend. You know, a girl could get paranoid being your girlfriend."

"Why?" Timothy said.

"I don't feel you will really talk to me," she said.

"I talk to you. What do you want me to say?"

Hoffen was working in the aisle next to the fire barrel within earshot of this conversation. He inched closer.

"No, you don't talk. You speak. You utter words, syllables, but you don't really talk. Timothy, I love you, and I want to be in your world, the good and the bad, the easy and the tough. You know, for better or worse."

Better or worse. Great, now she wants to talk about getting married. Just what I need today. Timothy saw Cheryl was getting upset and decided he didn't need to add to it.

"Cheryl, you're in my world—for whatever it is."

"No, I'm not. I'm on the outside of the fishbowl watching you swim and drown. I want to be in the fishbowl with you. Swimming. Helping you. Keeping you from drowning."

"Outside the fishbowl seems like a good to place to be. You won't get wet out there, and I can't take you down with me."

"Timothy, I want to get wet. I want to swim and struggle with you. I want to help."

"You want to talk? Okay. Here it goes. Dez wants an answer soon. The hospital is messing with me. Father Schmitt can't do anything for me. I'm broke. Hell, I'm broken—financially, physically and mentally. Do you want to hear about the ghosts that visit me in my dreams most nights or what it feels like to lose your best friend when he's trying to rescue you? You want to go down with me? Hang around, it won't take that long."

Tears welled. Cheryl heard the words, she saw them coming from his mouth, but this was a stranger standing in front of her. As her tears flowed, Timothy continued.

"Is this what you want? Do you want to hop in this fishbowl with me? Well, come on in. The water's fine. We can drown together."

Hoffen moved closer.

"I brought you lunch today. I thought you might be hungry. Here." She handed it to Timothy.

When he saw the impact of his words, he felt shame.

"I'm sorry. I didn't mean to jump down your throat. And thanks for this," Timothy said as he held up the lunch bag.

"Okay, you're forgiven." She leaned forward, gave him a peck on the cheek, and wiped her eyes.

"And this tree was cut down by elves," Kenny said, oblivious to the tension between Cheryl and Timothy just a few yards away.

They shared a smile.

"You better get back to work so Dez stays off your back."

"Thanks. Call you tonight?"

"Yes. You better."

Hoffen followed Cheryl to the parking lot.

"Cheryl, hold up," Hoffen yelled after her.

"Oh, hi, Hoffen. I'm sorry, I didn't see you," she sniffled.

"Is everything okay? You look upset."

"It's Timothy. Sometimes he feels like a stranger to me. He builds this wall around himself to keep everyone else out. He won't let me in, and he needs me in there with him. Sometimes, I feel like an intruder," she said.

"That's no good. I know he's feeling a lot of pressure, and most of it comes from him. He's trying to find answers but doesn't know the questions," Hoffen said.

"I guess. It's frustrating and disappointing. Is this what love is supposed to be about? How can something that is supposed to be this great thing feel so debilitating?"

Hoffen snickered. "I'm sorry, Cheryl. I don't mean to laugh, but it sounds funny the way you describe it. And yes, it is supposed to be confusing. Don't let yourself get discouraged. One discouraged person around here is enough, you know."

She nodded. "You're right. Sometimes I feel like I'm this weight around his neck."

"Has he said this to you?"

"No. He doesn't have to. When he shuts down, I don't know how to reach him."

"First things first. You're not a weight around his neck. From what I see, you're more like his anchor. You're keeping him steady when he bobs in the rough waters. When waves slap against a boat, the boat pushes back against the anchor. That's when it does most of its work, in stormy waters. That's what you're feeling right now. You're steadying, and he's pushing back."

"Oh, yes." She sniffled. "That's exactly what it feels like. I'm trying to help him keep it all together, and it's like he wants to rip it apart."

"Yes, that's a pretty good analysis on your part," Hoffen said.

"Thank you, that makes me feel better." She leaned forward and hugged Hoffen. She said, "Do you think you could have this talk with Timothy? It wouldn't hurt for him to hear this."

"I'll see what I can do. You take care. He's going to be okay. He's not all home yet," Hoffen said.

"What do you mean not all home yet?"

"This country does a good job of preparing men to go to war, but a lousy job of preparing them to return home and become good citizens. Some find their ways back by themselves and make mistakes along the way. Others, the lucky ones, have families and friends that welcome them home. They help them return and heal."

"That's a beautiful thought, Hoffen. We should welcome home these good soldiers, and ask them to become good citizens. I know Tim needs healing. Strangely enough, his injured leg is one of the healthiest parts of him. He can see the scars. He's adjusted to them. He knows what to expect from his leg and lives with it. It's the other wounds, the hidden ones, that cripple him," she said.

"Now you understand. He's not pushing you away as much as he is pushing away all of us. That's why he's close to the other veterans. They don't have to say a word to each other. They look at each other and understand in their souls what the other feels. Most of them are closer than blood brothers," Hoffen said.

"You're right. That's how I feel about Timothy and Scoot, and I must admit I'm jealous of it at times."

"Don't be ashamed of how you feel. You're learning how to understand, and it takes time."

"Thank you again, Hoffen. I think I know what to do," she said.

"Good. And don't worry. We can help him come home."

Hoffen watched Cheryl drive off. He turned and saw Dez looking at him.

"Well, well, old man. Do you really think you're that good? You've got to be tired of this. Why don't you give up and move on?"

"One of us should, Dez. How about you? Why don't you give up and move on?" Hoffen walked away.

Hoffen saw Timothy at the fire barrel as the crowds thinned. He knew Timothy wanted to talk—he had been staring at Hoffen since he returned from the parking lot.

"I saw you and Cheryl talking in the lot. I bet she gave you an earful, didn't she?" Timothy said.

"She's concerned about you. She really loves you," Hoffen said.

"I know. I know. This doesn't seem to be getting any better."

"What isn't getting any better?" Hoffen asked.

"Life," Timothy said.

"Is it that bad?" Hoffen asked.

"Yes. The way Dez looks at things is beginning to make sense. On some level, I know how insidious his thinking is, but on another level it connects."

"How so?"

"I've got all these ambitions and no way to make them happen. Every time I think I'm getting ahead—you know, gaining traction—I find out I'm spinning my wheels."

Hoffen nodded. "Most people feel that way from time to time."

"Yeah, but for me it seems that way all the time. Dez is right. Guys like me and him shouldn't even think in these terms."

"What terms? What are you talking about?" Hoffen asked.

"You know, dreams, ambitions, that stuff. Most of that stuff is out of my league."

"He told you that you shouldn't have any dreams and you believed him?"

"He didn't tell me that exactly. He pointed out how messed up my life is and told me to make practical choices," Timothy said.

"Like coming to work for him?"

"Yes."

"What about school? What about Cheryl?" Hoffen asked.

"School can wait, and Cheryl can do better than me."

"Says who?"

"Me!"

Hoffen raised his eyebrows. "Don't you think she has something to say about this?"

"Yes, I guess."

"Tim, we've talked about this before. You're going to regret the things you didn't do more than the things you did do. You have a right to dream. You have a right to hope. There is none of this 'guys like us shouldn't think in these terms.' That's lousy advice. Do you want Dez to be your career counselor?"

"No."

"Do you want to end up like him?"

"Hell no!"

"Exactly. Look, you have two voices whispering in your ears. One is the voice of hope, and the other is the voice of despair. You get to choose which one to turn down the volume on."

"Are you're saying Dez is the wrong voice?"

"I'm saying it's your choice."

They stared at the fire.

"Having this conversation and staring at this blaze reminds me of something I once read," Hoffen said.

"What's that?"

"A passage from Dante's *Inferno*, 'All hope abandon, ye who enter here.' Do you know what that means?"

"I'm familiar with the passage," Timothy said. "We studied it in a literature class."

"It was the sign hanging outside of hell. You see, hell is the absence of hope. When you're there, you figure there is no way out. You're stuck in your despair. You've stood at the door, haven't you, Tim?"

"Yes, and peeked in," Timothy said.

"I know you have. But you didn't walk through the door. Something inside of you told you to hang back. That was hope, the voice you never want to silence. That's the voice you must listen to."

"I guess I haven't thought about it in those terms. Thanks, Hoffen."

"My pleasure, Tim, and treat that young lady well. She is a big part of all that is good in your life."

"You're right. I hope to be a big part of what's right in her life."

"You already are, Tim. That's the point I'm trying to make."

CHAPTER TWENTY-FOUR

AFTER A FULL day of study on Monday, Timothy decided to show up at Cheryl's home unannounced to surprise her. When he arrived, he sat in his car and considered what to say about his behavior at the Christmas tree lot. Once he collected his thoughts, he rang the doorbell.

"Wow, this is a surprise," Cheryl said as she opened the front door.

"Yeah, I got to thinking about yesterday and what a jerk I was at the lot. I mean you brought me lunch and I . . . you know," Timothy said.

"Well, my mother taught me never to disagree with a man when he's trying to apologize. I accept your apology." She followed this with a hug and a peck on the cheek. "Come on in."

They sat in the living room. The rest of the family watched television in the den.

"I think the pressure is getting to me. The thing is, I have this attitude I should be able to handle anything life throws at me, but life seems to be winning this round. I've got all this stuff going on around me while I'm churning on the inside. It's weird. My bones itch, and I can't scratch them. I'm restless to get moving, but something is holding me back. I don't know. I'm rambling. I'm sorry." Timothy took a breath.

Cheryl smiled. "You're fine. I'm glad you're telling me this. I'm thrilled you're letting me in. You're too tough on yourself. You've created this sort of character for yourself that is unrealistic. Knowing and understanding that is a move in the right direction." Cheryl sounded like a counselor.

Timothy grinned. "I'll work it out with the help of a special person."

"I'll be here for you at every step along the way. Hoffen told me you're trying to come home. I want to help you make it all the way, Tim."

Timothy's eyes watered. He knew she understood. He felt uncomfortable talking about it with other people, but not tonight. He wanted to get *home*, and Cheryl could help. She played a role wives and girlfriends had lived since the first soldiers returned from battle.

"I know you will. You're good for me," he said. "The problem is that I'm not home yet—not all the way."

"What do you mean?"

"Everything around me reminds me of where I've been and what I've done. It rains, and I smell the monsoons. A tractor trailer passes, and the diesel smell reminds me of guys on a shit-burning detail. The neighborhood kids' fireworks send me diving for cover. When I can't sleep at night I hear every noise in the house. I look at the other students and feel like an outsider. It's like I'm out of my element, like I don't belong."

He paused and she hugged him. "That's the most you've opened up to me about this."

"Yeah, and I'm sorry. You had no idea what you were getting with me. You are good for me. Hell, you're great for me. I just wish I were great for you."

"You are." Cheryl smiled. "And another lesson my mother taught me is a woman should never interrupt a man when he's paying her a compliment."

Timothy laughed. "This should be a good week for me. I've got a few days of downtime. I'm going to use this week to take a break from everything that's pushing on me—work, money, classes—and study for exams. I feel like it's all up to me right now. I'd like to ace all of those exams, especially Leibert's. If I ace his, he has to give me a B for the semester, and I need that to get my 3.8 GPA."

"That would be wonderful. You deserve a break."

"Hey, let's go get a pizza and beer."

"My treat," Cheryl said.

"Okay, big spender let's go."

They drove to Shakey's Pizza & Ye Public House, where they ordered a large pie smothered in pepperoni, sausage, salami, ground beef, mushrooms, and black olives. They washed it down with two pitchers of beer—all for less than ten bucks. Families and college kids packed the place. The banjo and piano players served up live Dixieland jazz. Children stood on the riser in front of the kitchen window to watch cooks toss the pizzas. Timothy loosened up even more. Alcohol often lubricated his mind. Tonight, it seemed to soothe his restless spirit. He smiled, made silly faces, and attempted to sing along with the music with a voice more suitable for a sporting event. This was the man Cheryl had fallen in love with. They needed this night the way a sick patient needed medicine.

After dinner, Timothy took Cheryl home and made it a point to avoid any talk of work, money, or Nam. It took them twenty minutes to say good night. When he left, he drove on side streets, avoiding the main streets and police. He knew the better part of two pitchers of beer would be hard to explain to a cop looking to write tickets.

This was a great night. It felt good to open up to Cheryl. We needed this. It's the first time in a while I felt I could relax and be me. No pressure, just Cheryl and me. I know I've been acting like a jerk lately, and I'm glad she forgave me. I think I could use some sisterly advice.

Timothy hoped Ike and Leslie would still be up and headed to their house, carefully navigating side streets and intersections. Leslie answered the door.

"Hey, Sis," Timothy said.

"Well, look who it is. You smell like a brewery, little brother."

"I've been working on it."

"Ike, come here and see this."

"Hey, runt. Tying one on?" Ike said.

Ike gave Timothy this nickname when Ike dated Leslie and Timothy was not yet ten years old. He only used the nickname these days when he wanted to gig Timothy.

"Didn't think I was, but seems I got a start on it. Got a cold one for me?" Timothy said.

"Yeah, I think I can scare up a couple brews," Ike said as he walked to the kitchen.

Leslie motioned to Timothy to sit in the living room.

"So what's the occasion?" she asked.

"Do I need an occasion to take my girl for a couple of beers and pizza?"

"Tim, you seem looser tonight than I've seen you in a while. Must be the alcohol," she said.

"Must be. Ahh, here comes the rocket fuel."

Ike returned with two "Blue Cans," their code for Busch Bavarian, a local favorite.

"Here ya go, partner. Drink up."

"Cheers," Timothy said as he held up his can in a mock toast. "Tonight was the first normal night we've had in a while. I was beginning to worry there were no more of these in my life."

"Tim, you've got a great gal in Cheryl. Don't blow this," Leslie said in the way older sisters talked to younger brothers.

"Here, here," Ike said and held up his beer.

For the next hour, they sat in the living room and talked about Cheryl and school and work. Ike made a couple more trips to the fridge. Even Leslie commented that they didn't get many of these spontaneous nights since Timothy returned home. Life seemed to get in the way of living.

"Okay, boys. Time to wrap it up. Ike, you've got to go to work tomorrow, and I've got carpool in the morning early. And you, baby brother, if you're spending the week getting ready for exams, you need a clear head for that. Besides, you're staying here tonight. I already called Mom and told her."

"Hey, I'm not a kid who needs his mother's permission to stay out late."

"I didn't do this for you. I did it for us. Every time you stay out all night, she calls us at two in the morning to tell us she's worried. I want to sleep tonight," Leslie said.

"Okay, how about I park it here on the sofa?" Timothy said.

"Right. Ike, get a pillow and a blanket," Leslie said. "And Tim, if you feel sick, not in here. I just got the carpets cleaned."

Leslie made a vague reference to the time Ike and Timothy drank too much and Timothy puked all over the bathroom.

"All right, thanks," Timothy said.

Ike returned with the pillow and blanket, and Leslie came over to give Timothy a hug.

"Good night, baby brother," said Leslie.

The next morning, Timothy dragged himself into Leslie and Ike's kitchen, shaking the fog of a night of beer and conversation.

"Hey there, sleepy head. I was beginning to think you might sleep all morning," Leslie said.

"Not likely. What time is it?" Timothy said.

"A few minutes after ten," she said.

"What? I haven't slept that long in years," Timothy said.

"Last night you looked pretty tired and, uh—"

"Wasted?"

Leslie rocked her head. "That's one way to say it. How often do you drink like that?"

"Not often enough," he said.

"Not that often, really? How do you feel this morning?"

"Good. I think I needed that," Timothy said.

"The beer?"

"The whole night. Beer. Pizza. Talking. Cheryl. Time with you and Ike. And a good night's sleep."

"You were in a good place last night when you showed up. I was glad to see it," Leslie said.

"Me too. Is that coffee I smell?"

"Fresh. Made a few minutes ago. I stopped off at Rafferty's on the way home from carpool and picked up an apple fritter. Interested?"

"Oh yeah. I haven't had one of those since . . . I can't remember when," said Timothy.

"Cheryl was at the bakery when I got there, picking up doughnuts for some work function. We chatted a little while. She said last night was a great time for you guys. Like when you first met. She was relieved to hear you didn't drive home. According to her, 'My old Tim showed up at the doorstep last night.' She's a great gal, you know."

"I know. I have been a bit of a jerk lately to her. I'm letting everything get to me."

Leslie wasted no time weighing in on this. "Yes, you have and yes, you are. That girl is nuts for you. You're lucky to have her, and she's lucky to have you. A lot of people don't have as much as you two have right this moment."

"You're right. I know." *We do have a good thing going if I don't screw it up.* "Man, this thing is still warm," he said, cutting a piece of the fritter.

"Mrs. Rafferty had just taken it out of the oven when I got there. They don't come any fresher than that," she said.

Timothy took a big bite and washed it down with a gulp of coffee. He wiped his mouth and said, "The thing is, I was planning to get Cheryl a ring for Christmas. I managed to squirrel away some cash. This summer, we were at the mall, and she saw a ring that caught her eye. It was a long, narrow diamond. I think it's called a marquise. Show's what I know. Eight hundred dollars but it might as well be eight thousand now; the furnace burned up that money."

"It must have been beautiful," Leslie said.

"It was. I had it all planned out, but you know . . . life," he said.

"Tim, I wish we could have done something to help out on the furnace, but you know how tight things are around here."

"Oh, I didn't tell you this to ask for help. I was telling you what I had planned. I guess I'll have to wait."

Leslie looked disappointed knowing she couldn't help financially. Ike had a decent job at the post office, but with four kids and bills, they were strapped.

"Tim, Cheryl cares for you. She'll wait. I know she will. She understands," Leslie said.

"Waiting. I've been down that path before, and that didn't turn out too good, did it?"

"Are you talking about Connie?" Leslie asked.

"Yes. I mean, that's over. Has been ever since that letter, but it never really got started. That's what I mean. I don't want Cheryl to end up being one more piece of unfinished business in my life. Every one of these pieces of unfinished business in my life is like an open sore that never heals."

"She's in this for the long haul. I know. She's told me," Leslie said.

"This is why I must finish school. I don't want to add that to my list of things I started and didn't finish. There's too much of that already," Timothy said.

Leslie let this pass and redirected the conversation. "So, what are your plans for today?"

"As soon as I'm done stuffing myself with this fritter, I'm headed to the library to do some research for an English paper, and home to study for my other classes. That's my week. Lots of studying."

"Sounds like you have it pretty well mapped out," she said.

"Yep. As soon as I'm finished with exams and the holidays are over, I'll make a decision about next semester. I need a couple of weeks of downtime."

"You've earned some rest. That's for sure. Have you given any more thought to Ike's idea about you driving a truck on nights at the post office?" Leslie said.

"Yeah, I've thought about it. Here's the thing. Those trucks are big and tough to handle. The drivers need all their limbs to move those things. They take one look at the way I walk, and it's no deal. I don't need to hear that."

Leslie turned away. Her eyes watered. She bit her lip and then struggled to pick up the conversation. The whole family hurt for Timothy's war wounds.

"Hey, it's okay, Sis. No need to worry about me. That was a great offer, and I appreciated Ike thinking of me. Let it go. It's no big deal."

"Okay."

She gave her brother a big hug.

"I've got to get moving here," Timothy said. "Thanks for putting me up last night."

"That's fine, and be nice to Cheryl, little brother."

"I will. Love ya."

"Love you, too." She gave him another hug, and he left.

CHAPTER TWENTY-FIVE

TIMOTHY ARRIVED HOME from the library to begin hibernating. That's what he called his quiet time. Private time. A time to study and relax. It reminded him of R & R in Vietnam. Troops called it "rest and recreation" or "rest and recuperation" or "rock and roll."

The military gave the troops a few days off to rest and relax in Thailand, Hawaii, Australia, or in-country in cities like Vung Tau or Saigon. Timothy opted for in-country. He went to Saigon and shared a room with another pilot at the Rex, a luxury hotel known for the daily briefings by the military hierarchy. The cynical press corps named these briefings "The Five O'Clock Follies" because high-ranking officers delivered overly optimistic assessments of the war. The Rex had a rooftop bar frequented by the brass and correspondents. Timothy spent most of his days and evenings in the bar because his roommate spent most of his time in the room with local working girls. The choices for most GIs included sex, drugs, or alcohol. Some chose more than one option. Timothy chose alcohol as his antidote to the war and brought the thirst home with him.

He called his study space at home his *cave*, a small tool room in the corner of the basement. His father's tools were gone, but the memories lived. He spent countless hours here with his father during better times, tinkering, building, piddling, doing the kinds of guy things dads and sons do as a rite of passage, an initiation period into manhood. It smelled like a basement—damp but tolerable. It had plenty of light since the old man put in extra lighting, and in the afternoon and early evening, sunlight shined through the two windows. Most of the time, Timothy opened the windows.

Timothy built his desk out of an old wooden door supported on each end by two-drawer filing cabinets. He had few distractions on the desk—an old desk lamp that had been around about as long as he had, and a pencil cup with a dozen clear Bic pens, highlighters, and Ticonderoga pencils. On one end of the long desk sat his father's old Smith-Corona typewriter, which Timothy used for papers. Typing on it was an aerobic exercise. He imagined hitting the same keys his father struck for business letters. He sat in a straight-backed wooden banker's chair, a fact he found ironic since he was broke. He built the bookshelves with cinder blocks and pine boards. He filled them with books and memorabilia: two dictionaries, an *American Heritage* and a *Thorndike Barnhart Children's Dictionary* left over from grade school; a worn copy of *Roget's Thesaurus*; a high school grammar book with his freshman homeroom number in it; Bob Gibson's autobiography, *From Ghetto to Glory*; three novels, *Don Quixote, Huckleberry Finn, and A Farewell to Arms*; and every psychology book he ever read. Next to the books sat his childhood catcher's mitt, which cradled a baseball he caught during batting practice at the old Sportsman's Park, and a bowling trophy for rolling the highest game in a grade school Christmas tournament. He beat everyone with a score of 143. A beer mug he got for high school graduation from an old girlfriend sat between a picture of Cheryl and another of himself, Scoot, and Bobby in front of a helicopter.

No one bothered him in the cave, especially Mom. The blood clots in her legs discouraged her from making trips up and down stairs. And few others came by these days. Most of his high school friends graduated already from college and had careers. Scoot came by from time to time but not during the day because of his business.

Timothy loved being alone with his thoughts and books. He also wondered how someone majoring in psychology could value private time that much. He feared he had trust issues with people, which was terrible if he wanted to join that profession.

Today he had an English paper due on Joseph Heller's *Catch-22*, a satirical novel about a bomber group in World War II. Timothy connected with this book because it addressed the absurdities of war. In his war, they fought to win but suffered political pressure at home. *Catch-22* became a phrase Timothy often used to describe his options in life. *Damned if I do, and damned if I don't.*

By the end of the day, he had written a paper he viewed as his best work ever. Then he studied for a political science exam. It made sense to Timothy to tackle both in one day. Heller stacked one set of bizarre experiences on top of another. Lumping his own experiences in his political science class on top of Heller's made sense to Timothy. *Bizarre begets bizarre.*

In his paradoxical world, being busy with schoolwork calmed his mind. It struck him as odd that a week so filled with activities could feel this relaxing. In his cave, he had no bills, no shifts at the hospital, no pressure from Dez, and, most of all, no self-pressure to be some indefatigable hero. He came into this week distressed and planned to leave it de-stressed. He liked the play on words and wrote it in his journal for future reference. Timothy used his journal as a therapist. He viewed a blank sheet of paper as a patient and nonjudgmental listener. By Friday, he had studied himself into a state of confidence.

He and Cheryl planned to go ice skating to celebrate the end of study week. He had not done so in a few years. He thought his leg would make it difficult but agreed to give it a try. As he prepared to leave the house, Mom asked for a favor.

"Tim, before you leave, would you be a dear and take a load of wash down to the basement. I want to do a load of laundry. And please add some detergent and turn on the machine. I'll try to go down later and empty the machine."

"Sure, Mom. How's your leg?" he said.

"It hurts tonight. It must be the veins acting up. Oh, I made some oatmeal raisin cookies for you to take to work tomorrow."

"Thanks, Mom. Kenny will be thrilled. He bugs me about your cookies nearly every time I work."

"I'm glad to do it, Son."

Timothy took a load of wash to the basement and started the machine. He decided it would only take a few minutes for the load to wash, so he went to his cave and reread his paper on *Catch-22*.

I enjoyed writing this. It feels completely natural. I can't get over how easy this is for me. It's like the words are already in the pen, and my job is to get them on paper. I wish the rest of these subjects were that easy.

He was making minor edits and was deeply concentrating when the washer bell startled him. *Wow! Done already?* He unloaded the washing machine and hung the clothes on the line in the basement to dry. *One of these days, we need to get a dryer.*

"Mom, I finished the wash and hung it on the line."

No answer.

"Mom. Mom? *Mom!*"

Upstairs, Mom lay motionless on the floor. Timothy checked her pulse and breathing and called an ambulance, then Leslie.

The ride to the hospital with his unconscious mother seemed to take forever. Leslie and Ike lived close to the hospital and met the ambulance outside the emergency room entrance.

"What happened?" Leslie said after Mom was wheeled away.

"I don't know. I was in the basement, and when I came upstairs, Mom was on the floor. Unconscious but breathing. So I called the ambulance and you guys," Timothy said.

"What have you heard?" Leslie said.

"Nothing. The paramedic in the ambulance said it looked like a stroke but wasn't sure," Timothy said.

"Oh my God, how bad is this?" Leslie said.

"I don't know. We have to wait for the doctor to come out and talk with us. We need to keep our heads right and not go worst-case scenario yet."

Timothy felt more like the older than the younger brother. His military training kicked in. He learned in the war to compartmentalize in stressful situations to maintain his cool. Cheryl slipped into the waiting room while Timothy and Leslie talked. Timothy failed to notice her entering.

"Tim, what's going on?" Cheryl said.

"What? How did you get here?" he said.

"I called Cheryl after you called me. I thought it would be good for you to have her here," Leslie said.

Timothy remained silent for a couple of moments as he processed the series of events.

"Is this okay, Tim?" Cheryl said.

"Oh, yes. Yes. Of course. I'm trying to clear my head," he said.

"That's why I called Cheryl—to support you," Leslie said.

"Where are the kids?" Timothy said.

"My mom came over," Ike said. "We didn't know what we were dealing with here, and I wanted to be here in case . . ."

"I'm sure it's going to be okay, guys," Cheryl said.

At that moment, the door to the treatment room opened, and the doctor came out to talk to them.

"Hey, Tim. Can't get enough of this place?" The doctor's casual demeanor reassured Timothy.

"Apparently not," Timothy said.

"What is it, Doctor?" Leslie interrupted the small talk.

"This is my sister, Leslie, brother-in-law, Ike, and my girlfriend, Cheryl," Timothy said.

Leslie was getting more anxious. Timothy nodded to Cheryl, and she moved closer and grabbed Leslie's hand for reassurance.

"We think your mother threw a clot. We're still evaluating it. We have some tests to run, but that's the preliminary diagnosis. Her condition is stable. She's conscious and can move all of her limbs, but her speech is labored. I see a slight drooping of an eyelid. But we'll know more later," the doctor said.

"Oh, dear Lord," Leslie said. Cheryl placed her arm around Leslie's shoulders and squeezed her into a hug.

Timothy nodded to Cheryl.

"So what's the plan?" Timothy asked in a clinical tone as if he were on duty discussing a patient other than his mother.

"We will need to keep her here for a few days to observe what's going on. She'll be okay here but will need a lot of monitoring. Whatever is going on, we want to deal with it sooner rather than later. It looks like you got her here just in time. Tomorrow, the neurosurgeon will study the films to see what we should do next."

"You mean surgery?" Leslie said. Tears leaked down her cheeks, and Cheryl tightened her hold.

"We don't know yet. She did hit her head when she fell. We're keeping all options open at this time," the doctor said.

"Is there a window or critical time period for this type of situation?" Cheryl surprised Timothy by her calm demeanor and insightful question.

"Good question," the doctor said. "Yes. The next twenty-four hours are critical."

Timothy noticed the doctor's use of the word critical.

"I need to get back in there." The doctor tilted his head toward the treatment room. "The nurses will be out in a few minutes to update you on where we need to go from here."

"Thanks, Doc," Timothy said.

"Is my mom going to be okay?" Leslie asked.

"That's the plan, Leslie. We will do everything we can to make sure of that," the doctor said.

Leslie shook her head and closed her eyes. Timothy thought it looked like Cheryl was keeping Leslie on her feet at this point.

"Okay, thanks, Doc. We'll stay out here until we hear from the nurses," Timothy said.

"Folks, once you hear from the staff, go home and get some sleep. It's going to be a long weekend, and you'll need your rest. You can't do her any good staying up all night," the doctor said.

"Thanks." Timothy knew he had to take charge of this situation, like every other situation. He suddenly resented his father for leaving him this responsibility. With Cheryl here, he knew he could rely on her.

The doctor returned to the treatment room, and the family sat looking at each other and decompressing. Finally, Ike offered to get some coffee, and Cheryl said she would go with him.

When they got out of sight, Timothy looked at Leslie. "I can't believe you called Cheryl. I don't want to pile my baggage onto her."

"Don't you get it? This isn't about you, Tim. It's about all of us. This is what it means to have someone in your life. Cheryl's not a spectator. If she's going to be in this family, she needs to be in your life. Cheryl has to see the whole picture, not the one you want to paint for her. It's unfair to keep her out of this—unless, of course, you want to keep her out of your life," Leslie scolded.

She's right. He took a deep breath before responding.

"Of course I want her in my life. I don't want her to think I'm some loser whose life is screwed every way possible," he said.

"She doesn't think that, and stop making this about you," Leslie said. "This is Cheryl's life, too."

Cheryl and Ike returned with the coffee.

"What did you two decide?" Ike said.

Timothy and Leslie looked at each other. Timothy didn't want to go into their conversation, so he manufactured something. "We decided to wait and hear what the nurses have to say and take the doctor's advice to go home to get some sleep."

"Yes, I think that's the best thing to do at this point," Leslie said.

"Here, Tim. I think you need this," Cheryl said and handed him the coffee. She cupped his hand affectionately. Leslie saw this and smiled at Timothy. He nodded at his sister.

"Thanks. You're right," he said.

They sat for a few minutes, sipping coffee and making the kind of small talk people make when they're nervous. Ten minutes later, none of them would remember what they discussed, but it didn't matter. The nurse came out of the treatment room.

"Hi, Tim. Sorry about your mom," the nurse said.

"Thanks. What's the verdict?" he said.

"We're transferring her to Three-Main, and she'll be there for a few days. Tomorrow, they will run some tests. I can't tell you anything more about her condition other than what the doctor told you. I think it would be best for all of you to go home and get some sleep," the nurse said.

"Okay, you're right. Can we see her before we leave?"

"Sure. Come on in."

They went into the treatment room to visit Mom. The staff had sedated her, so they couldn't tell if the medicine or the stroke affected her speech. They stayed long enough to reassure her they would be back in the morning. She asked Timothy to hang back.

"Timmy, I don't want you to feel guilty about this," Mom said. "This is not your fault. I would have fallen whether or not you were there to catch me."

These words stunned and stung.

"Mom, are you saying this is my fault?" he said.

"Oh, no, dear. And I don't want you to feel that way. I know sometimes you feel you don't do enough for me. You should not feel bad about this."

He decided to let this slide. "I'll see you tomorrow."

Always the dutiful son, he held her hand and bent over to kiss her forehead. He left the treatment room and went to the lobby where the others waited for him.

"How about I give you a ride home?" Cheryl said.

"Thanks," Timothy said.

"So what are your plans for tomorrow?" Cheryl said.

"I'm supposed to be at Dez's in the morning, but I'll call him and tell him I'll be in later in the day."

"Will he be okay with that?"

"No, probably not, but what's he going to do? Send me back to Nam?"

Ike laughed. He had heard other Vietnam vets use this false choice at the post office.

"Okay, I guess I walked into that," Cheryl said.

"Sorry, didn't mean to be flippant. How about that ride?"

She locked her arm in his. He didn't know if he supported her or the other way around. It didn't matter. Either way, he liked it. They all said good night and Timothy and Cheryl walked to her car.

"Want to spend the night tonight?" he asked.

"Sure. I planned on it."

CHAPTER TWENTY-SIX

THE DRIVE TO the hospital on Saturday morning gave Timothy the time to think about his week. What began as light and hopeful turned darker. He spent most of the week studying for exams and last night with Mom in the hospital. He was running late this morning because he wanted to stop at the hospital. He knew Dez would be irritated with him. With the parking lot at the hospital full, Timothy parked on the street. He saw no pickets out this morning. This gave him one less thing to think about. He walked through the main entrance and up the stairs to Mom's floor.

"How did she do last night?" Timothy asked Sandy, the charge nurse on Three-Main.

"She had a bit of a tough night last night. Her breathing was labored but settled down by early morning. Wasn't she recently here for a breathing issue?" Sandy said.

"Yes. It was a reaction to furnace fumes in the house. Do you think this is connected?"

"Oh, I don't know. We have her scheduled for more tests this morning."

"Sandy, you've been at this awhile. How bad do you think this is?" Timothy said.

"I really don't know. The doctors are being cautious at this point.

During the night when she was having trouble breathing, the house doctor increased her blood thinner and that seemed to help. I'm thinking there's another clot in there somewhere obstructing the breathing. But we won't know until later today."

"Okay, can I go see her now?" Timothy said.

"Sure, as soon as the aide is finished with vitals, but don't stay too long."

"Got it, thanks. Who's the aide?" Timothy asked.

"Ginny."

"Good, she's a good aide. Going to be a nurse, right?"

"That's what she says," Sandy said.

Timothy waited outside Mom's room for Ginny. He knew second-guessing the previous diagnosis made little sense at this point. *Is this a sign of what's coming? No use going there—I'm not a doctor, but it is a good question for later.*

"Hi, Tim. Your mom is stable and resting. Going in?"

"Yes. Thanks for your help."

"That's what we do, you know."

"I know, but it helps having people you know involved," he said.

Ginny squeezed his arm and walked away. He stood at the door and stared at Mom lying there. She looked pale. He put on his game face and went in. He leaned over and kissed her clammy forehead. She stirred and opened her eyes.

"Hey, Mom. How did you sleep last night?" he said.

"It was rough, Son. I had some breathing problems, but they got it under control with some medicine. It kind of feels like last week when I was here, but they said something about a blood clot." Some of her words sounded lazy and even labored, which led him to believe she threw a clot.

"Yeah, I talked to the nurse and she brought me up to speed. It sounds like things are stable now," Timothy said.

"Yes, but it's still . . . a lot of work . . . breathing."

"More tests today, I understand. Then we'll know for sure."

"Yes," Mom said. "I already feel . . . like a pin cushion. In all night . . . sticking me. Hard to sleep . . . when people are working on you . . . all night."

"No one gets any sleep in the hospital, Mom. Have you eaten breakfast?" Timothy asked.

"Yes, I had a piece of dry toast, and some tea with lemon. My stomach's upset . . . that's all I could handle."

"It's probably unsettled from some of the pills, but you must keep your strength up."

"I know, Timmy. You've been good to me. They told me you rode in the ambulance last night . . . and here you are early this morning. Every mother should have such a good son . . . I don't know what I would do without you."

"That's not anything you need to think about now, is it? I'm here now and Leslie will be up with the kids later. I talked to her this morning before I left home."

"Would you hand me some ice chips? My mouth is dry."

"Sure, it's probably the meds. How about a 7 Up? That should settle your stomach," he said.

"Yes, good idea."

Timothy went to the nurses' station to get the ice chips and 7 Up. This gave him an excuse to tell the staff what Mom said about her stomach being upset. They already knew about it and told him she complained of her throat hurting from the tubes they put down it.

"She didn't tell me about that," Timothy said.

"She probably didn't want to pile on," Ginny said.

"You don't know Mom," he said and grinned.

Timothy went back into her room and Mom greeted him with one of her more pitiful faces. He thought she must practice these in the mirror to create the right effect. He laughed, but part of him felt guilty thinking that. Mom had a unique talent for eliciting an eclectic mix of emotions from people. He fed her the ice chips, as a dutiful son would do.

"Thank you, dear."

"Is your throat hurting?" he asked.

"Yes. I thought it was parched from being dry, but apparently they put some tubes down my throat last night . . . and irritated my throat. That's another reason I have trouble eating this morning," she said this as she took a sip.

They sat silently for a couple of minutes, Mom treating her dry mouth with ice chips and sips of soda. *What would she do if I weren't here? Leslie can't be here. Frank doesn't care. How did I end up with all of this responsibility? It's like I'm the last man standing. Shit, now*

I'm being dramatic. Timothy did not allow himself the luxury of asking these types of questions without feeling guilty. He dealt with his guilt the only way he knew; he felt it and stuffed it.

"Mom, how about I go to the snack bar and get you a chocolate shake? You like those when your stomach is upset."

"Would you do that for me, Timmy?"

"Sure, I'll be back in a few minutes."

Timothy walked to the snack bar on the main floor. He threw a leg over one of the stools and sat down at the counter. Penny, a waitress, came over.

"I'd like a chocolate shake, please," Timothy said.

"What! You can't even say hello to a girl?" Penny said and smiled.

"I'm sorry, Penny. I'm preoccupied. Hi."

"I don't see you down here much anymore," she said.

"I got moved to evenings and now nights," he said.

"I heard."

"How did you hear?" he said.

"Please, this is the smallest big hospital anywhere. Everyone knows everyone else's business. That's the favorite pastime around here," she grinned.

"I'm here to see my mom. She's up on Three."

"Is this for her?" Penny asked.

"Yes."

"I'll make it extra special for you," she said and winked.

Timothy thanked her. Penny was a sweet girl, a few years younger than he. He heard from other employees she had a crush on him. That surprised him. He never did anything to encourage her. She normally gave him a heaping serving of fries with his burger and a large soda when he ordered a medium. Sometimes, she even threw in a piece of lemon meringue pie. She made up some bogus excuse that she cut it for someone else by mistake and couldn't put it back in the tin. Her attentiveness embarrassed him, especially when he sat there with coworkers. She returned with two shakes with lids and straws. He shook his head in amusement.

"Thank you, but two?" he said.

"Oh, yes. I put too much ice cream in the cup for one and didn't want to throw away the rest so I decided to make two shakes. You only have to pay for one. The other is compliments of the house."

She smiled and handed him the shakes, making sure she touched his hand as she gave them to him. He flinched.

"No need to jump. I don't bite," she said.

"Sorry. I'm jumpy today. Lots going on. Thanks a bunch. I appreciate it."

"Anytime, Tim," she said and smiled.

As he turned to walk away, he nearly bumped into the director of nursing.

"I'm glad I ran into you, Tim," Monica said. "When I took census this morning, I saw your mother's name on the admission list. I understand she may be here a few days?"

"I don't think we know yet. Waiting for some more tests this morning. Thanks for saying something."

"Oh, that's okay." She paused. "You know we have a policy that prohibits employees from working on the same floor where family members are patients?"

"Yes, I seem to remember that," he said. "I guess that means I go back to nights on Psych until she's discharged?" he said.

"No. Doctor Faro prefers that you not work on the floor. He thinks Psych is not for you."

"Does he have some special power that enables him to read minds?"

"I know this is a trying time for you, mother and all—"

Timothy didn't want to hear any phony sympathy, so he cut her off mid-sentence.

"So what's the plan?" he pushed.

"The good news is you can keep your Tuesday and Thursday nights schedule, but we will need you in the ER."

"ER?" *They are trying to get rid of me.*

Timothy had worked a few weekend shifts in the ER and had a bad experience after a bloody night. It took him back to a place he didn't want to go. He did not look forward to the sights and sounds of the ER. He felt trapped. He took a deep breath and calmed himself.

"Do I start with my next shift?" he asked.

"Yes," Monica said.

"Okay, if that's what I have to do, fine. Will I go back to the third floor after my mother is discharged?"

"Not immediately, but yes."

"Okay." *End on a positive note and keep your job.* "Thanks again for mentioning my mom."

"Of course. We're interested in our employees' problems. Thanks for understanding, Tim. And don't let Dr. Faro's comments discourage you from your studies," she said.

Why would I let that discourage me? That was nowhere in my mind. That guy is a button-happy pill-pusher. There's no way I'd listen to him.

Timothy took the shakes up to Mom's room. Between gulps, she managed to say how nice of him to take such good care of her and that the shake soothed her scratchy throat. After he had enough of the shake, he kissed Mom on the forehead and told her he would be back later today after his work at Dez's.

"Timmy, you work too hard. I wish you didn't have to push yourself this hard. If you want to take some time off . . . it's okay. Everyone would understand. I'm sure even Cheryl would understand."

"Okay, Mom. Thanks. Bye."

Time off. Time away. Time to myself. All of that would feel good at this point.

The pickets were now out on the sidewalk as Timothy walked to his car. He picked up his pace and reached his car a little winded. With his leg, a brisk pace tired him quickly. His car started on the second attempt.

Now I get to deal with Dez.

CHAPTER TWENTY-SEVEN

TIMOTHY ARRIVED AT Schoen's and headed for the shop. He needed to talk to Dez.

"Well, well, Ed, look what the wind blew in," Dez said. Edna coughed up the pack of cigarettes she already smoked this morning.

"Hey, Dez. You got my message this morning, right?" Timothy said.

"Yeah, the ol' lady told me. What happened?"

Timothy told him the whole story.

"They gonna be able to help her?" Ed asked.

"I don't know. They're running some tests this morning. We'll know more this afternoon."

"Boy, leave it to those old penguins to suck the last dime out of a sick person. Tests. They always do more tests. It's like taking your car to the repair shop, and the mechanic finds all kinds of shit to fix. More dough for them," Dez said. "Boy, you ain't as smart as you think you are."

"They're trying to figure out what's going on," Timothy said.

"Keep tellin' yourself that, boy," Ed chimed in. "And we're jus' tryin' to sell more trees."

"You gonna be late tomorrow, too? Can't nobody in your family help ya out?" Dez said.

"Not really," Timothy said.

"All right, but ya better take me up on my offer. It's about the only thing you got goin' on right now. Those hospital dames will stick it to you. Sock you with big bills you're gonna have to pay," Dez said.

"Yeah, well, for now I better get out there and sell some trees. They're not going to move themselves off the lot. Besides, it looks like those guys can use some help."

"You bet they can. That dope is tellin' every kind of lie he can think of to move trees. I don't care what he says as long as it gets a tree on the roof of a car. And the old man can barely lift anything taller than himself. Get out there and help those two charity cases," Dez said.

Timothy nodded and walked outside. He brought with him a bag of the oatmeal raisin cookies Mom had made earlier in the week.

"Hey, Chester. About time ya showed," Kenny said.

Chester was a deputy on the television show *Gunsmoke* who walked with a limp.

"Those for me?" Kenny said, pointing his cigar toward the bag of cookies.

"Yeah. My mom made these for you, Kenny."

"Tell your mama I said thanks." Kenny stuffed two cookies into his mouth. "Better go in there and get a carton of milk to wash these down. Hope Ed's busy and don't see me so I can get one and not pay." He spit as many crumbs as he swallowed.

"Do what you have to do, Kenny."

Hoffen saw Timothy come outside and held back until Kenny went into the shop. He had his work cut out for him today. He had been in the shop when Edna got Timothy's call this morning explaining why he would be late. Edna couldn't contain herself when she hung up the phone and gave Hoffen an earful of sarcasm between hacks. He knew Timothy must have been running dry on hope. *I hope he didn't spend too much time in there with Dez and Edna. Their attitudes stink so bad they would knock a buzzard off a manure wagon.*

"Those two deserve each other, don't they?" Hoffen said to Timothy as he approached him.

"Huh? Morning, Hoffen. You mean the two in the shop?"

"Yes." Hoffen didn't want to talk about Dez and Edna. He redirected the conversation quickly. "How's your mother this morning?"

"You heard?" Timothy said.

"Yes, I was in the shop when you called earlier, and Edna told me."

"She's stable. Good for now. Rough night. Breathing issues. More tests today."

The short, machine-gun-burst answers were uncharacteristic for Timothy. It sounded like statements on a police incident report. Hoffen knew many people used cool detachment as a defense mechanism. It was how they kept things together, and Timothy appeared to be trying to hold it together.

"So, how are you doing?" Hoffen said.

"Okay."

"Just okay?"

"That's about all I got right now," Timothy said.

"Well, 'okay' will get you through the day. That's all you have to do. Get through the day," Hoffen said.

"Hope so."

"Boy, we've really thinned the herd here, haven't we?" Hoffen said, referring to the number of trees they've sold.

"Yeah, we may be able to empty the lot this weekend. That ought to make Dez happy," Timothy said.

"Anything that puts money in Dez's pocket makes him happy," Hoffen said.

"You seem to have caught onto him pretty quickly in the past few weeks. Ever study psychology?" Timothy said.

"No, not formally. But I've known people like Dez for a long time."

Timothy started to loosen up, and Hoffen dug deeper.

"So, what happens when the lot's empty? Back to more hours at the hospital? Work here for Dez?" Hoffen asked.

"I don't know, Hoffen. This thing with Mom has complicated things a bit. I'm the only one that's in any position to help her. Leslie can't help, and my brother doesn't care. If I worked here and blew off school for a while, I could make enough money to get us out of the hole we're in, and with her in the hospital, the hole is getting deeper."

"What about school?"

"I'm damned if I do and damned if I don't. You know what's funny? I just wrote a term paper on a novel, *Catch-22* by Joseph

Heller, and I'm thinking the whole time I'm writing this that I'm living a *Catch-22* life. School is a dream and a nightmare at the same time for me."

"How so?"

"It's my dream to become a psychologist, but getting there is proving to be a nightmare."

"That's a little dramatic, isn't it?"

"Maybe, but you asked what I'm thinking."

"You know why Heller wrote that book, don't you? He was a bombardier in World War II and discovered that being declared insane was a legitimate way out of the war. Those who wanted to fly were thought to be insane and therefore didn't have to fly. But anyone who claimed insanity because of the war was really sane. In other words, acting crazy was the sanest thing you could do," Hoffen said.

Timothy laughed at this. "Yeah, well, I feel like I know about insanity. Maybe that's why I want to go into psychology. To understand a crazy world."

"Or maybe yourself." Hoffen paused to let his words sink in.

"Have you read *Catch-22*?"

"Oh, heavens yes. I met Heller once."

"What?" Timothy said.

"Yes, I told you, my son was in World War II as a bombardier. He and Heller were stationed together. When my son didn't come home, Heller came to see me. We talked about the craziness they experienced and how their reaction made them sane. Heller said he wanted to write about the war. Twenty years later, I was browsing in a bookstore and there, in the best seller stack, was his book. I bought a copy and enjoyed it, especially the craziness of life. I still have it."

"That's an amazing story. You really have had some interesting life experiences," Timothy said.

"That's one advantage of having been around for a while—you see a lot of things. For example, I've seen that life is difficult but not impossible," Hoffen said.

"Yeah, it seems like I'm still stuck on the impossible side."

"Give it time. And here's the real paradox—be patient. Let some things happen. Your dreams may be in the process of reshaping themselves a bit right now, and maybe you're pushing too hard,"

Hoffen said.

"That's my *Catch-22*? Be patient even though I'm running out of time?" Timothy said.

"Yes. And you're not running out of time. You're young, ambitious, and hardworking. That is a great combination."

"It doesn't feel that way."

"Did you enjoy writing that term paper?" Hoffen said.

"Yes, I did. A lot, in fact."

"Why?"

"Because I understood what was happening. I could identify with it."

"Have you found that same insight in your other studies?"

"Not really. Not yet," said Timothy.

"Then I would keep reading good books and writing good term papers. Others' life experiences are good teachers for curious students. You may find you can work out a lot with pen and paper."

"I could do that," Timothy said.

Hoffen nodded. "And as far as this thing with Dez, you don't have to make that decision today."

"That's true, but I feel like I'm running out of choices."

"There are always choices—some you see, and others you don't," Hoffen said.

"Yeah, I wish I weren't blind to other choices. And I have to consider Cheryl in all of this. She didn't bargain for all of my problems."

"What do you have to decide about Cheryl?"

"Whether or not to cut her loose. I love her enough to cut her free from my problems."

"What! You mean break up with her because you have problems? Doesn't she have a say in this?"

"You sound like my sister."

"Then maybe you should listen. It's like when you're driving down the street and another car honks at you. You look around to see what's wrong. If you see nothing, you think the other guy is wrong. But if more cars start honking horns, you should look closer. Maybe you're causing it," Hoffen said.

"I don't think it's fair for her to have to put up with all of this. You know, life in my world."

"Timothy, that's life. Pain. Joy. Hope. Despair. All of it. It's just life," Hoffen said. "Pain is as much a part of life as joy. Hope is as much a part of life as despair."

"Yeah, well, some days, life isn't that special. . . . I better go help those people with their tree."

Hoffen watched Timothy walk away and saw despair taking root. Hoffen recognized the confusion and frustration people experienced as they approached life-changing events. He knew fear, doubt, and the pull of the status quo kept people stuck in whatever circumstance they found themselves. He understood Timothy struggled with a simultaneous calling and resistance. This tug-of-war of opposing forces—positive and negative—meant Timothy was on the edge of something big in his life. Hoffen wondered if he had enough time to help Timothy make his transition from feeling helpless to hopeful. He decided to pay Dez and Edna a visit.

He walked back to the shop. Dez and Edna stood there smoking and grinning smugly. Kenny stood in the corner guzzling milk from a pint carton.

"Hey, pea brain. Did you pay for that?" Edna said to Kenny.

"Oh, forgot. Sorry, Ed." Kenny said.

Hoffen knew Kenny neither forgot nor felt sorry he took it. Kenny paid for the milk and walked out of the shop grinning at Hoffen.

"Ain't it enough we give someone like that a job? It's charity, I tell ya," Dez said.

"There it is," Edna said. "Then the simpleton steals from us. Shows how stupid he is."

"It's downright charity givin' him a job," Dez said.

Hoffen knew they laid it on thick for him. They wanted to see what he would say. Dez and Edna stood there grinning and smirking.

"I guess you two are proud of yourselves," Hoffen said.

"Well, looky here, Ed. Huff 'n Puff's got somethin' to say. Say it, old man. What's on your mind?"

"It's bad enough you two give Kenny a tough time. I know why he's here, but Timothy? This young man is trying to build a life, and you two are making it as tough as possible by confusing his thinking," Hoffen said.

"Hey, you do what you do, and we do what we do, old man. You're lucky we let you in the game."

"You didn't let me in. You had no choice, and you know it. It's the way the game is played. I'm here to do a job, and I'm not finished yet."

"Us neither, old man," Edna hissed at Hoffen.

"It looks to me like you brought out the whole team for this one? This win must be important to your side. What happens if you fail?" Hoffen asked.

Dez grinned, a gaping hole in his face exposing a nasty set of yellow-brown stumps and breath so foul it stunk up the entire shop. Ed coughed a cumulous cloud of cigarette smoke toward Hoffen.

"Don't plan to fail, Huff 'n Puff."

"Yeah, we got this one in the bag," Edna added.

"You haven't won yet. I've got a pretty good idea why this one is important to you," Hoffen said.

"You don't know squat," Dez said.

"I know you're keeping score and losing," Hoffen said.

"We ain't losing nothin," Edna said.

"Get outta here, old man, and sell some pine. That's your job, ain't it?" Dez said.

Hoffen walked to the back door of the shop and turned to them. "Hope will prevail."

He didn't wait for a response. He walked back to the lot and stood there watching Timothy talk to a family about a tree. He knew Timothy faced a tough few days. Timothy was approaching that critical point when the pull of opposing forces was strongest. Hoffen prepared to take bold action.

CHAPTER TWENTY-EIGHT

TIMOTHY'S ROOM FACED east, and the early morning sun hit his pillow at the right angle to awaken him. Growing up, Timothy loved Sunday mornings. In those days, he slept in, ate a big breakfast, read the paper, and went to church. Those memories seemed more distant than they were.

He lay there for a few minutes thinking about the past week, especially the past couple of days. He spent last evening with Cheryl at her house. He did most of the talking, and she did most of the listening. School, Mom, the hospital, Dez, and Hoffen. He opened up like a ripped sail.

He hoped this week would turn out better than last week. He planned to take advantage of this last study day before exams. A knot in his gut told him it might not work out exactly as he planned. *When does life work out for me as I planned? I didn't plan to get shot down. I didn't plan to lose my best friend. When do I get to drive the bus? I'm tired of being a passenger.*

He mentally ran through his day—a trip to the hospital, Mass in the chapel, Schoen's for a couple of hours, and home by midafternoon to study the rest of the day. He wanted his exams behind him so he could make decisions about his future.

He took a shower, shaved, and gobbled a couple of hard-boiled eggs and toast. No coffee. He forgot to buy some. *No problem. I can get a cup at the hospital.* He hopped in his car and gave it a few pumps of the gas pedal. It woke up on his third attempt. The car hated cold mornings more than his leg did.

He drove to the hospital by way of the doughnut shop. Mom liked a particular jelly doughnut they had, and he didn't want to wait for coffee at the hospital. He visited with Mom for about half an hour. She seemed about the same as the day before, though her breathing sounded better. The nurse told him they still didn't have the results of the tests but should have them by Monday morning. He thanked her and left for the chapel and then Schoen's.

He arrived at Schoen's on time and Dez met him in the lot.

"Why don't you get rid of that piece of junk and get yourself something decent. I can see the smoke from that thing a block away. You're polluting all of Brentwood."

"It started, Dez. That's about all I can expect at this point."

"I'll tell ya what I told the mole head and the ol' man. I want all of those trees gone today. Do whatever ya gotta do to get rid of them. That's what I pay you morons for—to move pine. Anything left after today I'm burnin' in my woodstove at home."

"Really? Your woodstove?" Timothy asked. "Is it safe?"

"Hell yeah. Pine burns good after it sits for a couple of months, and it's cheap fuel. Now, get back there, and help those schleps sell some trees."

As he walked away, he heard Dez mutter under his breath about charity cases, retards, and retreads.

"Hey, next time I see ya I want an answer about working those hours we talked about. You're lucky I'm still willing to give you that job," Dez yelled after him.

Timothy nodded and walked away. He wanted to say no at this moment but couldn't. The economy teetered on the edge of a recession, and jobs were tough to find right now, especially ones that paid a decent wage. He couldn't say no to Dez without having something else to say yes to.

Maybe Dez is right. College isn't for everyone.

About that time, a brand-new 1973 Chevelle SS pulled into the lot and parked next to Timothy's heap. Timothy wanted to laugh at the contrast, but he didn't have it in him. The Chevelle had a midnight-blue, metallic overcoat with rally wheels and enough chrome to blind a person on a sunny day. Timothy looked at the car like a poor child looks in the window of a toy store. The door opened, and Timothy couldn't believe his eyes.

This is the last person I want to see today.

He quickly walked over to a family comparing two fir trees to avoid helping the driver of the Chevelle.

Dez came over to Timothy and said, "See that guy over there with the fancy overcoat? Take care of him."

"I'm busy here with these folks, Dez."

"Go. I'll finish up here. I want *you* to deal with this guy," Dez said.

"What about Kenny?" Timothy said.

"No. I got that idiot doing somethin' else, and the ol' man's in the shitter. Now go. No more back talk," Dez said.

Timothy turned and walked slowly toward the man in the cashmere overcoat. *Of course this asshole's wearing cashmere.* He hoped if he walked slowly enough the man would leave before he got there. No such luck.

The man saw him and approached Timothy. "O'Rourke. I'll be damned. What are you doing here? Do you work here? Of course you do."

"Goodenough?" Timothy said.

"Yes, old man. How are you?"

Old man. You pretentious asshole.

"Fine. You?"

"I'm fine, just fine, and Constance is fine, too."

"Constance? You mean Connie?" Timothy asked.

Timothy did not want to talk about Connie. That bus left the station a long time ago.

"Yes, of course. She no longer goes by Connie. She decided her full, given name is more sophisticated. She thought Connie sounded too bourgeois," Goodenough said.

"Really? What can I do for you?" Timothy said, though he didn't want to do anything for Goodenough except punch his Jodie face.

"I'm here for a tree. Constance and I just returned from a two-week ski trip at my family's cabin in Utah. We forgot to get a tree before we left, and Constance insists on a big spruce. Can you help me?"

"Sure. We're running low, as you can see, but we have a few

spruces left. Follow me."

Timothy led him to the back of the lot to the spruce trees.

"Best you've got. Money's not an issue. Can't disappoint the little lady," Goodenough said.

"I'm sure. What do you think about this one?"

Timothy pulled the tallest and fullest spruce out of the tree stand.

"Perfect. Constance will love it. What do I owe you?"

How about an apology for stealing my girl while I was in Vietnam? How about apologizing for being an arrogant asshole? How about an apology for sucking the same air I breathe?

"Twenty bucks," Timothy said.

"Sounds like a bargain. Can I get some help carrying it to the car?"

Goodenough handed Timothy a twenty.

"Sure. I wouldn't want to see you get some tree sap on that cashmere coat."

Goodenough walked behind Timothy. The cold air and the weight of the tree pressed hard on Timothy's leg. Though he tried not to limp, he couldn't escape the pain.

"Say, old man, I heard about your accident in the Army," Goodenough said awkwardly.

"It wasn't an accident, Goodenough. The VC shot me down."

It's only a little worse than getting shot down at home.

"Yes, I heard that. Whew! That must have been scary. My draft number was forty, but with my 2-S deferment, I was able to avoid that mess."

"We missed you," Timothy said with piercing eye contact. "There was plenty of room for you guys that had deferments."

Goodenough let it pass.

"So, what are you doing these days? Is this your full-time job?" Goodenough asked.

"I work here part time during Christmas and part time at the hospital. I'm a full-time student," Timothy said.

"Sounds tough. I can't imagine going to school full time and working, too," Goodenough said.

"Well, Goodenough, some of us have to pay our own way, and that's how we do it."

Goodenough let that pass, too.

"This is my car here—the new Chevelle. Picked it up before our ski trip. It's a four-speed, 350 cubic-inch screamer. Good thing it has bucket seats to hold us in when I wind it out. Constance wanted me to get the jade green, but I had to put my foot down on the blue. You know, it's a guy thing."

Timothy looked at Goodenough and wondered if he had a clue how he sounded. *This guy could be the biggest asshole I've ever known.*

"Say, careful, if you don't mind. Don't want to scratch the paint," Goodenough said.

"No problem, I'll tie it down tight so it won't fall off when you accelerate," Timothy said.

"Ha, that's a good one. Here, for you," Goodenough said.

He handed Timothy another twenty.

"No, that's okay, Goodenough. I don't accept tips. If you don't mind, put it in the collection plate on Christmas."

Goodenough's face turned red. Timothy knew this guy didn't have the guts to be mad, so it must have been embarrassment.

"Oh, I didn't mean anything by that offer. I hope you're not offended," Goodenough said.

"Not in the least," Timothy said.

A few moments of awkward silence passed as Timothy tied down the tree.

"Have you ever thought about applying for work at the railroad? My father and I have some influence there and might be able to help you."

"Thanks, but I'm working around my class schedule."

"Of course. Even though you don't have a degree, there may be something in one of our entry-level hourly positions—the mailroom or something. Many of our folks get their start in those lower-level jobs."

"Is that where you started, Goodenough?" Timothy couldn't resist the jab.

"Oh, heavens no. I began in the management development program, but you need a degree for that. I'm now in charge of scheduling for the Tri-State Region."

Timothy held onto his cool while this bag of arrogant chattering bones talked to him, but he had his fill by this point.

"You're set to go. Have a nice Christmas," Timothy said.

"Thank you, and you too. I'll tell Constance I ran into you,"

Goodenough said.

"You do that."

Timothy walked back toward the lot. Goodenough's car roared to life on the first turn of the key. He refused to turn around and look at it.

Of course his car started right off. Of course he's the manager of some bullshit department in a bureaucratic cubicle farm. Of course they went skiing at the family ski lodge. Of course he's married to someone named Constance.

As Goodenough pulled out of the lot, he jerked the clutch, killed the engine, and the car abruptly stopped. Timothy grinned. *Karma.*

Timothy did not see Dez approach him.

"I see you took care of him," Dez said, grinning mischievously. "Big tip? Do you know that guy? Seems like you know him. An old friend?"

"No tip and sure as hell no old friend, but he gave me some good advice," Timothy said.

"Yeah, what's that?" Dez asked.

"He told me to get an education, or I would end up working in a mail room or a tree lot for the rest of my life."

"What the hell does that mean?" Dez said.

Timothy walked back to the trees.

CHAPTER TWENTY-NINE

TIMOTHY WOKE EARLY with anticipation. He had studied hard all semester and prepared for the challenge. As he lay in bed, Timothy thought about his plans for the week. *Ace this poly-sci exam today, get my B for the semester, and I'm done with Professor Leibert. Next, I can focus on my other exams. I'll be done with all of them by Wednesday. Then, I can make decisions about the future.*

He planned to eat a good breakfast and leave early to arrive at school with enough time for some last-minute cramming. He was surprisingly upbeat considering the past couple of days. *Maybe Hoffen was right. Things can get better if I hang onto a little bit of hope.* Hope was a good traveling partner. Timothy compartmentalized the events of the past few days—even the interaction with Goodenough. Denial or compartmentalizing worked for him.

He showered, shaved, and ate like he was fueling for an athletic contest. He planned to get coffee at the Student Union. When he opened the front door, a thirty-degree northwesterly wind slapped him in the face. He went back into the house to get a warmer coat and gloves. He had to walk a few blocks when he got to school.

His car was stubborn this morning. *Come on, not this morning. Not today.* Timothy coaxed it to life. He turned onto the entrance ramp and gunned it. The Fairlane roared back. He amused himself with the thought, *This may not be a Chevelle SS, but this old baby still has some life in it.* He pushed the Fairlane to the red line and, before the automatic transmission could shift, he heard a clank and a grind, and the engine started missing.

"No, not today. Not today. Not this morning," he screamed at the car, hoping it would cooperate. He looked out the rearview mirror to check traffic and saw a cloud of black smoke in the car's wake. "Come on, I need a break today, please."

The car limped up an exit ramp to a Texaco service station. One last push on the gas pedal nudged his car into the station. He shut off the engine as soon as possible. A full-service attendant approached.

"That doesn't sound good. What happened?" the attendant asked.

Timothy stepped out of the car and told him what happened. The attendant said he would get a mechanic to look at it. Timothy stood there, thoughts racing. *How long is this going to take? How do I get to school? Will I be late? What about work? What's this going to cost?* For a guy who could compartmentalize, his mind ran wildly from one worry to another.

The mechanic came outside, wiping grease off his hands on a shop towel and said, "What's the problem? The other guy told me this thing is making some noise."

"I don't know," Timothy said and rubbed his neck. "I got on the highway, opened it up, and heard this clank and grind."

"Did you red line it?"

"Yeah, probably."

"You can't do that with an old engine, especially in this weather. It doesn't wake up that fast. Crank it up and let's hear what you got." The mechanic sounded like a doctor talking to a patient.

Timothy started the engine.

"Yeah, what I thought. Rods, bearings, or rings. Sounds bad anyway. You can't drive it like that or the engine will seize up on you, and you might as well salvage it."

"Can you fix it?" Timothy asked.

"Sure, we can fix it, but it ain't gonna be cheap. Probably take a week or so."

"A week? You're kidding! What are we talking about money-wise?"

"To tell you the truth, if it was me, I'd sell it for parts and get a new car. This will probably set you back a thousand bucks, and for that, you could get a good used car without too many miles."

Timothy froze. *A thousand dollars! I just spent my last thousand on a new furnace.*

"You okay, fella? Sorry to give you the bad news," the mechanic said.

"Yeah, sure. I'm okay. Thanks. Look, I have to get to school to take an exam. Can I leave this here until I figure out something later in the day?"

"No problem. Let's push it out of the way over there by the side of the garage."

The mechanic called to the attendant and the three of them pushed the car along the building.

"I'll be back later to figure this out," Timothy said.

"I'll figure what it'll cost and be able to tell you then," the mechanic said.

"Thanks. You got a phone I can use?"

"Sure, inside." The mechanic pointed to the garage office.

Timothy got the phone book and looked up a number.

"Political Science Office, please."

"One moment, sir," the operator said.

The woman answered on the third ring. "Political Science Office."

"Can you connect me to Professor Leibert?" he said.

"He's not in his office. He has an exam in a few minutes. Would you like to leave him a message?"

"Yes, I'm one of his students, Timothy O'Rourke, and I'm supposed to be in that exam. I had car trouble this morning, and I'm at the gas station trying to get to school as soon as possible. Can you get this message to him, please?"

"Sure, I'll send someone over to the class right now," the secretary said.

"Thanks."

"Sure."

Okay, now how do I get to school? I don't have enough for a cab, and I don't know the bus schedule.

Timothy thanked the attendant and mechanic and walked to the eastbound entrance ramp. He slung his book bag slung over his shoulder to look like a student. He stuck out his thumb and stared at passing drivers. By the time someone picked him up, the exam had already started. He hoped Professor Leibert had received his phone message and understood. The first students to finish the exam exited the classroom as he arrived. Passing them quickly, he failed to return their solidarity nods.

Winded from the long walk and standing there like a child trying to catch his breath, Timothy said, "Professor Leibert, I just got here."

"I see that, Mr. O'Rourke."

"Did you get my message?"

"Obviously not, since I have no idea to what you are referring," Professor Leibert said.

"I called your office about an hour ago and talked with your secretary. I explained to her my predicament, and she said she would get word to you."

"Like your fellow students who were here on time for this final, I was in this classroom handing out the exams. I've been here the whole time," the professor said.

"I'm sorry. I had car trouble." Timothy explained the chain of events including his hitchhiking a ride.

Professor Leibert appeared disinterested in Timothy's explanation. "I'm sorry for your troubles, Mr. O'Rourke, but what do you want?"

"I want a chance to take the exam. I've studied a lot of hours for this."

"I'm sorry. You've missed the exam time. How can I allow you a makeup and be fair to the other students? It would require me to design a new exam, and I don't have that kind of time."

"But I studied hard for this. I'll take a tougher exam if needed."

"I'm sorry. It's not that I'm unsympathetic to your situation, but I have a class of fifty other students to consider."

"Do you think they care that I'm late?"

"Maybe not, but that extra time to study might give you an advantage," Professor Leibert said.

"My extra time to prepare was spent at a gas station and on Highway 40 hitching a ride to try to get here on time." Timothy's tone became aggressive.

"I'm sorry, Mr. O'Rourke. Those are the rules."

"What rules?"

"My rules," Professor Leibert said.

Timothy's face turned red. His lips tightened, and the veins in his neck throbbed. He could see himself grabbing the professor by the scruff of the neck, but his better sense prevailed.

"Your rules? That sounds arbitrary to me. If they're your rules, you can change them," Timothy pushed.

"That's a fairly cogent argument, Mr. O'Rourke, but everyone must operate by the same set of rules. A failure to operate in that manner results in chaos. It's the only way for this class to be fair."

Fair? That's what you call the way you treated me this semester because you don't like my military service? Is that what you call demeaning any student's opinion that differs from yours? There's nothing fair about your classroom, you hypocritical asshole. Timothy wanted to say all of this, but again his good sense prevailed.

"So, what now?" Timothy asked.

"As I said, I'm not unsympathetic to your situation. Here's what I am willing to do. Normally, I would assign an incomplete grade for a student who missed finals, and you would have to repeat the course next semester."

"Take it again?"

"Yes, but the reality is I don't want you in my classroom next semester. Your political views are not something to which I want the other students exposed. They're impressionable at this time in their lives. They lack your life experiences and may be seduced by your adventures and exploits."

Seduced? Adventures and exploits? You little prick. Timothy wanted to laugh, shout, or both. He opted for self-control. He didn't want to give the professor any more reason to push back.

"I don't want to be in this class next semester, either. I guess we agree on something, finally."

"Apparently so," Professor Leibert grinned. "As I was saying, you have completed all of the course work to this point and already have a grade."

"Yes, a C at this point," Timothy said.

"Right, whatever it is. I will have to look at that. I will give you that grade without penalty for missing the exam."

"So all of this study and prep has gone to waste," Timothy said.

"Not if your goal was to get an education," Professor Leibert said and smirked. "You're not here for tests, Mr. O'Rourke. You're here for an education."

Timothy hated this rational response. It made too much sense. He calmed a bit. "I was hoping to get my grade up to a B with this exam. I'm trying to boost my GPA to get into grad school. Clinical Psych is tough to get into."

"Look, Mr. O'Rourke, do you want to know why I'm willing to do this?"

"Why?"

"Apparently, some of your classmates think I have been especially hard on you and the other veterans in the class. I don't think I was, but they thought it and went to Father Schmitt and complained—"

Timothy cut him off. "You don't think I was part of that, do you?"

"No, in fact I know you weren't. Father told me so. Since I don't want to have to deal with him or you again, I am willing to be flexible in my incomplete rule and give you the grade you have earned this semester. I think that's accommodating."

Timothy couldn't bring himself to thank the professor. He nodded his acknowledgement of this consideration and repeated mentally, *Take yes for an answer.*

"Also, the last paper you wrote on the Vietnam War . . . I disagreed with every point you made in that paper, and I understand you saw it from a different perspective . . . but that was the best-researched and most well-written paper I have seen from an undergraduate. I showed it to a couple of others in the department, and they concurred with me. They disagreed with your premise but respected your writing and rhetorical talent, as did I."

Timothy, amid his confusion, managed to say thanks with a nod of his head.

"Look, I don't have to agree with you to respect your work. After all, I am an educator. I appreciate a well-reasoned argument even if it fails to persuade me."

The professor's comments weighed heavily on Timothy's mind. He didn't like this guy but didn't mind the compliment. *This is the worst kind of appreciation—a victim thanking the oppressor for taking it easier on him. This is insanity.*

"All right, thanks for hearing me out," Timothy said.

"That's why I'm here. You know, there are a lot of good psychologists in this school, but there are not many good writers."

Walking to the Student Union, Timothy considered his situation. *A damn C in that class is not going to help my GPA, which means no financial aid. Shit, that's only one of my problems. What about the car? I don't have a thousand dollars to repair or replace that thing. I don't even have five hundred dollars for that. I have no money and no transportation—a fitting combination for someone going nowhere. I'm tired of this shit. If I drop out now, no GI Bill money. How can dropping out make me broker than I am? I'm living in a Catch-22 world. Heller could have written these choices for me. Maybe I am crazy for dreaming of a better life.*

Timothy walked to the Student Union for a cup of coffee but wanted something stronger. Forget beer; straight vodka sounded better because it would get him there quicker. He had an experimental psychology exam on Tuesday—not one of his favorites, but he knew he would do well on it. He had abnormal psych and statistics scheduled for Wednesday. He liked both of these. He would turn in his final paper on *Catch-22* for contemporary American literature on Tuesday. Though disappointed with the outcome of his political science exam, he remained confident about the rest of his week.

He needed a ride home and called his friend.

"Hey, Scoot," Timothy said.

"What's up, Tim?"

"Exams, you know."

"Another reason I never went to college. I hate tests. They ask questions I know nothing about," Scoot said.

"Yeah, I hope that's not the case for me. You got any time this afternoon?"

"Sure. What's up?"

Timothy filled him in on the car. "I have to go back this afternoon and wanted someone to go with me to translate all that mechanics jargon you guys speak."

"Yep, we have a secret language we talk," Scoot said. "What time and where?"

"I'm at school now and need to study for a few hours. How about five o'clock?"

"Sure, where?"

"At the Texaco station at 40 and Brentwood Blvd."

"How are you going to get there?" Scoot asked.

"I'll take a bus or hitch."

"Bullshit. I'll pick you up."

"Nah, you don't have to do that," Timothy said.

"I want to. We're bros, you know."

"Okay, there's a Shell station right off the highway at Grand. How about I meet you there at four-thirty?"

"Got it. See ya."

Timothy walked to the school library. He passed a Students for a Democratic Society demonstration. This left-wing, anti-war group protested regularly on campus. He recognized a couple of students from his political science class and nodded. They returned the courtesy. He never sensed animosity from the other students, only Professor Leibert.

When he got to the library, he went straight to the third-floor study booths. He figured a few hours here and he would be ready for the exam. He studied through lunch and into the early afternoon, until his eyes could no longer stay open. He laid his head on the table. A couple of coeds laughing loudly woke him at four. He gathered his books and left.

It hadn't warmed up much, and his leg remained stiff from earlier. He pushed through the pain and made it to the station on time. Scoot had arrived first.

"Am I late?" Timothy asked.

"Nope." Scoot shook his head. "I'm early. Had to go downtown to pick up some parts, so I decided to make one trip."

"Man, I appreciate this."

"I told ya, no problem. All that education and you can't speak to a mechanic, huh?"

"Right. Pathetic, isn't it?"

"It's how we keep our secrets to ourselves," Scoot said.

As they drove, Timothy rambled nonstop—Mom, his car, Cheryl, the hospital, bills, and Dez.

"You want to work full time for that guy? He's a world-class asshole," Scoot said.

"Only as a last resort. I've got to let him know by this weekend."

"Lots on your plate, bro," Scoot said.

"Too much. I feel like a glutton."

Scoot shifted gears in his truck and the conversation followed the lead. "Still haven't heard anything about Bobby or any of those other guys, and I'm listening for it."

"Me neither," Timothy said. "With everything else going on, I feel guilty not giving it more time."

"Hey, don't beat yourself up over that. You've got plenty of other stuff to deal with," Scoot said.

"Yeah, maybe too much."

Focus on the pressing thing of the moment. Focus on the pressing thing of the moment. Focus on the pressing thing of the moment. Timothy continued his mantra.

"Comin' up on our exit," Scoot said.

Timothy pointed to the service station. "Over there—the Texaco."

"Yeah, got it."

They exited and pulled into the lot next to Timothy's car.

The attendant met them. "How ya doin'? Take your test?"

Timothy had no interest in pleasantries. "Is the mechanic around?"

"No, he left about an hour ago. He works the early shift, but he left an estimate in the shop for ya."

Scoot leaned over to Timothy and said, "Don't commit to anything until I talk to the mechanic." Timothy nodded. The attendant gave him the estimate.

"Wow, $915! Did you guys plan to rebuild the whole thing?" Timothy asked.

The attendant shrugged. "Sorry, man. I dunno, I guess. I just pump gas here."

"When will he be back so I can talk to him?" Timothy asked.

"Tomorrow morning. Comes in at seven."

"Okay, thanks," Timothy said.

Scoot jumped in the conversation. "Tell ya what. I'm going to send a truck over here tomorrow to pick this car up and take it to my place until my friend here decides what he's going to do with this thing."

"Uh, okay. I'll let 'em know," the attendant said.

"Ain't Frank your mechanic?" Scoot asked.

"Yeah. Know him?"

"He rides with our group sometimes. We call him Cave Man—

he looks like one with his hair and beard," Scoot said.

"Come to think of it, he does. Good to know. We may start calling him that around here," the attendant said.

"I know he'll appreciate that," Scoot said and laughed.

As they walked back to Scoot's truck, Timothy said, "What do you mean you're going to pick it up?"

"Look, man, if you leave that thing here, you got no negotiating power. He'll figure you're stuck. I'll pick it up and park it at my place until you figure out what you're gonna do."

"Okay, that makes sense, but I have to do something for transportation," Timothy said.

"I got you covered on that. You know that old red shop truck I got? It's a pathetic sight but runs like a top. Mechanically, it's strong as can be. You can drive it until you decide how you want to handle your stuff. That way all you got to worry about is your tests."

"That's a good thought." Timothy nodded. "The exams are the most important thing this minute. I need to get through this week. Okay, thanks, Scoot."

"See, things are already lookin' up."

"I've been looking up lately and only seeing clouds. It's nice to see a little light break through." Timothy smiled.

Scoot hadn't exaggerated the condition of the truck. The fenders didn't match the color of the body, one door came from another truck, it had more rust than paint, and Timothy could see the street through the passenger floorboard. But, as Scoot promised, it started on the first crank and sounded strong. And that sound was exactly what Timothy needed at this point. The heater even worked.

CHAPTER THIRTY

TIMOTHY LEFT SCOOT'S shop and arrived at the hospital to see his mother. He waited in the truck until a few pickets left.

"How's she doing, Sandy?" he asked the charge nurse.

"Oh, hi, Tim. She's about the same. Her breathing is occasionally labored, but her lungs sound clear. The doctors are still trying to figure out the right mix of meds for her. For now, it's wait and see how the blood thinner works. Sort of touch and go." This sounded more like a report given to a staff member than a family member.

"Touch and go—that's not what I expected to hear," Timothy said.

"I'm sorry. That sounds worse than I meant," Sandy said. "We are cautiously optimistic, and those are the words the doctor used earlier today."

"Optimistic? That sounds a little better."

"Yes. I should have said that the first time," Sandy said.

"Okay, I'm going in to see her. Thanks."

He walked down the hall to Mom's room. "Hi, Mom. How are you?"

"Timmy, I'm glad to see you. I've been worried about your exams. I hope you did okay. How did it go?"

He wanted to tell her about the car and the conversation with

Professor Leibert, but he saw no point adding those problems to the mix of Mom's issues.

"It went fine today. I should get the grade I need. I talked to Sandy, and she said you're in a holding pattern right now."

"Yes, the doctor said I needed time for the medicine to work. I don't understand a word they say. Doctors and nurses might as well be talking Greek or some secret language."

"Mechanics, too," Timothy said before he could catch himself.

"Huh?" Mom said.

"Nothing, Mom. Making a joke."

"Oh yes, I do what they tell me to do. I figure they know what's best."

"You're a good patient, Mom, and that's what it takes around here."

"Lord knows I've had a lot of practice."

"Yes, you have. Has Leslie been up to see you?" Timothy quickly changed the conversation, not wanting to travel down the path of all of her sicknesses.

"She came up during her lunch hour today. Wasn't that nice? She and Ike have a lot going on."

"Yes, they do. Four kids will do that to you. Can I get you anything?"

"No, I want to lay here and rest my eyes," Mom said.

"Okay, I'll sit here with you for a while. Go ahead and try to rest."

Mom closed her eyes and drifted off. Timothy watched and thought she wasn't putting up much of a fight, at least not like she usually did. He saw this in other patients who began to accept their illnesses or diseases. It wasn't a bad thing necessarily, but it made a difference since it was his mother. *Part of the recovery process I guess.*

When Mom started to snore, he went back to the nurses' station to test his observations with the staff. They affirmed she was weak from the experience, and once she began eating and moving around, her energy would return. He thanked them, walked back to her room, and sat for a while until she stirred.

"Mom, I think I need to get going. Studies and all."

"Oh, I'm sorry I'm not home to fix you a good dinner. A man needs a good meal at night."

"That's fine, Mom. I'm pretty self-sufficient."

"Yes, you are. You've had a lot of practice, haven't you?"

"Nothing wrong with that." He leaned over and kissed Mom on her cold forehead. She grabbed his hand and held tightly, as if she didn't want to let go.

"I work tomorrow night, and I'll be back up here then. Get some sleep and eat something. You need to get your energy up."

"Okay, honey. I will. Always looking out for me, aren't you?" Mom said.

"Yeah. Good night."

He left feeling a bit depleted. Mom could do that to him, intentionally or not. He prepared himself for the usual heaping of guilt, but not for this. Her lack of fight caught him off guard, and it worried him.

Scoot's truck sprang to life at his first command. He liked feeling in control. In the Fairlane, turning the key was a request.

On the drive home, he thought about Mom. He worried she might not recover from this, and it saddened him to think about life without her. He jarred himself back into the moment. He hated when he thought worst possible outcome—WPO, as he called it. When he got home, he made a ham sandwich and grabbed a Pabst. He wanted more than one but knew he had a few hours of study left, so he drank just enough to wash down his dinner. *I've got to call Cheryl.*

"Hey, it's me," he said.

"I hoped you would call. I was going to wait until later and call you if you hadn't called. How was your exam?"

"I don't know. I didn't take it." Timothy paused to let this sink in, and told Cheryl what happened.

"Okay, you've got Scoot's truck for transportation, right?"

"Yeah, for the time being, anyway. I've got to get through these next couple of days. Then I'll decide what to do. First things first, you know." Timothy sounded more in charge than he was. He liked putting up a front for Cheryl. For Timothy, self-delusion was a poor man's pride.

"Timothy, I know how you feel about this, but will you please let me help you? I've got some money saved—"

He cut her off in mid-sentence. "I'm not taking your money.

What kind of man would that make me?"

"Okay, okay, I'm sorry," Cheryl said. "I'm not trying to offend you. I can drive you if you need help or you could borrow my car."

"I'm covered with the truck," Timothy said defiantly. "It'll work short term, like I said."

Cheryl switched topics quickly. "Okay, how's your mom?"

Timothy told her about his visit and the nurses' comments. He rambled like someone with more thoughts than words.

"So what test is tomorrow?"

"Experimental psych—not my favorite, but I should do okay. I've got a solid *A* going into it, and I'll need it after today. Wednesday is abnormal psych and statistics. Then, onto Mister Pabst. I can use an evening with him."

"You sure can. Will you call me tomorrow after your test to let me know how you did?"

"Sure."

"Timothy, you know I'm here for you. You have big shoulders, but you don't have to carry the weight of all of this yourself." She paused. "I love you."

"Yeah, me too." He paused for their private joke to register. "I know you're here for me." He softened his tone.

"Okay. Get some good study in and a good night's sleep."

Timothy hung up and stared at the empty can of beer. He wanted another beer, or two or three or more, but decided studying would do him more good. Studying was the only thing in the way of a bad hangover. *Making the right decisions can be a burden.*

CHAPTER THIRTY-ONE

TIMOTHY WOKE UP Tuesday morning hoping it would be a better day than Monday. Scoot's truck started on the first turn of the key. With light traffic, he got to school earlier than he anticipated and had even more time for a last-minute review.

He took the exam and finished early. It was easier than he anticipated. Preparation made the difference. He went to the Student Union for another cup of coffee and to review for Wednesday's finals. He called Cheryl to deliver the good news. He liked calling her with something positive for a change. It seemed like every time he called her lately he felt like a loser.

He left school and went home to study for a few more hours and to catch a nap before going to the hospital for the night shift. Even though he would take Wednesday's exams on a few hours' sleep, he knew he could handle it if he got his nap in today. His plan succeeded. He got about six hours' sleep before leaving for work.

Driving to work he thought, *Today's turning out a whole lot better than yesterday. Maybe things are beginning to turn around in my life. I'll stop by to see Mom before starting my shift.*

Mom was asleep when he checked on her. Timothy spent an uneventful Tuesday night working in the ER. He even got in a couple of hours of study. He knew Wednesday's exams would go well, even though he struggled with statistics during the semester. He wanted it behind him. Then, he had abnormal psych, which he knew he could ace. He didn't want to break a good morning routine, so he went to the snack bar for a big breakfast. He had plenty of time for the fifteen-minute drive to school.

"Hey, early bird," Penny said as he walked in the snack bar.

"Hi, Penny," Timothy said.

"I heard you worked in the ER last night. Busy?"

"No, pretty quiet."

She knows that. This place is a rumor mill.

"How's your mom?"

"I poked my head in, and she had a stable night. That's a good thing, I guess," Timothy said.

"Glad to hear she's stable. You take your blessings where you can get them, I guess. Want a milkshake for her?"

"No, it's breakfast and off for exams—my last two and I'm done."

"Yea, freedom. You sound relieved," she said.

"We'll see."

"I think that calls for a celebration," Penny said.

"I think I'll visit Mister Pabst this evening and discuss things," he said.

"It sounds like a fun time. Do you want—" She stopped mid-sentence, and Timothy was glad because he knew it could have gotten awkward.

"Yeah, it'll be fun," he said quickly.

She changed the conversation. "So, have you figured out your plans yet for next semester?"

"That's part of why I want to meet with Mister Pabst tonight. I need to do some real thinking and make some decisions. There's a lot going on right now. I want to take my exams and catch my breath."

"It sounds like you have a lot of responsibilities. I'm sorry if I come across as nosy."

"No, that's fine. Yeah, I do have a lot on my mind right now, but that's just life."

"I think you need a vacation," Penny said.

Timothy laughed at the suggestion.

"A vacation? That's a pipe dream for a guy like me," he said.

"Why?"

"Like you said, too many responsibilities."

"Doesn't that get old? I mean, being that responsible?" Penny asked.

Only the young and naïve could ask that question.

"There are days," he said.

"Maybe you need to get away and clear your head. Things may look simpler then," she said.

She's starting to make sense.

"Are you a therapist?" He laughed.

"No, a concerned friend. Can I call you a friend?" she asked.

"Sure."

"Good. Here's an idea. You know Ginny on Three?" Penny said.

"Yeah, she's taking care of my mom."

"She and I leave in February for her uncle's condo in Fort Myers, Florida, for six weeks. It's our last hurrah before nursing school starts. She and I will be roommates in the summer. Bill from maintenance is going. He's kind of sweet on Ginny, and she likes him, too."

"It sounds like you guys will have fun," Timothy said. *Okay, this sounds like somewhere I don't want to go.*

"Carefree and single. How good does it get? Oh, did I mention it's free?" she said.

"Carefree and free sound great. I bet you guys will have a good time," he said.

"Wanna find out? You could go with us," Penny said.

Whoa, I set myself up for that one. Okay, I need to get out of this fast.

"Penny, I've got a girlfriend, you know."

"Well, I know you're too old to be going steady, so are you two engaged?"

"No, not exactly."

"Not exactly means no, doesn't it?" she pressed.

"Maybe you should go to law school."

"Am I persuading you?"

"Tempting? Yes. Persuading? No. Look, I hope I haven't been giving you the wrong impression," Timothy said.

"Oh, no. Just the opposite. You've made a great impression on me. Any girl would be thrilled to have you as a—friend." She laughed.

"That's not what I meant."

"I know. Where's your sense of humor?"

"Good question," he said. "How about some breakfast?"

"What's your pleasure?" Penny said playfully.

"Pancakes, two over easy, and bacon."

"Coming right up," she said.

He opened his statistics book for some last-minute review, but his mind drifted.

Six weeks away from responsibilities. God, that sounds good. It sounds like R & R—getting away from the action. Is this the same as running away from home as a kid? Something like this may get me away from responsibilities but not obligations. This comes with strings. No way. What about Cheryl? What would she think? What would I think if the situation were reversed? I wouldn't like it a bit. It sounds innocent, but I know it's not. But man, six weeks away from decisions and problems is tempting. Leslie would have to take care of Mom. About time. I've been pulling the wagon long enough. I deserve a life, right? And Frank, he's done nothing to help. It's about time he stepped up.

"Here ya go, hungry man," Penny said as she delivered the breakfast.

She leaned over with the platter and rubbed against him. He would have been lying to himself if he said he didn't feel a reaction to it.

"Thanks, and thanks for the offer, but I need to stay here. Responsibilities, you know," he said.

"Sure, the offer stands. Bill and Ginny are serious, and I will be their third wheel. I thought it might be fun to have a friend to hang around with. Bill plans to join the Marines when we return. I thought you'd be a good influence on him. He knows your background and respects you," Penny said.

"Oh, I didn't realize," Timothy said.

Could I have misread this whole thing? My radar must be bad these days. Maybe it was simply a friend thing. I hope I think more clearly in my exams.

"Enjoy your breakfast." She smiled and walked away.

Timothy gobbled the breakfast, left enough money on the table for the meal and a generous tip, and managed to slip out without saying goodbye to Penny. He thought rude was better than awkward. He could square it with her later.

She'll be fine—she likes to play the game.

He decided to check on Mom before leaving. Since he had exams, he knew he could use it as an excuse to get out of there in a hurry. She was sitting up in bed with her breakfast tray, sipping tea and eating toast.

"Hey, Mom. You're eating." he said.

"Yes, dear. I'm hungry this morning. It must have been that activity yesterday, making me get up in the chair."

"That's a good sign. Just got off work and thought I would peek in on you. Got exams this morning."

"Yes, dear. Go. Take your tests and do well. I know you have studied hard for these," Mom said.

"Thanks, Mom."

He leaned over and kissed her forehead.

"I'll be back later to check on you," he said.

"Goodbye, honey, and good luck."

CHAPTER THIRTY-TWO

AFTER HIS WEDNESDAY exams, Timothy walked to the Student Union to call Cheryl. The Student Union buzzed with post-exam euphoria. Music poured from the jukebox, laughter filled the air, and groups of students sat around talking. This painted a different picture than a few days ago.

"Hey, I'm done," he said.

"So, how did you do?" Cheryl asked.

"Good, I think. I know I aced the abnormal psych final, and I thought the stats exam would be tougher. The professor grades on a curve anyway, so I should get my grade. I'll need it after Monday's experience with Comrade Leibert."

"Congratulations. I'm proud of you. One more semester under your belt. I think a celebration is in order, and it's on me."

"Okay, girl. What do you have in mind?"

"A special occasion like this can mean only one thing: Mantia's," Cheryl said.

"You're on. You know how to make a guy a deal he can't refuse. How about I come by your house after you get off work? Say six o'clock?"

"I'll be waiting," she said.

Timothy left the Student Union and headed to the truck. It started on the first try. That added to his euphoria. *Life is good today.*

As he drove home, he sang along with the radio, drumming his fingers on the wheel. Timothy hadn't felt this good in a while. Even with his responsibilities and the decisions he faced, finishing the semester today and celebrating tonight with Cheryl offered needed relief. He decided to swing by the hospital and see Mom again before heading home for a short nap. He wanted to rest for their big night of celebrating. When he got to the hospital, Leslie was already there.

"Hey, Mom," he said.

"Hello, dear," Mom said.

She sounded weaker than a few hours ago. Leslie's eyes looked red.

"Tired, Mom?" he said.

"Yes. They made me walk this morning. I think it wore me out."

"Well, that's good you're up."

He looked at Leslie and nodded hopefully.

"Hey, Sis. What's up with you guys?"

"Work and kids, what else? I hear you finished your exams today," Leslie said.

"I took my last two this morning. I'm off for a couple of weeks, and I think I will catch up on some sleep," he said.

"That's good, dear. You deserve it."

"What about your car?" Leslie said.

Timothy gave Leslie a pleading look.

"What happened to your car?" Mom said.

"Oh, Scoot's doing some work on it. He let me use his truck," Timothy said.

"That's nice. He's a good friend, isn't he?" Mom said.

"Yes, he is," Timothy said.

Mom closed her eyes and breathed heavily. Timothy motioned Leslie toward the hall. They went outside Mom's room to talk.

"Why are your eyes red?" Timothy said.

"Can't you see?"

"See what?"

"Mom—she looks terrible," Leslie said.

"She looks tired to me. They got her up earlier. That's a good thing. She's probably tired from the exercise," Timothy said.

"Maybe. I haven't seen her in a couple of days, and you've seen her every day. It's more dramatic for me."

"I understand. She's stable. That's something to be grateful for," he said

"You're right. What are your plans to celebrate exams being over?"

"Cheryl is treating me to dinner at Mantia's."

"Whew, fancy. You'll love that."

"Timmy, are you still here?" Mom called out.

"Yes, Mom. We're in the hallway," he said.

"Could you get me some ice chips?"

"Sure."

Leslie went back inside as Timothy went to get the ice chips.

"Mom, I'm leaving. I need to go home to be there for the kids when they get home from school. I'll come back tomorrow to see you," Leslie said.

"Okay, dear. Thanks for coming up. I'm lucky to have you children. I don't know what I would do without you."

"You don't have to do anything. We're here," Leslie said as she leaned over and kissed Mom.

"Okay, dear. Thanks for coming by."

Timothy met Leslie at the door.

"God, I feel guilty every time I come up here," Leslie said. "She looks pitiful."

"Mom can do that to you, you know," Timothy said. "She is the master." He grinned.

"You're better at handling this stuff than I am," Leslie said.

"I've had more practice." He smiled. "Look, you have nothing to feel guilty about. You have your hands full."

"So do you," Leslie said.

"Yeah, but I don't have four kids depending on me."

"You're a good little brother."

She leaned forward and hugged him.

"And don't say anything else to Mom about the car. I didn't tell her. Besides, how did you know?"

"I think you know." Leslie smiled.

"Cheryl, right?"

"Timmy, do you have those chips?" Mom called.

"On the way, Mom." He fed her the ice chips.

"Do you know how lucky I am to have children like you and your sister?"

"Yeah, I do. You keep telling us that," he said.

He laughed loud enough for her to hear. Mom returned the laugh.

"Listen, Mom. I need to get going. I want to go home and take a nap before we go out tonight."

"Yes, I understand. How's your friend?" Mom said.

"If you mean Cheryl, she's fine. She asks about you all the time."

"Does she? She's a sweet girl. I think she's good for you."

Timothy said nothing. Mom never called Cheryl sweet. This sounded out of character for her he didn't know what to say. Mom looked at his dumbfounded face and smiled.

"Okay, Mom. See you tomorrow. I work tomorrow night, so I'll come up earlier in the day."

"Okay, Timmy. I love you."

"I love you too, Mom," he said.

Timothy drove slowly home, thinking about this semester and the relief of having it behind him. He wondered if he had the energy for the next semester.

Maybe Penny is right. Packing up and taking off for a while sounds like a tempting offer.

The adolescent Timothy missed that part of life because of the war. Penny's invitation simply echoed his longstanding thoughts. He experienced the same emotion all young soldiers confronted when they came home—that they skipped several grades in school and never had the opportunity to live that carefree life.

If I take off a semester to regroup, I could work the sixty hours for Dez, quit the hospital, and still save some money. If I did that through the end of summer, I could start back next fall with money in the bank. That two hundred and twenty a month from the VA doesn't even cover tuition, fees, and books. All right, I'm not going to think about that today. I'm going to celebrate. Besides, I need to check with Scoot when I get home.

He drove slowly the rest of the way, enjoying the pace. Not rushing felt therapeutic. The lack of urgency relaxed him. When he got home, Timothy called Scoot to check on the car. Scoot told him he wasn't able to talk to the guy yet but would try again later. He told Timothy he picked up the car on Tuesday and had it at the shop. It could sit for a couple of days until Timothy figured out what to do. Scoot didn't need his truck, so Timothy could drive it until he got his car fixed.

CHAPTER THIRTY-THREE

TIMOTHY DROVE PAST Cheryl's house and parked Scoot's truck down the street.

"Hi, I didn't see you drive up."

Timothy poked his head inside the door and looked around for her parents. He whispered, "I didn't want anyone to see me pull up in my reliable heap."

"Oh, please. Who cares? My parents wouldn't think a thing of it. They know what's going on with you and respect how you're facing up to all of this. My father likes to contrast you to all the hippies he sees on television. He calls you a real man. No, you wouldn't embarrass them."

"Okay, enough serious talk. I'm here to have fun tonight," Timothy said.

"Long overdue. Let's go," Cheryl said.

"Will you drive?"

"What, the truck again?" she said.

"No, I'm thinking about drinking my fair share tonight."

They walked to Cheryl's car, and it started right up. Timothy smiled.

"Why are you smiling?"

"I don't know. Nothing, really. It's kind of silly. Since I've been driving Scoot's truck, every time it starts on the first try, I smile. It's a different experience from my car. You know, the simple things in life."

"That's funny. Well, tonight smile all you want," she said.

They drove to the restaurant. Mantia's was special to them. Good food. Romantic. Private. A good place to celebrate special events. An immigrant couple owned Mantia's. They came from the old country and brought family recipes with them. People could get Italian food in a lot of restaurants in Saint Louis because of the Italian area called The Hill, but there was only one place to get Mama Mantia's recipes. The hostess sat them in a booth in the back of the dining room. Timothy and Cheryl liked to sit close to each other. They ordered a couple of beers and studied the menu.

"I don't know why I'm studying this thing. It's either spaghetti or cannelloni. No one makes cannelloni like Mama Mantia," Timothy said.

"You're right. I want both," Cheryl said.

"How about I order one, and you order the other, and we share?" he said.

"Good call. It's nice to see you in such a good mood. You're under so much pressure I worry about you." Cheryl cupped her hand over his.

The waitress delivered their drinks and said she would return for their dinner order.

"I feel good. It started this morning after exams. At this point, I've got a couple of decisions to make, which I will not make until tomorrow. Tonight, it's all about us."

He held up his beer and tapped her bottle.

"To another semester under your belt." Cheryl returned the toast.

They sat there in silence for a few moments until the waitress returned to take their orders. As planned, they ordered one of each, spaghetti and cannelloni.

"What if I decide not to share?" Timothy said.

"Then you would probably need to find a ride home," Cheryl said.

He laughed.

"How's your mom today?" she asked.

"To me, she looks about the same, but Leslie thinks she's worse. I see her every day, so I don't notice small changes. Leslie does."

"I know she's worried. I talked to her yesterday."

"Is that when you told her about the car?"

"Yes. You don't need to be that secretive with your family," Cheryl said.

Timothy stared at the label on his beer bottle before nodding his agreement.

"Mom asked about you before I left," Timothy said.

"Really? That's nice."

"Yeah, I told her you asked about her, and she was pleased to hear it."

"Well, bless her heart. She's probably scared to death," Cheryl said.

"A little, I think," he said. "She doesn't say she is, but it's natural for her to be."

"Of course," Cheryl reassured him, something at which she excelled.

The waitress brought their salads and a basket of fresh bread.

"Thanks," Cheryl said to the waitress. She looked at Timothy and said, "This bread is my downfall. I could eat that whole basket myself."

Timothy reached for it. "Do you want me to move it?"

"Not unless you want to draw back a stump." She laughed.

They ate in silence until Timothy broke it between bites of salad.

"I think I've made my decision about Dez's offer. I'm going by tomorrow to talk to him about it.

"Really? What did you decide?" she said.

"I don't want to say anything tonight. I want to sleep on it one more night and wake up to one less set of things to deal with, but I'm leaning in one direction."

"Which way?"

"I'll let you know as soon as I talk to Dez. I know this sounds cryptic, but I don't mean it that way," he said.

"That's not fair. You're teasing me."

"Absolutely. What happens if I wake up tomorrow with a hangover and change my mind? You'll think I'm fickle."

"You are fickle," she said.

"About some things but not about you."

She leaned over and kissed him on the cheek. They finished their meal and sat for a while enjoying their drinks. They decided to cap off the evening with pistachio-flavored gelato and a cappuccino. Old-country style.

Cheryl drove back to her house to give Timothy time to absorb his alcohol.

Cheryl's parents were already in bed when they got home, which meant they had the kitchen to themselves. They talked some more over the cocoa. Timothy did most of the talking. She smiled as he shared his feelings. Alcohol loosened his tongue.

"I needed this tonight to clear my head," he said. "Thank you."

"I know you did, and you're welcome."

"You seem to know what I need more than I do," he said.

"That's pretty common in good relationships," Cheryl smiled. "One partner knows what's good for the other, even if the other doesn't agree or see it."

"Again, you're right," Timothy said and leaned forward to kiss Cheryl.

They said good night, which took a while, and he drove home. When he got home and changed for bed, he lay there for a while thinking about the past few days and the conversation he would have with Dez.

What would it feel like to have a few weeks of this? No work. No studies. No one to answer to. No bills. No problems.

Restful thoughts to carry him to sleep.

CHAPTER THIRTY-FOUR

THE SUN BROKE through the window—not directly in his eyes but close enough to wake him. Timothy lay in bed for a while. Having nowhere to go and nothing to do fit him nicely. No responsibilities. He discovered morning greeted the rested differently than the weary.

What a great night. A nice way to cap off a tough semester. Shave and a shower and I'm off to see Dez. He had the confidence of someone who'd made an important decision about the future. One less thing to think about. He anticipated things would change today for him. On his way to the bathroom, the phone rang.

"Hello?"

"You need to get up here fast."

"What? Where? Leslie, what's going on?"

"Ike and I are at the hospital, and Mom has taken a turn for the worse. You need to get here fast, but be safe. The priest will be here in a few minutes."

"Priest? What the hell happened?"

"Just hurry up. Mom's asking for you," Leslie said.

Timothy took charge. "I will. Call Frank."

"Okay."

Timothy didn't bother with a bar of soap or a razor. He slipped on his clothes from last night and ran to the truck. *Lord, I don't*

know what's happening, but please let me be there when it happens.
He repeated this silent prayer twice. It was one part prayer and one part white noise preoccupying his mind.

When he got to the hospital, he parked directly in front of the main entrance. He didn't care about real parking spots today. He ran through the door as fast as his bad leg could move. He didn't bother to look around and didn't hear the director of nursing say good morning to him. He had one thing on his mind, and nothing would slow him down.

He took the stairs two at a time, pushing through the pain to the third floor. He opened the stairwell door and saw the chaplain coming from Mom's room. As he passed the chaplain, the priest said, "She's still with us, Tim."

"Thanks, Father."

When he reached Mom's room, Leslie and Ike were at her side. The charge nurse and resident checked her vitals. Ginny, the aide, stood at the foot of the bed, waiting to do whatever the nurse told her to do. When they saw Timothy, they stepped aside and let him get next to Mom's face.

"What's going on?" His voice broke.

"Everything's shutting down, Tim. There's nothing we can do but make her comfortable," the resident said.

"She's been waiting for you," the nurse said.

Timothy grabbed Mom's hand and leaned over inches from her ear. "Can you hear me, Mom?" He sensed a slight pressure on his hand. "I'm here, Mom. I'm going to stay here with you."

Leslie sobbed in Ike's arms. Ike's eyes were red and wet. The resident and the nurse moved closer to the door. Ginny sniffled.

"I love you, Mom," Timothy said. She squeezed his hand slightly and he sat with her for several minutes.

"Did you get hold of Frank?" Timothy asked.

"Yes, I got him on the phone, and he talked to Mom. It made her smile," Ike said. Mom squeezed Timothy's hand again. She had all of her children here this morning.

Ginny stroked Leslie's arm. *She'll make a good nurse.*

"Is Frank coming?" Timothy looked at Leslie.

"Yes, he'll be on the first flight this morning," Ike said.

"Did you hear that, Mom? Frank's on his way. You'll have all three of us pestering you before long." Timothy used humor to take the edge off things. His father told him it was an Irish thing. His father said, "When you're Irish, if you can't laugh, you'll cry your way through life." Timothy took that advice to heart.

He felt the faint squeeze from her hand, and a tear ran down her face. Her breathing became shallower now and irregular. Timothy knew what was coming. He'd seen it before. Mom sounded congested and rattled a bit. Timothy looked at the doctor and nurse, and they moved closer to the bed, still giving the family their space.

"How about we say the Lord's Prayer?" the nurse suggested.

Timothy on one side, Leslie holding Mom's other hand, Ike holding onto Leslie, and Ginny at the foot of the bed, they began the prayer. As they finished the prayer, the nurse looked at Mom and said, "It's okay, Dorothy. You can go. It's all right. You can go home."

Timothy dropped his head. Oftentimes, people needed permission to let go. He knew the routine, but it was not routine for his family. He looked around. Ike held up a shaking and sobbing Leslie. The doctor folded his hands and held his eyes down out of respect. Ginny wiped her eyes while the nurse remained composed, as did Timothy. He compartmentalized his emotion as he had done many times in the recent years. Letting himself feel nothing became a controlled response or a defense mechanism. It also kept people out of his inner space.

The last bit of strength left Mom's hands, and her eyes opened slightly. She was looking somewhere beyond this room.

"Doctor, pronounce?" the nurse said.

"Yes." The resident placed his stethoscope on Mom's chest and listened in a couple of spots. He shined a small light into her eyes to examine her pupils. He removed his stethoscope slowly, looked at the clock on the wall, nodded, and said, "Mark TOD at 9:56 AM."

Leslie sobbed loudly. Ike was crying, too. Ginny left the room with the resident, and the nurse stayed behind. Timothy sat next to Mom and looked at her, mirroring her expressionless stare. He was slowly processing this. He appeared to be somewhere else. He felt alone even with others in the room.

"Tim, take as much time as you and your family need. I'll be at the nurses' station. Once you've said your goodbyes, we'll move the body. God bless all of you. Your mom's no longer in pain." The nurse placed her hand on Timothy's shoulder, and he accepted the act of compassion. Ginny returned to the room and stood in the background in case the family needed something.

They sat for a while, and when it was time to leave, Leslie and Ike both hugged Timothy, who still had not broken down. He told them there would be paperwork to sign, and he would take care of it. He knew the nurse would be back with it in a few minutes. He wanted Leslie out of there for that formality. There was something too final about paperwork, and he wanted to be here alone for that.

The nurse returned with the papers, and he signed them. She left, reassuring him he could stay. He sat down again next to Mom and grabbed her hand.

"I love you, Mom. I hope I was a good son." He buried his head in the mattress and sobbed. He felt empty. Hollow. The piece of him that was missing lay in front of him. He sat for a few more minutes gaining his composure. He stood to leave.

"Tim, we're sorry for your loss. I know this must be difficult for you," Sister Mary Margaret said. She and Loretta stood inside the doorway. He didn't hear them enter.

"Yes, Tim. We're sorry," Loretta said.

"Thanks."

"I know you have a shift tonight, but don't worry about it. We have it covered. And I know this doesn't mean much now, but our bereavement policy ensures your salary is not interrupted during the next week. You won't have to come in next week either, but you will still be paid. I know it's a small thing, but it's one way to show we understand and care for our employees."

This caught Timothy off guard. He didn't know which surprised him the most—the policy or their compassion.

He went back to Mom's side and sat and wept, "I'm here, Mom." He replayed the death scene over in his mind, as if he could change the outcome. He knew it was a fool's folly to think he could change the past. He'd tried this before.

CHAPTER THIRTY-FIVE

TIMOTHY WENT HOME to an empty house—the emptiest and loneliest it had ever been. He suffered aloneness in a way he never imagined. He searched for familiar living memories. He imagined Mom in the kitchen making her rolls. He envisioned her in her rocking chair in the living room—she called it the front room. He saw her in his mind's eye sitting at the dining room table reading her Bible. He remembered family dinners. He recalled the day he left for the Army, and she didn't want to let go of him. He relived the day he returned home from Vietnam, and she met him at the front door. He visited all of these familiar places. He already missed her pitiful expressions, and that made him smile. He sat in the chair and rocked. Death strips time of urgency. Lost in time, Timothy sat and rocked until the phone startled him. He had little desire to answer it or talk to anyone but knew it might be important—something about the funeral arrangements. The responsible Timothy went to the phone.

"When did you get home?" Leslie asked.

"About an hour ago. How are you?"

"Sad. Really sad."

"I hear ya."

"Ike went to get the kids from school. We are taking them out early today. They need to know. This is going to be a tough afternoon."

"It's already a tough day," he said.

"Frank changed his flight and will come in on the red eye tomorrow morning. I asked Ike to pick him up when he gets in. Is that okay with you?"

"Sure." Frank was the least of Timothy's concerns now.

"Do you want to come over later for dinner? You don't have to be by yourself, you know."

"Thanks, but I think I'll stay here. This place feels pretty empty right now, and I better get used to it."

"Okay, but if you change your mind—"

Timothy wanted to change the conversation. "Where is Frank staying?"

"He's got a hotel room."

"He could've stayed here with me," Timothy said.

"I think he felt awkward since he never called much."

"That's a shame. I'm sure he feels this in his own way. How could he not? This was his mother that died," Timothy said.

"Yes, I'm sure he does in his own way."

"Tomorrow, we have some things to take care of at the funeral home and church. We should probably start at church and then go to the funeral home. How about we meet at the rectory after Ike gets Frank?"

"Okay." She paused for a long moment. "I can't believe she's gone, Tim. I didn't see this coming."

"None of us did, Sis. Let's talk in the morning, and don't worry, I'll be fine," Timothy said but didn't believe it. He hoped he sounded confident.

Timothy went to the refrigerator for a beer. He popped open a can of Pabst and returned to Mom's rocking chair. This first beer went down smoothly and quickly. He decided to have another and a third to keep the second one company. Time of day meant nothing to him at this point. He liked the way it soothed his pain. *If one is good, two is better, and three's not enough. Cheryl hates that saying.* The doorbell rang, and he answered it.

"Oh, Tim, I'm sorry," Cheryl said. "Why didn't you call me from the hospital?"

"I'm sorry. I should have. I don't know. I wasn't thinking real clear. I was kind of in a fog. Still am."

She leaned forward and hugged him. He hugged her like a stiff tree. She cupped his face in her hands and looked into his moist red eyes.

"You look sad."

"I feel sad. How did you hear? Leslie, right?"

"Yes, she's worried you want to be by yourself. That's why she called."

"I have this great big hole in me right now. I'm empty. There's nothing here," he said, pointing to his gut. "It's like there's a part of me missing. I hurt when my dad passed but not like this."

"It's different when your mother dies. At least, that's what people tell me," she said.

"I feel like I've lost my biggest fan in life."

"You still have a pretty big fan in me," she said.

"Thanks." He kissed her forehead. "Let's go sit. Want a beer?"

"No, I'm fine," she said. "How many have you had?"

"Lost count after the last one."

"Is it helping?"

"I'll let you know."

They spent the next couple of hours talking about nothing in particular but Mom in general.

Cheryl was a good listener. Patient. Nonjudgmental. Accepting. He laid open his grief the way a repentant sinner seeks forgiveness in a confessional. She offered an occasional smile and nod, enough to encourage him to continue.

"You probably didn't want to hear all of this," he said.

"I want to hear anything you have to say."

The doorbell rang.

"Okay, I wonder who this is," Timothy said as he walked to the door and opened it.

Scoot stood on the porch. "Hey, bro. I'm sorry."

"Thanks, Scoot."

They exchanged a male hug—close but not weird.

"Come in. Cheryl's here."

"I know. She called me earlier."

"Really?"

"Yep."

"I'll be damned," Timothy said.

"You probably will be." Scoot couldn't resist.

"Want a beer?" Timothy asked.

"Always."

"Hey, Cheryl. How's it goin' girl?" Scoot said as Timothy went for the beers. Cheryl hugged Scoot.

"I'm glad you're here," she said.

"Me too," Scoot said.

Timothy returned with a couple of beers, which they quickly drained, and went for a couple more. They sat for a while and told Mom stories. They told war stories. They told Bobby stories.

"Time for a girl to leave, boys," Cheryl said.

"Thanks. This means a lot to me you came over." He kissed her.

"I know. I'll call you later. See you later, Scoot," she said.

Scoot nodded and held up his can.

Timothy and Cheryl hugged and kissed and said their goodbyes again. He returned and sat across from Scoot.

"You gotta good woman there, man," Scoot said.

"I know. Probably too good for me."

"Probably." Scoot smiled again.

"Scoot, I don't know what I'm going to do. I want to run as far and as fast as I can and keep running until I've got nothing left. I feel like I'm ripping at the seams."

"Dude, you said the same thing when Bobby went missing. It's your life unraveling. At least, you think it's unraveling."

"That's exactly what's happening. It's coming apart a thread at a time. I want to run away from it all. Take a break. Have no responsibilities."

"Hell, that sounds good. We can take a couple of shop bikes and split this summer for a while. I know a place in the hills of South Dakota that don't put up with foul moods. They heal ya real quick. Let's get another beer," Scoot said. He often said there were few things in life another beer couldn't fix. They were about to test out how true that was.

CHAPTER THIRTY-SIX

TIMOTHY WOKE SLOWLY and painfully. Cotton mouth. Head vibrating like a jackhammer. Stomach raw as a fresh abrasion. He dreaded the morning after a night of drinking. That's why he often said, "The best part of staying sober on Saturday night is Sunday morning." He managed to sit up on the side of his bed. *How much did I drink last night? Too much.*

He smelled coffee, which his nose liked but his stomach didn't. He ambled toward the kitchen trying to muffle the sounds of his footsteps. Any noise was too much. He stopped for the necessary relief at the bathroom, and even that was too loud.

"Morning, sleepyhead," Scoot said with a smile.

Timothy grunted, "How?" pointing to the coffee.

"I had to go to the store this morning. Don't you ever go shopping? I got us some doughnuts and orange juice."

The thoughts of doughnuts and orange juice turned Timothy's stomach, and he wanted to empty its contents, though he'd failed to fill it with anything other than the liquid that gave him this hangover. He didn't respond, fearing he might bring up more than words.

Scoot handed him a glass of fizzing water. "Drink this. It's Alka-Seltzer. Got that at the store, too."

Timothy grunted and gulped the bubbling contents. He stared

at Scoot, who gobbled his second doughnut and washed it down with juice. Timothy never saw Scoot hungover. Regardless of what he drank the night before, Scoot had this enviable ability to get up and function the next day. Most people saw this as an admirable trait, but a couple of years of working in psych units caused Timothy to think Scoot operated as a functional alcoholic. Timothy would settle for functional this morning.

"How do you do that?" Timothy asked.

"Do what?"

"Eat and drink like that the morning after."

"It don't bother me. Guess I'm used to it. Here, coffee's done. Drink it." He handed a large mug to Timothy.

Timothy smelled it and sipped it like it was a spoonful of hot soup.

"Man, you threw 'em back last night. Kill any pain?"

Timothy shook his head carefully. "Created more than it killed. Traded one pain for another."

"Yeah, you needed that. Got a lot out of your system. You always need alcohol to loosen your tongue and your grip on stuff."

"So, how bad?"

"Oh, you said plenty of stupid stuff, but, dude, you get a pass on that. Your mom just died. That's a get-outta-jail-free card any day."

Timothy nodded.

"The only thing you said that bugged me was about Cheryl. You talked about taking off and leaving her here, saying she'd be better off without you—that she deserves someone better than you."

"It's true, isn't it?"

"Hell no. You said something about some people at work getting ready to bolt for a few weeks, and they asked you to go with them. You said it sounded good to get away from all this shit."

Everything started to come back to Timothy as Scoot talked. Though most of it made sense to Timothy, he regretted saying aloud what he thought privately. He learned long ago that he shouldn't make public stuff that ought to stay private.

"Yeah, I'm a lousy drunk."

"I heard that. I can tell ya, if you're thinking about ditching Cheryl, there'll be plenty of guys lined up to take your place, like Jodie back home," Scoot said.

"Did I talk about that, too?"

"Yep. You talked about some asshole coming to the lot to show off his car. You called it his latest trophy. I didn't get it all, but I suspect it had something to do with that broad that Dear Johnned you in Nam. Am I right?"

Timothy shook his head as if to rid himself of that memory. "Yeah, but there's nothing there. Just a few unsaid things that would make me feel better."

"Yeah, you need to release your grip on that, too. You carry too much shit around with you. That load gets heavy, don't it?"

"Yeah, too heavy at times. I wish I could let go of some of this stuff. It would lighten my load. That's for sure."

"Look, man, there's all kinds of shit floating around your head right now. You don't never make decisions about life when life is this messed up. The bottom line is you're gonna feel like shit for a while and then you won't."

Timothy knew Scoot was right but didn't show it.

"Here's a prescription from Doctor Scoot. You can't run from this crap. It's traveling with you. You ain't leaving it in Saint Louis if you take off with a bunch of kids. It's gonna follow ya. And then what? You're a thousand miles from home and still feelin' like shit. You can't travel away what you're feelin'. You gotta stay here and face it like a man."

Timothy managed to nod.

"You need to come home every day to this empty house and feel empty sittin' here. Then, one day when you ain't feelin' empty, you'll begin livin' again. In the meantime, have a couple of beers or joints, whichever gives you less of a hangover."

"That's pretty good advice, mostly." Timothy managed a slight smile.

They sat and drank coffee for a while.

"God, what did you make this with? It tastes terrible."

"Hundred-weight. No weak coffee for you, bro."

"Okay." He sipped. "About your truck."

"Man, don't even think about that. Keep it until you can figure out somethin' else."

"Thanks. I'll get through the next few days and then we'll talk about it."

"That's cool. I gotta go. Got an engine waiting for me to do a Lazarus move on it. You take care today, and I'll check back on you later."

"You're a good friend, Scoot. You've always got my back."

"Brothers forever, right?"

"Forever."

Scoot left. Timothy sat at the kitchen table, drank the motor-oil-weight coffee, and stared at a plate of doughnuts. Even though they still turned his stomach, he grinned, thinking of the nickname he and others gave coffee and doughnuts in Nam— "slop and slugs." His head cleared enough to realize there were some things the family must do today, hungover or not. He mentally made a short list, which was all his throbbing head would allow. *Item one, Excedrin.* He walked to the cabinet, opened a bottle of the painkiller, and downed three of them with the heavy coffee. *God, this is terrible slop.*

Leslie called and told Timothy that Frank would arrive at her house soon and they should meet about noon to discuss everything they needed to do today. They could all drive together to take care of things. It sounded like a good idea to see Frank at Leslie's house before they went to the rectory and funeral home, just in case Frank wanted to act like his normal obnoxious self. They could get that out of the way. He showered, dressed, and drove to Leslie's house.

She greeted him on the front porch with a hug.

"How are you doing today?"

"Functioning. How about you?" Timothy asked.

She studied his face. "About the same as you. Looks like you had a rough night."

"Yeah, Scoot came over and, well, you know."

"I know. Cheryl called and told me. I figured you two would—"

"Yeah, we did. Get any sleep last night?"

"A little. I was up with the kids until midnight trying to get them settled down. They are struggling with this, as you might guess. Come on in. Ike's in the kitchen with Frank."

Timothy followed Leslie into the kitchen where Ike and Frank huddled around a pot of coffee.

"Hey, little brother." Frank stood to greet Timothy with a handshake. They gave each other a perfunctory hug, like the type of hug strangers would offer under these conditions.

Frank stood six-foot-three, towering over his younger brother.

He exploited the age and height difference every chance he got and had done this from the moment Timothy became aware he had a big brother. Timothy appreciated this toughening up the way a patient appreciates a good drilling from the dentist. Timothy knew this treatment made him tougher. The only thing Frank ever gave him was a hard time.

"You finally woke up, huh?" Frank said.

"Yeah, tough night. You?"

"I slept pretty good. I was tired from the long flight and the time difference, but I'm good this morning."

"Right," Timothy said.

"Tim, want some coffee?" Ike held up the pot.

"Sure. Scoot made coffee this morning, and it tasted like motor oil. How long you here for, Frank?"

"I figure we bury her on Monday, and I can get the red eye for Tuesday."

Timothy had no energy for this. Normally, he would have seized on his brother's cavalier attitude but not today. Leslie shot Timothy a look begging him not to go after Frank. He understood the look and honored the request. *Not here. Not today.*

"Busy, huh?" Timothy said with no particular interest.

"Oh yeah, lots of irons in the fire at work, and Mary is still struggling with her recovery, but I think she has things under control. I'm proud of her. It's a whirlwind, I tell you. But thanks for asking."

Timothy thought, *Can he be this self-consumed? Yes.*

"How do you guys think we should handle all of this today? It seems like there are a lot of moving parts to this." Frank sounded like a mid-level business manager in a staff meeting getting ready to delegate to his subordinates. He automatically assumed the role of the older brother.

"All of what, Frank? Do you mean Mom's wake and funeral?" Timothy said. His face reddened and tone sharpened.

Leslie looked at Timothy again with her pleading look. As usual, Frank sat tone-deaf to these types of things.

"Yes, of course. That's what I mean," Frank said the way a politician corrects the record or clarifies his position.

"We need to go to the funeral home at one-thirty to meet with the manager and make arrangements for the wake and funeral." Leslie entered the conversation. "We don't need to go to the rectory because I've already talked to a lady at Mom's church, and she told me ten on Monday morning was good for the Mass."

"Good," Timothy said.

"Yes, that works for me, too," Frank said.

Timothy ignored this, and Ike rolled his eyes.

"I contacted the funeral home Mom used for Dad," Leslie said.

"Which one was that, again?" Frank said.

"That's right—you weren't here for that, were you, Frank?" Timothy said, and Ike smiled.

"It's Blauman's, and they said Sunday evening is fine for the wake," Leslie said. "This gives us enough time to contact everyone. The only out-of-towner is Bill, and I called him yesterday. He'll be in tomorrow. We've still got plenty of time to get the obituary in the paper."

"Thanks, Sis. It sounds like you've got things under control," Timothy said.

"Yes, thanks, Leslie. We appreciate all of the hard work you've put into this," Frank said.

This is a fucking committee meeting to him. He cannot be this detached from reality.

"We can get all of this done this afternoon," Leslie said. "I'll swing by the house later today or tomorrow to pick out a dress for Mom."

"It sounds like we have a plan. When do you think we should read the will and check the insurance policies?" Frank asked.

Timothy felt grateful for his hangover because it kept him from leveling his brother. Though, if Frank kept this up all weekend, the tide might change to a storm. That possibility made Timothy grin.

"I already checked the insurance policy, and you'll be relieved to know it will cover the funeral expense. As far as the will is concerned, how about we take care of Mom's arrangements first? We can read the will tomorrow," Timothy said.

"Splendid. Yes, that makes sense," Frank said.

"Ike, can you drive us?"

"Sure, Tim."

They left the house and took care of the wake and funeral details. Frank had little to contribute except for his annoying habit of stating the obvious. It was his lame attempt to sound relevant. A few hours with Frank reminded Timothy why he was glad Frank lived on the other side of the country.

Timothy spent Friday evening with Cheryl at her parents' home. He stayed late and sober. Cheryl listened as her typical understanding self. She said she understood he had to cut loose with Scoot the night before. "Best friends do some things better than anyone else." Timothy appreciated her understanding.

On the drive home, he thought about his conversation with Scoot. He knew he sounded like an adolescent wanting to run from his responsibilities. War stole the innocence of youth. It robbed the warrior of the adolescent silliness others got to enjoy. Sometimes warriors got lost in *arrested development*—the official psychological term. In Timothy's case, his reaction to everything was a blend of guilt, fear, and insecurity. He opened up to Scoot about his feelings for Cheryl. He recalled their talk about Penny's offer. Timothy would have felt guilty having this conversation with anyone other than Scoot.

CHAPTER THIRTY-SEVEN

TIMOTHY AWOKE WITH a hole in his heart from Mom's death. While she was in the hospital, Timothy still felt her presence at home. Not this morning. Today, it was more like Mom's house than Mom's home. In spite of the heap o' living they did here, a vital part was missing. He experienced this aloneness one other time—when Bobby got shot down and went missing.

He decided to get up and make some decent coffee and a hearty breakfast. He wanted to be at the top of his game today for the reading of the will and Frank's inevitable and inappropriate comments. If Frank started up, Timothy would shut him down quickly. Clean-shaven and showered, Timothy sat at the kitchen table and sipped coffee while reading through yesterday's mail. There were a couple of utility bills and donation requests. He made a mental note to write each a small check in Mom's memory and ask them to remove her name from their mailing list.

The doorbell rang about eleven. Leslie and Ike stood there with Frank in tow. They'd picked him up on the way.

"You look better this morning than yesterday," Leslie said as she pushed her way through the door.

"Better living last night," Timothy said.

Ike grinned and Frank walked through the door like he was

eyeballing a house to buy.

"Just like I remember it," Frank said. "Hasn't changed much."

"That applies to people, too," Timothy said.

Frank grinned. Timothy raised his eyebrows and returned the grin.

"Do I smell coffee?" Ike said.

"Yep, just made some. In the kitchen. Pour yourselves a cup."

Timothy followed Leslie into Mom's bedroom and stood at the door as Leslie went through Mom's closet for the burial dress.

"This one," she said. She held up the dark-blue dress Mom wore to Dad's funeral. "It was the only time she ever wore it. Seems appropriate to me," Leslie said.

"Me too, I guess," Timothy said.

Timothy walked to the kitchen and topped off his mug. Leslie followed him to the kitchen and placed Mom's dress on a chair. She also selected some simple jewelry for Mom at the wake.

"I'll make another pot. We may be here a while," Timothy said. He dumped the coffee in the basket without measuring and filled the percolator with water, the creamer with milk and put more sugar in the bowl.

"I see you're still using that old relic," Frank said.

"Pardon?" Timothy looked up from the sugar bowl.

"The coffee pot," Frank said.

"Oh, yeah. We never got around to getting a new one," Timothy said. "Are you guys ready for this?" Timothy pointed to an envelope on the table.

"As ready as I'm ever going to be," Leslie said.

"Let's do this," Frank said, as if he were encouraging teammates in an athletic competition.

Timothy sliced open the large manila envelope labeled with a return address for the Law Offices of Hart and Associates. They handled all of Mom's legal matters, as minor as they were. The envelope looked official, and Timothy didn't open it before they arrived because he wanted no criticism or suspicion. Its contents were unknown to him as well as to the others.

"How about I read this out loud?" Ike offered.

"That's a good idea, Ike," Timothy said.

Frank agreed. "Yes, that makes sense."

For the next few minutes, Ike read the customary legalese lawyers got paid to write—a boilerplate will. "Being of sound mind and body . . . I direct my executors to pay my enforceable unsecured debts and funeral expenses, the expenses of my last illness, and the expenses of administering my estate . . ."

It all sounded official and legal. It directed the disbursement of family heirlooms. Everyone agreed Mom put some thought into this. She already had written names on slips of paper and attached them to items around the house. It had been a source of humor over the years over who got what. She named Timothy the executor, and Frank winced at this, being the oldest. He let it pass. The three-way split of everything met everyone's expectations until they got to the house. Ike read the passage silently at first, paused, and read it again aloud.

"At the time of the writing of this will, Timothy is neither married nor has a home of his own and therefore lives with me. If my death precedes his marriage or moving out, Timothy may remain in this home until he determines when, how, and why to sell it." Ike stopped reading and put the will on the table.

Leslie nodded her approval. Timothy sat expressionless, not knowing if this would be a burden or a blessing. He needed time to process what he heard. Frank wasted little time expressing his opinion.

"This goes to show she wasn't of sound mind. How could she bequeath an asset like that to only one of her children, leaving the other two out of it? That's not right. I knew you were her favorite, Timothy, but this is insulting."

"Frank," Leslie said.

"Yeah, Frank, calm down," said Ike, who never commented on O'Rourke family matters.

"No, I'm not going to calm down. This isn't fair. I grew up in this house, too. It's like we're distant cousins or something. Tim, how can you sit there and say nothing? You can't think this is fair, do you?"

Timothy sat for a while and thought before he spoke.

"Frank, did you bring your checkbook with you?"

"What? Of course I did. What are you getting at?"

"You want a third of this place, right?" Timothy said.

"Absolutely, it's only fair."

"Good, I agree with you," Timothy said. Leslie sat up and Frank smiled. "Take out your checkbook and write a check for one-third of the cost of this home. I need your share of the mortgage and your piece of the taxes and insurance and, while you're at it, add in there your third of the furnace I paid for last week. By my count, you can write me a check for four thousand dollars as your share of the bills. Does that work for you, Leslie?"

Leslie smiled and grabbed Ike's hand. "Of course it does. It's only fair." Ike gave her hand a squeeze. Timothy smiled at them.

"Come on, Frank. Let's see your check. Now, damn it. Write the fucking check. And then, when Mom's hospital bill comes in, I'll send you a bill for one-third of that, too. Come on, big brother, let's see your goddam checkbook."

Frank sat speechless as Timothy stared him down. No more baby brother here as big brother stammered a response.

"Look, I don't have that kind of money. I told you that when you called a couple of weeks ago. I want what is mine—what I'm due."

"Oh, I think you're getting what you're due, Frank," Ike said.

"Hey, there's no need to gang up on me and get hostile. I'm sure we can put our heads together and come up with a solution." Frank returned to his business mode.

"Here's the solution, Frank. If you want your third of the house, you have to write a check to help us dispose of the house. And besides, I'm the executor. You know what that means, right?"

"There's no need to get nasty and make this personal. You agree, don't you, Leslie?" Frank said.

"Yes, I do, Frank. Write him a check for your third, and we'll do the same. We'll take out a second on our home to get the money. You could do the same. That will give him some room to do what he has to do with the house," Leslie said.

"I can't do that. I don't have any equity in my home. I don't have the money. Can't you see that?" Frank sounded panicky. "I'm broke, damn it!"

"Do you think I can afford it, Frank?" Timothy said, staring through Frank, who struggled to make eye contact with his younger brother.

"What do you want to do, Tim?" Leslie said.

"I don't know for sure at this moment, but I think we should sell it. I need to look into this," Timothy said.

"Yes, that's a good idea. Sell it, pay the bills, and divvy up whatever's left over," Frank said.

"What about Tim?" Ike said. "Mom wanted him to have a place to live until he can get out on his own. You had that chance, Frank, and so did Leslie. It's only fair Tim gets the same chance—if you're all about fairness, that is." Leslie smiled at her husband and Timothy winked at him.

"I . . . I . . . I don't know. Let's think about this. We don't need to make that decision today. Bill's coming in town. Maybe he'll have some ideas. We can decide tomorrow. I like to sleep on big decisions," Frank said.

"Tomorrow's Mom's wake," Timothy said. "How about we bury her before we start haggling?"

"Fine, we can wait until she's buried, but you're going to be responsible for the bills. You're the executor, remember?" Frank said.

"That's right, Frank. I'm the executor, and I'll do what's fair," Timothy said.

Nothing else in the will needed discussion. It allowed for a straightforward dissolution of the estate. They made plans to meet on Sunday before the viewing for the public. It would be their private time with Mom.

Frank walked ahead of the others to the car. Leslie gave Timothy a hug and whispered in his ear, "I think little brother just taught big brother a lesson in life." Timothy smiled.

Ike leaned over and said, "Well done."

"Thanks, guys. See you tomorrow."

CHAPTER THIRTY-EIGHT

THE FAMILY MET at the funeral home on Sunday before the wake. It was customary for the family to have their private time for viewing and grieving. The obituary made it into the paper, but that didn't mean everyone saw it. People who read obits read them every day so they didn't miss someone. They read Mom's name at Mass on Sunday morning so her fellow parishioners would know of her passing. Timothy visited a few of Mom's neighbors and told them firsthand. Leslie called Mom's friends by phone. Uncle Bill arrived in town on Saturday and stayed at the same hotel as Frank. They rode together to the wake.

Timothy and Cheryl arrived first. He picked her up on the way. He needed her strength and support today. The funeral home staff escorted them to Mom's parlor. They had a few minutes before anyone else showed up. He thought he was cried out until he saw Mom in the casket. The tears streamed down his cheeks. He discovered that preparing yourself to see someone in a casket and seeing them were two different things. He felt relieved to have Cheryl at his side.

"She looks so small in there, doesn't she?" Timothy said.

"Yes, she does," Cheryl said.

"I thought I was ready for this, but I'm not. How do you prepare for this kind of thing?"

"You don't," Cheryl said. "You have to go through it. It is sad, though. You had a good relationship with your mom. You're lucky. A lot of people cannot say that with loved ones. You'll grieve for the life you had with her. Others have to grieve for the life they didn't have with a loved one."

Timothy looked at his girlfriend, the therapist. *God, that sounds rational. She's better equipped than I am for dealing with this stuff.*

"I know, but I think that makes this loss hurt more. I miss her already," Timothy said.

"That's how it's supposed to be." Cheryl sounded confident and stable despite the tears in her eyes.

"Hey, guys," Leslie said as she and Ike came into the parlor.

Timothy and Leslie hugged and hung onto each like two orphans.

"She looks small, doesn't she?" Timothy said.

"I think all people look smaller when the life leaves them," Leslie said.

"You know what's going to happen here today. It's going to be typical funeral parlor chitchat. 'Tragic, too soon, unexpected. It's such a shame.' People are going to come in and say how great she looks, how natural she looks, how peaceful she looks. It's all bullshit. She's dead, and she looks dead," Timothy said.

"They say that because they don't know what else to say. It's their way of trying to comfort us," Leslie said.

"They mean those things in a good way, Tim," Cheryl said.

"I know, they're paying their respects. They're here to say goodbye to Mom, also. It's awkward for me."

"All you have to do is thank them," Cheryl said.

Timothy knew Leslie and Cheryl were right. What they said made sense, but he suffered this loss with his heart, not his head. He processed everything through pain and loss.

"Do you want to hear something weird?" Timothy said. "Last night, as I lay in bed, I kept thinking about Mom and hoped she didn't feel lonely or abandoned in the funeral home by herself."

"It's grief, Tim," Cheryl said. "It's okay."

"Yes, you're grieving. Tim, you never need to worry about Mom feeling alone or abandoned. You made sure she wasn't when she was here," said Leslie, the reassuring older sister.

By the time Bill and Frank showed up, guests began to file in. Bill and Frank approached the coffin and said a silent prayer. Leslie and Ike's children alternately laughed and cried. They dealt with grief the way children process such things. Tim offered the children words of comfort that seemed to help for a while. Bill and Frank hung back close to each other as Timothy comforted the children.

"Tim, it's good to see you. I'm sorry it's under these conditions," Bill said, offering him a familial hug.

"Thanks, Bill. Good to see you, too," Timothy said as he returned the hug.

"I know this is tough on you, being the youngest and all."

"Bill, I thought this would be tough on all of us. Frank, Leslie, and you, since Mom was your sister and all." Timothy found it difficult to conceal his irritation with Bill and Frank. *They could have helped when Mom was alive.* Once raw emotion surfaced, it had a mind of its own. Timothy's was on display for everyone to see.

"Oh yeah, of course, it is tough on all of us. Say, listen, I'm sorry I couldn't do anything to help out with the furnace when you called. You know, setbacks and all," Bill said.

"That's fine, Bill. I know you would have helped if you could." Timothy didn't believe a word he just said, but Mom's wake was no place to call out Bill as a phony. He restrained himself out of respect for Mom.

"Tim, Frank and I were talking on the way over here, and he told me you were thinking about selling the house. I think that's a splendid idea. It will raise some cash to settle the estate, and who knows, there may even be some left over for the rest of you. Frank's got a good business head on his shoulders. I think you ought to listen to him," Bill said.

"Yeah, that's pretty much what he said to me." Timothy's blood rose and his patience waned. *Okay, Bill, if you and Frank have such great business heads, why are you both so broke that you couldn't help us when we needed it?* Timothy walked away and greeted arriving visitors. Bill and Frank looked at each other.

For the next couple of hours, people came and went, mostly Mom's friends and acquaintances. The church women showed up and told Timothy the Bereavement Committee planned a lunch for the family in the church basement for after the burial. He thanked them and felt relieved because he had given no thought to this at all. In an awkward attempt to make small talk, one of Mom's neighbors asked Timothy what he planned to do with the house. Relief arrived when Timothy saw a familiar face at the entrance.

"Tim, I'm sorry about your mom. I know how dedicated you were to her. I read about it this morning in the paper and wanted to pay my respects," Father Schmitt said.

"Thanks, Father. It means a lot that you came by. I guess you've seen more than your fair share in life," Timothy said.

"My share, that's for sure. Fair? I don't know about that."

"Do you ever get used to it?"

"No, not really. Mostly because someone is hurting. I never get used to seeing people hurt. I don't know that I would ever want to get used to that," Father Schmitt said.

"Good point."

"Are you doing okay?"

"I'm making it," Timothy said.

"That's all you have to do today—just make it. Your grief will settle over time once it finds a space to rest in your mind. At least the semester is over, and your exams are behind you."

"Yeah, that's a relief."

"Speaking of school, Professor Leibert came by to see me the other day, and your name came up in the conversation."

"Really?"

"Yes. When things settle down over the next few days and you get a chance, come by my office and see me, will you?"

"Sure, Father. What about?"

"Let's not talk about it tonight, Tim. It's not the time or the place."

"Sure, Father. Thanks for coming. Would you lead us in a prayer for my mom?"

They walked to the coffin, and Father Schmitt silenced the room as he led them in prayer. After a few moments of silent reflection, Father Schmitt met the rest of the family, offered his condolences, and said his goodbyes.

Timothy stood by himself in the middle of a crowd, alone with his thoughts. *Leibert. What's he doing, snitching on me? Big deal, I missed an exam. It's not like I committed a crime. At least Father had the decency not to go over it here.*

"Hey, soldier boy." This greeting startled Timothy, but he recognized the voice.

"Hey, Kenny. Thanks for coming." Kenny knew how to clean up for a wake. Under his wool peacoat, he wore a nearly white shirt, black pants, and a tie with a knot as big as his fist. The small end of the tie hung longer than the fat end. Timothy appreciated the effort.

"Sorry about your mom. She was a nice lady. Always treated me polite. Made me those cookies, you know."

"I know, Kenny. How did you hear?"

Cheryl walked up.

"Hi, pretty girl," Kenny said.

"Hi, Kenny. Glad you came," Cheryl said.

"Yeah, me too."

Timothy knew Kenny didn't read the paper, so he asked again, "How'd you hear?"

"Oh, yeah, Hoffen came by this mornin' to talk to Dez about somethin' and told me. Boy, I don't know what they was talkin' about, but Dez sure was pissed when Hoffen left. Dez and Ed was red-faced as hell when I went into the shop," Kenny said.

"Oh, Hoffen. Gosh, I forgot to call him. I bet he's disappointed I didn't call."

"Oh, he probably understands, Tim," Cheryl said.

"God, I forgot to call Dez and tell him too. I was supposed to go in today and talk to him," Timothy said.

"Yep, he ain't happy about it but knows your mama died," Kenny said.

"Okay, I'll deal with that later," Timothy said. "Would you like to see my mom?"

"Nope." Kenny shook his head. "Dead people scare me. I wanted to come by and pay respects."

"Okay, thanks for coming, Kenny."

"Yes, thanks, Kenny," Cheryl said.

"Alrighty, see you two." Kenny left without looking at the coffin.

Bill and Frank pressuring me about the house, Father Schmitt talking about Leibert, and Dez mad at me for not stopping by. What else can I fit on my plate today?

"Pretty good turnout for the old gal. What do you think, little brother?"

"Yeah, Frank. It's nice. Mom would be proud," Timothy said.

"I'm sure she would. Listen, Bill told me he talked to you about selling the house to pay the bills. He thinks it's a good idea, and I agree with him. Have you given it any more thought?"

"Not for a moment, Frank," he said. Timothy wondered how much of this he could listen to. Cheryl squeezed his forearm. He saw this as her way of asking him to show some restraint. Leslie saw the brothers talking and came over to join the conversation.

"You boys okay?" she said in a way that really wasn't a question.

"Yeah, we're fine. Frank wants to talk about selling the house right here in front of the coffin and all of these visitors," Timothy said—in a measured tone, thanks to Cheryl.

"Frank, how could you, for goodness sake?" Leslie said.

"I thought since we're all here we could—"

"Frank, how about we bury our mother first. Then we can deal with the business side of this," Timothy said and looked away. At that moment, Scoot showed up. "Gotta go, Frank."

After viewing Mom, they walked out into the hallway for privacy. Timothy unloaded on Scoot. Leslie and Cheryl stood at the doorway and watched the two of them.

"It's hard to imagine, sometimes, that Timothy can tell Scoot anything, but it feels like he's holding back from me," Cheryl said.

"Those two have been through a lot. Timothy doesn't feel he has to impress Scoot. They take each other as they are," Leslie said.

"I hope we get to that point, someday."

"You will."

The crowd thinned as the evening wore on. Only the immediate family remained. Timothy looked tired, physically and emotionally.

Cheryl approached Timothy and asked, "Are you doing okay?"

"Yeah. We made it through tonight and have to get through tomorrow. After that, Frank and Bill will be gone, and Leslie and I can get back to normal, whatever that is."

"Do you want to talk about it?" Cheryl said.

"No thanks, I'm talked out."

"How about we go get a bite to eat? You haven't eaten in hours," Cheryl said.

"I'm not hungry, just tired."

"Do you want some company tonight?"

"No, thanks. I think I want to be alone for now. You understand, don't you?"

"I guess I do. Are you ready to leave or do you want to stay for a while?"

"I think I want to stay with Mom for a while. Leslie and Ike are leaving. You could hitch a ride with them if you want," he said.

"Sure. That's fine. I know you want to be here alone with Mom. Would you like me to come by tomorrow and get you before the funeral?"

"No, we're going to meet here first and go to the church. You can meet us here if you like."

"Would you like me to ride with you to the church?" Cheryl said.

"Sure, if you want."

"What I want to know is if you *want* me to be with you?"

"Yeah, why not?"

"Okay, I'll be back here in the morning." She leaned over for a hug and kissed his cheek. He returned a strong hug and held on long enough to reassure her he wanted her there in the morning.

"Goodnight. Thanks for being here with me today," Timothy said.

"Goodnight, Tim," she said.

Timothy stood in the middle of the room. Frank and Bill left. Cheryl left with Leslie and Ike and the children. Timothy and Mom were alone again. He stood for several minutes staring at Mom. He approached the coffin and knelt down on the kneeler provided at Catholic wakes. He prayed silently for a few minutes and said goodnight to Mom. He stood to leave.

"How are things?"

Timothy turned around. "Hoffen, how long have you been here?"

"A few minutes. I didn't want to interrupt. Let's talk."

They sat in a couple of chairs.

"Hoffen, how do I deal with all this?" Timothy asked.

"You know that life is not fair or unfair—it's just life. It's difficult but not impossible. Despair and hope are largely the result of the choices people make. I know you will choose the right path. It's who you are."

Timothy pushed back. "What about this pain?"

"Feel it. Don't fight it. This is supposed to hurt. Go home to your empty house. Listen for the voice that is silent. Smell the meals Mom used to make. Enjoy those memories. Then, feel the loss. Grieve. People don't really get over things. They just get on with life. Moving on is the magic because it is the natural rhythm of life. Getting stuck in time is unnatural. Live the memories, love the memories, and loosen your grip on the pain. That hole you feel right now will fill with new experiences and memories. That is the natural rhythm I'm talking about. That's your mom's final gift to you—the empty space to fill with new life."

Timothy put his face in his hands and cried. Hoffen rested his hand on Timothy's shoulder and said, "Someday you will be able to talk about this without a tear on your cheek."

CHAPTER THIRTY-NINE

CHERYL DROVE HERSELF to the funeral home and arrived first. Ike dropped off Leslie at the front and parked the car. Cheryl and Leslie greeted each other with sisterly hugs at the door to Mom's parlor.

"Hey, early bird. How long have you been here?" Leslie asked.

"Hi, Leslie. I've been here a while. I was hoping to talk with Timothy before everyone else arrives."

"Why? What's up?"

Cheryl welled up at this question.

"Like I told you on the way home last night, I'm worried about him. I thought he would be the first to arrive this morning and we could talk. He looked alone yesterday, even with other people here. He didn't want any company at home last night. It was like he was on this island all by himself."

"I know what you mean. There are times when you're talking to him he seems to be somewhere else. It's like his body is here, and his attention is a thousand miles away."

"Yes. Has he always been like that?" Cheryl asked.

"No. Growing up he was the most focused person I've ever met. When he played sports, the only thing that mattered to him was the action on the field at that moment. It was the same way with schoolwork. I would walk into his room when he was studying and try to startle him as a joke, but he remained locked in. I used to tell him that a bomb could go off next to him and he wouldn't notice. Now, he's jumpy and distant. That's what's disturbing."

"What happened?"

"He went to war. When he came home, part of him never returned. He went inside himself and shut the door. He sat in front of the television during the evening news and drank his beer. It was like he wanted Walter Cronkite to tell him the rest of a story that had no ending. Mom didn't know what to do, so she left him alone."

"That's so sad. I get that feeling at times—that we're together but not really together. He's there, and then he leaves for a while. I feel like I'm losing him. Like he's slipping away." Cheryl began to cry, and Leslie hugged her.

"I know. That shell he's built is more like a cell. He went over there young, idealistic, and innocent. He came home with little, if any, of that," Leslie said.

"I want to fix him, but I don't know where he's broken," Cheryl said.

"That's the problem. Timothy doesn't even know where he's broken. He's got all of these things he's dealing with—money problems, school, car, furnace, work, and now Mom's death. In the middle of all of this, I think there is something still eating at him, and all of these other things are distractions. I think he keeps himself busy to avoid thinking about his real pain. Can I share something with you, Cheryl? Will you promise me not to say anything to anyone?"

"Yes, of course."

Leslie said, "I've always wondered if Timothy's interest in psychology was more than academic."

"How? You mean like he's using it to figure out something?" Cheryl asked.

"Maybe. I've never asked him about it because I don't want him to withdraw more. I don't know. Growing up, he never talked much about psychology. He always had this warrior thing going. He was like Don Quixote, tilting at windmills. You know, fighting battles, rescuing damsels. Sorry. That sounds bad. It was no surprise when he went into the Army," Leslie said.

"I think he's looking for answers and doesn't even know what questions to ask. Whenever I try to bring this up, he slams shut the windows to his mind and nothing gets in or comes out," Cheryl said.

"I think something is trying to make its way out. It's just not what or how you want."

"What do you mean, Leslie?"

"He has something to say. He wants to give voice to something. He wants to share with others but doesn't know how to go about it. That's why he and Scoot are close. They both probably feel that way and don't have to say much to understand each other."

"I see that, too. And I have to admit, I'm a little jealous of that."

"That's a girlfriend thing, Cheryl." Leslie smiled.

"You're probably right."

"One time he was over at the house, and he and Ike had a few too many beers. Ike went to bed early. Timothy spent the night, and we talked into the early hours of the morning. I told him to write down what he was feeling in a notebook."

"What did he say?"

"He didn't say no, if that's what you mean," said Leslie.

"That's interesting. Do you think he's been writing down these thoughts?"

"Maybe, I don't know. I remember that when he was about eight or nine, he would sit in his bed at night with his Big Chief notepad and a pencil and write things down. I would ask what he was doing, and he said he was telling a story to Chief, his imaginary listener."

"His therapist in those days, right?" Cheryl said.

"I guess. I never thought about it like that. But, yes, you could be right." Leslie nodded.

"I wonder if he has been talking to Chief all these years."

"Mom told me one time she found a box of notebooks under his bed while cleaning. Of course, she said she didn't read them, but I know Mom. She read every one of them but never told us what they said. It was her way of respecting his privacy. Got to give her that."

"Wouldn't you like to know what's in them?" Cheryl said, curious.

"Absolutely, but that's not for me to ask. Speaking of little Timmy, guess who just got here?" Leslie nodded to the door.

"I'm glad we talked. I feel like you're my sister," Cheryl said as she leaned into Leslie for a hug.

"Me too. I'm glad Timothy has you. You're the light in his life,"

Leslie said.

"Thank you."

Timothy stood at the door and looked at the two women talking. Cheryl walked over and gave him a hug.

"Did you sleep last night?" Cheryl asked.

"A little. The house is so empty and lonely. It feels hollow. That's a silly word to use, isn't it?"

"Not at all. I'm sorry you're hurting so much," Cheryl said.

"What were you and Sis talking about?"

"Just things. You know, girl talk."

"Right. I see Frank and Bill aren't here yet. I guess they said their goodbyes last night." Timothy shook his head.

"I wouldn't give that much thought. You've got to grieve your way, and they have to do it their ways." Cheryl shifted back to therapist mode.

"You're right. I've been way too judgmental lately. I think I'm trying to make myself look better by making everyone else look bad," he said.

"You don't have to make yourself look better. You look fine to me." With that, she hugged Timothy again and kissed his cheek.

"Can we all gather to say a prayer before going to Mass?" the funeral director said to the handful of people in the parlor.

They gathered around the casket for a prayer before closing the lid for the last time. Timothy dropped his head at the same moment, as if he were sealing the lid himself. Cheryl clenched his arm. A solitary tear fell from his cheek.

At the church, candles flickered, and the flowers smelled like those at every funeral he'd ever been to. The music was classic funeral dirge—flat and somber. He didn't notice the people in the pews. His eyes locked onto the coffin, and it guided his every step. Others in the church didn't matter to him at this moment.

Weddings, funerals, and baptisms. These all happened here, sometimes in the same day. Timothy's parents baptized him and his siblings here. Leslie got married here. The family buried his father here. This familiar church did not seem like home for him. He didn't want Mom's funeral Mass to feel like home. That would make it too routine for him.

The service was solemn. The music was good and predictably

Catholic: "How Great Thou Art," "Holy God We Praise Thy Name," "Amazing Grace," and "Let There Be Peace on Earth" to lead the crowd out. The priest's eulogy showed he had known Mom for a long time. It had all the right platitudes. An occasional sniffle interrupted the solemnity of the service. Timothy sat in the front row with Cheryl and Leslie and her family. Frank and Bill sat behind them, which Timothy thought suited them perfectly.

Timothy didn't cry. He had cried his last tear at the funeral home when they closed the coffin lid.

As they proceeded out of the church following the coffin on its cart, Timothy scanned the crowd, making a mental note of those who attended. It might be useful for later when he wrote thank-you notes. He saw neighbors, Mom's friends, Leslie's in-laws, Cheryl's parents, church people, and in the last pew he saw a steely-eyed Scoot. At the other end were Penny and Ginny. Both nodded their condolences. *That's odd, but nice.* On the other side of the aisle, he saw Hoffen, smiling at him. *How can you smile at a time like this?*

They rode in the funeral parlor's limousine to the cemetery with a queue of headlights trailing them. Timothy smiled at the rain and cold—appropriate weather to bury an Irish mother. At the gravesite, the family sat beneath funeral parlor umbrellas. *They seem to be ready for all contingencies,* he thought. Timothy stared at the box and nothing else. He heard the Scripture readings and sympathetic words from the priest, but his gaze never left the box. The woman who brought him into this world, changed his diapers, wiped away his tears, and prayed him home from Vietnam lay in a simple box for all of time. *A simple box for a simple person; how appropriate,* he thought.

The priest said, "It's never an easy day for friends and family to say their goodbyes to a loved one, but it is always a glorious day for a good person to meet her Maker." This brought sobs from Leslie and her children. Ike hung his head. Cheryl wiped her eyes. Timothy stared straight ahead. There was more, but he didn't hear it. His mind drifted unashamedly elsewhere.

At the conclusion of the gravesite service, the priest invited everyone to a luncheon in the church basement. The bereavement committee did their job. As the crowd dispersed, Timothy remained seated. Leslie and Cheryl stood twenty paces behind him, waiting for him to move.

"He's gone again, Leslie," Cheryl said.

"I know, honey. Be patient. Let him grieve the only way he knows," said Leslie.

Timothy stood, took one last look at the box, and turned. From the corner of his eye, he saw a lone figure standing in a copse of trees. Hoffen gave Timothy a broad smile and slight nod. Timothy returned the smile and raised his hand to wave.

As he turned to walk away, Leslie said, "Who are you waving at?"

"It's Hoffen, by the trees," Timothy said. "Don't you see him?"

Cheryl and Leslie looked at each other.

"We must have missed him. Shame, he's such a nice man. Do you think he'll be at lunch?'

"I hope so," Timothy said.

"Let's go. The others are waiting for us." Cheryl took charge.

As they walked back to the limo, Cheryl looked at Leslie with widening eyes. Leslie returned the puzzled look. They reached the limo, and Timothy never looked back. He'd seen enough of the box. They drove to the funeral parlor to pick up their cars and then to the church basement for lunch.

Salad, fried chicken, roast beef, macaroni and cheese, mashed potatoes, green beans and apple pie. Comfort food for those who needed comforting.

"Mom would have enjoyed this, Tim," Leslie said.

Timothy looked around and nodded. "Yes, she would. There are a lot of people here who cared about her. She would have loved that. A shame she couldn't see it."

"What makes you think she's not looking down on all this right now, Tim?" Cheryl added.

"You're right, she probably is," he said.

"Hey, little brother. Are you hanging in there?" Frank said.

"Yeah, Frank, I'm okay. You?" Timothy didn't really care if it was a question.

"Oh sure. I knew it would be harder on you, being the youngest and still at home," Frank said.

"I think this is tough on everyone, Frank," Leslie said.

"So when do you think we should powwow and discuss our options?"

"Options, Frank? You mean like what to do with the house? Do you think Mom is even in the ground yet?" Timothy could not hide his contempt for his brother.

"Hey, take it easy. I know you're upset. We can deal with this later," Frank said.

"Frank, you need to back off. We'll get to it when we get to it. Let's thank all of these people for coming," Leslie said.

"Yes, of course. I can arrange to stay over." Frank walked back to the table to sit with Bill.

"Can you believe this?" Timothy said. "That greedy bastard is worried about his cut—"

"Timothy, it's okay. It's okay. Do you hear me? It's okay," Cheryl said.

"Yeah, I hear you. It's okay, but it doesn't feel okay," he said.

They stayed for about two hours until the last guests left and the bereavement committee ladies nudged them out like waiters clearing a table to prepare for the next seating. The family said its goodbyes. Leslie and Ike headed home with the children. Frank and Bill headed to the airport so Bill could get back home. Timothy and Cheryl drove past the cemetery. Timothy wanted to make sure Mom's gravesite was taken care of.

Timothy dropped off Cheryl at the funeral home for her to pick up her car. She offered to spend the evening with him, but Timothy said he wanted to be alone.

"Timothy, please let me help you," Cheryl said.

"I'll be fine. This is something I need to do by myself," he said.

"Do what?" Cheryl said.

"Grieve. Think. Plan. Whatever you do when you bury your number one fan in life," Timothy said.

"Remember, you still have a pretty big fan in me, you know," she said.

"I know. Thanks for being with me throughout this. You sure didn't bargain for any of this."

"That's what people do when they love someone." She leaned over to kiss him. "Call me later?"

"Yes. I promise."

"Okay. I'll be waiting." Timothy watched Cheryl drive away. When he got home, Timothy sat in front of a blank television screen, drinking beer, in the same chair he sat in when he returned from Vietnam. This nearly-the-same routine—beer, TV, sitting, and thinking—had one significant difference. Mom was gone from this echo-empty house. Notebooks lay scattered on the coffee table in front of him—each filled with his musings as a kid. A pile of empty beer cans on the floor next to his chair kept him company. After a couple more beers, he went to his bedroom for more notebooks.

He opened the nightstand drawer and on the pile of notebooks rested his Colt 1911, standing guard over his memories. He won this .45 caliber pistol in a card game in Vietnam and carried it for the rest of his tour instead of the standard .38 caliber revolver the Army issued to helicopter pilots.

Timothy carried the .45 the day he got shot down and the last time he fired it. He shot a Viet Cong who charged the crash site. He saved Scoot's life with that shot. He traded one life for another in a zero-sum game. At times, he wondered why he experienced no guilt over this. It felt transactional to him. A simple trade. The other life didn't matter. That he thought in those terms bothered him. It seemed uncharacteristically cold for Timothy. The shooting didn't haunt him, but his lack of feeling did. That part of him kept trying to connect with the rest of him.

He stared at the pistol for few minutes, thinking about the card game, the crash, and Bobby. Alcohol unlocked the vault in his head. He gathered the notebooks, carried them back to the living room, and placed the 1911 on the stack. He stared at both while popping the top of another Pabst.

Timothy liked the weight of the gun in his hand. He removed the magazine and cocked the slider, ejecting the round from the chamber. He picked up the bullet and studied it. This round weighed about 15 grams and packed a punch of 21,000 psi with a muzzle velocity of 1,000 feet per second. Its stopping power made the 1911 a military staple for over sixty years. Timothy shot one for the first time in training, and its recoil surprised him. This no-nonsense solution had the power to stop all attackers—the two-legged kind and the memory kind. One small pull of the trigger and whatever got in its way became instant history. No problems, no bills, no guilt, and no memories. Timothy stared at the bullet as he placed it back in the magazine and inserted the magazine into the pistol. He cocked the slider and chambered the round.

The phone rang, and he let it ring. He had no conversation in him this evening. He had only decisions to make, and he had to make them by himself. He sat on his chair, the 1911 in hand, and replayed the life events that brought him here.

What did Hoffen say to me? Why can't I remember?

The phone rang again. Timothy aimed the 1911 at the phone and alternately at the television set. He knew it would be an easy way to stop the ringing.

CHAPTER FORTY

THE SHOP PHONE rang, and Scoot answered it. "Scoot's Cycle Shop."

"Scoot, I'm concerned," Cheryl said.

"Hey, pretty lady. What's wrong?"

"I called Timothy last night several times, and he never answered the phone."

"He's probably trying to figure out a couple of things," Scoot reassured her.

"He promised me he would call. It's not like him. I have a bad feeling about this. He was depressed when I dropped him off yesterday, and he said he didn't want anyone around. What does that mean?"

"Probably that he wants some time to himself." Scoot maintained his cool.

"What if he's not okay?" Cheryl said.

"I'll drop by later and check on him."

"Could you do it sooner than later, and call me right away?"

"Sure. I'll head over there right now," Scoot said.

"Thanks, Scoot." Cheryl hung up.

Scoot sat at his desk staring at the phone. He placed the receiver on the cradle and grabbed his keys. *What's he up to? Doesn't he know he's got a great gal trying to make his life better? This is bullshit. I need to go talk some sense into this guy. He saved my life. Now it's time for me to try to help Cheryl save him.*

Scoot hopped in his truck and drove to Timothy's house. It was Timothy's house now, at least for a while. A lot of things ran through his mind this morning after talking with Cheryl. He knew how hard Timothy took Bobby's status. Timothy tried to keep his hopes up, but Scoot knew each day brought them closer to reality. Scoot trimmed the ten-minute ride to five minutes. He wasn't sure what to say to talk some sense into Timothy, but he knew he had to deliver the message fast. Words were Timothy's strong suit, not Scoot's. Scoot was good at fixing things that involved gasoline and combustion but not at fixing people.

He turned onto Timothy's street and saw the shop truck parked in front of the house. *Good, he's home. Now we can have a talk about this stuff.*

Scoot stopped in front of Timothy's house and looked in his work truck, wondering if Timothy decided to sleep one off on the front seat. It wouldn't be the first time. Scoot remembered the time they went to an all-night party and both of them slept in the front seat of Timothy's car outside of the party house. It brought a smile to his face. *Better times.*

Things looked quiet. He knocked on the door. No answer. He rang the doorbell. No answer. He knocked on the back door. No answer. He cupped his hands to look inside. *No one's moving around. Too quiet for me. He's usually up by now.*

Scoot walked around the rest of the house checking windows. When he got to Timothy's bedroom window, he stood on a wooden beer box Timothy had lying around the yard. Again, he cupped his hands to see inside the house. *All right, this is strange.*

As he walked around the side of the house, Scoot saw Rob.

"Hey, Scoot. Looking for Tim?" Rob said.

"Yeah, seen him around?" Scoot asked.

"No, can't say I have this morning. His truck's out there."

My truck, you mean. "Yeah, I saw it. He came home last night after burying his mom yesterday, and I thought I would come by to check on him today," Scoot said.

"I saw him at the funeral. Sad," Rob said. "I liked his mom. She was nice to me and the other neighborhood kids."

"Have you seen anything?" Scoot had enough small talk.

"I saw his living room light on pretty late last night but didn't think anything about it. Figured he was watching TV."

"Did he ever turn it out?"

"Don't know. I went to bed about midnight, and it was still on," Rob said.

"Did you hear anything?"

"Come to think of it, I did. A little before midnight I heard like a firecracker or something pop. I figured it was those kids down the street. Those little brats do that kind of shit all of the time."

"All right, thanks, Rob. I'll check it out," Scoot said.

"Let me know if you need anything."

"Okay."

A pop? Who shoots off firecrackers on a school night in the middle of winter? And just one pop? What the hell is that?

Scoot went back at the front door. This time he stood on his tiptoes to look through the stained-glass window and saw a light on but no other movement. Nothing.

Man, don't tell me you did something stupid. C'mon, Tim, answer this fucking door. Scoot pounded until his fist hurt. He pounded until the old man across the street with a bag of groceries stopped to watch. He pounded to wake the dead.

Scoot continued to pound away on the front door, nearly breaking his fist.

Timothy sat there for a few seconds getting his bearings. He opened his eyes wide and made his way to the front door. He opened it to a frowning Scoot.

"What the hell, man?" Timothy said.

"Man, you gave us one hell of a scare," Scoot said.

"What do you mean 'one hell of a scare'? C'mon in."

Scoot went into the house and looked around the front room. Beer cans and notebooks littered the floor. The 1911 sat on the edge of the coffee table. A spent casing sat on the floor. Scoot spotted a hole in the floorboard where the bullet had entered.

"Rough night, pal?" Scoot asked.

"Sort of. Don't remember everything, but I do remember trying to shoot a mouse that ran across the floor," Timothy said.

"A mouse!"

"Yeah. I hate those things. Ever since that bar girl in Nam gave me a piece of rat wrapped up in a leaf to eat," Timothy said.

"Are you shitting me? You shot a mouse because of some gook broad in a bar?" Scoot said.

"No, because I didn't want to shoot myself."

"Huh?"

"Yesterday, when I got home, I started drinking. I thought about all the stuff I've got going on right now. Cheryl, school, work, this house. Everything. It got to me. It's like everything I am dealing with ganged up on me, and I couldn't see a way out. I started going through these old notebooks I kept while I was growing up. I went back in my room to get some more when I saw the .45 sitting there. Remember this thing?"

"Uh, yeah. It saved my life," Scoot said.

"I thought about using it to end mine last night. With the stopping power of this thing, I thought it might stop the pain. Wait a minute. Why are you here?" Timothy said.

"What? You gotta be shittin' me, man. Cheryl called me this morning to tell me she hadn't heard from you. She called you several times last night, and you never answered the phone."

"I figured it was her," Timothy said.

"Why didn't you talk to her?" Scoot asked.

"Didn't know what to say."

"So you got drunk and shot up your house? Are you fuckin' crazy?"

"Probably, but that's not the issue," said Timothy.

"What's the issue?"

"Last night I had a lot of thinking to do. I kept looking for the easy solution to tough problems. I went through my old notebooks. Found some old entries that made sense, even though I wrote them years ago. I drank myself into a stupor, and of course I shot the mouse."

"No, you didn't. The little prick got away. All you did was put a hole in the floorboard and scare the shit out of me. I saw Rob, and he told me he heard a firecracker go off last night," Scoot said.

"You talked to him?"

"Yeah, he was outside in his yard when I walked around the house to see if I could see any movement. I rang the bell and knocked on the door. You didn't answer."

"What time is it?"

"Noon," said Scoot.

"Holy shit. I slept twelve hours."

"You probably needed it."

"I think I slept through the hangover. I feel pretty good."

"Glad to hear it." Scoot dished out a heaping dose of sarcasm. "So why did you shoot at the mouse instead of yourself?" Scoot pressed.

"I was sitting here feeling sorry for myself. Drunk, which needs to stop, by the way. I read a couple of things in my old notebooks I hadn't thought about in a while. I've dealt with a lot of shit in my life and never let it take me down this far. I remember something Hoffen said to me."

"Like what?"

"When I was growing up, all I ever wanted to do was write. I thought I had something inside of me that wanted to make its way out. I went to Nam and kept a diary of what we did there. I knew we were doing something important even though most people here didn't understand it."

"I heard that," Scoot said.

"I got out of the army and enrolled in school. When they asked what I wanted to major in, I thought psychology would be good because I could get in people's heads to understand them," Timothy said.

"So what did you discover?"

"It occurred to me maybe I was trying to get inside my own head—trying to figure me out. As I sat here last night, the answer was lying on the table in front of me. My whole life is in those notebooks. The ups and downs. Good times bad times. My hopes and dreams. Things that make me sad. More importantly, things that make me happy."

"Yeah, okay. Where's this headed?" Scoot asked.

"Hoffen said something to me at the funeral parlor the other night. He said something about life being difficult but not impossible, that hope and despair are largely the result of choices we make. If we make the right choices, hope will take us down the right path. Bad choices and we end up on the wrong path. And here's the kicker—once we decide to do something, if it's the right thing for us, Providence steps in and things begin to happen to make that path easier for us. My path has been tough the past year. Maybe I'm on the wrong path," Timothy said.

"So what does this mean you're going to do?"

"First things first. I need to square things with Cheryl. She deserves the best I have to give, and I've been shortchanging her lately."

"About time you pulled your head out of your ass," Scoot added.

"Then, I will go to school and talk to Father Schmitt one more time. I know there's another answer there. Once I do that, I'll figure out something with the hospital to pay off Mom's bills and give me more hours. After all, they can't fire me if they want their money. I am going to tell Dez I'm not taking his offer. He'll be pissed, but he'll get over it. Frank plans to stay over a couple of days, and we'll work out the sale of the house. He's a prick, but he's still my brother. If I can keep your truck for a little while longer, I'll figure out something for transportation."

"Speaking of that, I'm going to need the truck this week. Can you swing by tomorrow morning and drop it off? I've got something else you can drive," Scoot said.

"Sure, that's fine. I appreciate it. You know, Scoot, as bad as I felt yesterday, I feel that much better today. It's like I stepped onto the right path—whatever that path is," Timothy said.

"Okay, I got a business to run. I'll see you tomorrow when you drop off the truck, and call Cheryl," Scoot said.

"I will. As soon as you leave. Thanks, bro, for keeping an eye on me."

"I got your back, and you got mine."

They bumped fists and gave each other a half-hug.

Timothy grabbed the phone and dialed Cheryl's number.

"Hey, I heard you were worried about me."

"Thank God, you're okay. I was worried. You sound good," she said.

"Yeah, my guardian angel just left. I heard you called him this morning."

"Why didn't you answer the phone last night?"

"I was in the middle of a conversation when you called."

"With who?"

"Myself."

"What does that mean?"

"I needed to figure some things out, and I did. I woke up this morning feeling a lot better than when I went to sleep," Timothy said.

"Will you come by later?"

"Yes. I need to do a little house cleaning around here, but I'll be by this afternoon and we'll hang out. Okay?" he said.

"Yes. Of course. Thank God you sound better."

"For a change, I feel like I have a few more answers than questions."

"Okay, see you later. Love you," she said.

"Love you, too."

Timothy hung up and dialed Leslie.

"Leslie, have you talked to Frank today?"

"Good afternoon to you, too, little brother. And yes, I have talked to Frank. He's staying over until Thursday, and we can figure out some things."

"Good. Let's get together tomorrow afternoon and talk about it. I had this thought. Since we can't do much for a year anyway because of probate, all we have to focus on is taxes and insurance. I can sell my baseball card collection and pay that off. That way I can live in the house until we sell it, and you guys won't be out any money," Timothy said.

"That's really nice, Tim. Are you sure you want to do that? We can take out a second mortgage on our home—"

"No, you're not going to take out a second mortgage on your house to resolve this, and yeah, I am fine selling that collection. It means no more to me than a savings account. Kind of a rainy day fund."

"All right, I'll call Frank and set this up for tomorrow. How about four?"

"Sure. I'll be there. Bye."

"Bye," she said.

Timothy hung up the phone and collected his thoughts. *This feels good. It's like I'm in control again.*

He cleaned up his mess in the living room and attempted to repair the hole in the floor from the shot he fired. After that, he cleaned up to meet Cheryl. He had a lot of cleaning up to do in his life.

CHAPTER FORTY-ONE

WAKING UP WEDNESDAY morning felt different to Timothy. No pounding at the door. No fogginess. No guilt.

Today, he had to drop off Scoot's truck and pick up something else to drive. Scoot was a great friend. Always there. Whatever Scoot had for Timothy to drive would be fine with him. And he needed transportation to meet with Father Schmitt. After that, he was to meet Leslie and Frank to work out the details for the house. Timothy was discovering the difference between having problems with solutions versus problems by themselves.

As he pulled into the lot at the shop, Scoot came out to meet him. He motioned Timothy to park on the side of the building.

"Hey, dude. You look better today."

"Feeling better, too. Listen, man, I appreciate you letting me use your truck. If it puts you in a bind to let me borrow something else, I can figure out something else," Timothy said.

"No problem at all. I've got something else for you. It's around back. Let's go get it."

As they walked around the corner of the building, Timothy saw a jade green Ford Fairlane shining like new money.

"Looks good, don't she?" Scoot said.

"What happened? What is this?" Timothy asked.

"This is your old heap with a few changes. A buddy of mine owns a body and detail shop. He owes me big time, so I asked him to do a rush job fixing it up. Did a nice job, too. I got a deal on the tires. Our tire guy is a Nam vet, and when I told him about your situation, he sent these over. My guys did the engine work. Wasn't as bad as the guy at the station said; it was worse, but it's all good now. She runs like new," Scoot said.

"Scoot . . . I don't know what to say." Timothy's eyes leaked, and he bit his lower lip.

"Just say you'll take care of it," Scoot said.

"I will. Hell yeah, I will. This is amazing. I've never seen this car look this good. I don't know how you got all of this done in a couple of weeks."

"All we did was adapt to the situation, bro. You remember that, don't you?" Scoot said.

"Yes, I do. I don't know how I will ever repay you."

"You already did. Remember, you saved my ass. I'm the one still payin."

Timothy opened the car and sat inside. His smile filled the car. "It even smells new," Timothy said.

"This should last you for a while, buddy," Scoot said.

"Scoot, thanks." He got out of the car and gave Scoot a bear hug. Scoot nodded. "I have to go see Father Schmitt. How about we get together later and have a beer? On me," Timothy said.

"You know me, I never turn down a cold one. Now, go see the priest."

"Thanks again, man."

"Always," Scoot said.

Timothy turned the key and the engine roared to life, answering his call. Timothy no longer requested it to start, he commanded it. He drove away like a sixteen-year-old who just got his license. He punched the accelerator, and the Fairlane lunged like a youngster. He couldn't wait to share his good news with Cheryl. He thought she needed it as much as he did. He drove to school and parked away from the building, ensuring no one would park near his reborn Fairlane. He looked back at it several times as he walked to the administration building that housed the College of Arts and Sciences and Father Schmitt's office.

Father Schmitt walked through the office door a little winded. "Tim, good to see you. C'mon in." They sat across from each other in Father Schmitt's office.

"So how goes it? Missing your mom?" Father Schmitt asked.

"Yes, Father, I am. I'll make it. What option do I have?"

"Good thinking. No other option. You feel it. Let it work its way into your life, and keep going. You never want to forget, but you never want it to hold you back, either."

"Thanks, Father. Makes sense. Why did you want me to swing by?" Timothy asked.

"It's about Professor Leibert. He came to see me."

Ah, shit. Just when I thought things were getting better for me.

"Why?"

"He told me about your grade and how you missed the final, but he wasn't complaining. In fact, just the opposite. He was singing your praises."

"You gotta be shitting me. . . . Sorry, Father."

Father Schmitt smiled.

"That guy hates me."

"Not so much, as it turns out. It seems a paper you wrote impressed him more than he let on. He told me he disagreed with nearly everything you said, but loved the way you argued your point. He said he recognized great talent when he saw it."

"He kinda said the same thing to me; it's why he gave me a passing grade. Guess it wasn't good enough to let me take the exam, Father. I really needed a B in that class."

"He took the liberty to show it to a couple of folks in the English department. It seems one of the professors in that department was so impressed with your style that he wants you to TA for him next semester. That's a position they reserve for grad students, but, in your case, they made an exception. How about them apples?"

"I don't know what to say," Timothy said.

"Say yes, son."

"Yes."

"Good, because he told me if you have a good semester with them, they will be able to help with tuition next year. In fact, he said that tuition bills should not get in the way of a talented student getting an education," Father Schmitt said.

"Father, I'm stunned."

"Tim, I know plenty of good psychologists. We have them in our department, but we don't have many talented writers in this school. Have you ever considered that path?"

"Uh, maybe at one time," Timothy said.

"Maybe it's time to dust off those thoughts. You never know— we may have a budding Hemingway here."

"I don't know about that, but I sure want the TA position. Who do I need to see?" Timothy asked.

"You will get a formal offer letter in the mail next week. It will have all the information you need to get the ball rolling on this."

"Thank you, Father. Why didn't you tell me this the other night?"

"Tim, there's a time for sorrow and a time for joy. You needed to grieve. Now, you need to celebrate."

"I have the perfect person to celebrate with," Timothy said.

"I thought you might. And since part of your tuition will be taken care of with the TA position, enroll next semester, and we'll figure out the payment schedule."

Timothy jumped up and shook the priest's hand vigorously. "Father, I don't know how to thank you."

Father Schmitt looked straight into Timothy's eyes and said, "Yes, you do, Tim. Write good stuff."

"I will. I promise I will."

Leaving the office, Timothy was awestruck by the sudden changes in his life. Two days ago, he lived in cold darkness. He had few options. Today, hope and warmth illuminated his path. He drove his new car to Leslie's house. When he got there, Frank's rental car was gone.

"Hi, little brother," Leslie said as she greeted him at the door. "What's that you're driving? It almost looks like—"

"It is," Timothy said. He filled her in on Scoot's resurrection of his car.

"He's a special friend, isn't he?"

"Yes, he is," Timothy said. He then told her about his conversation with Father Schmitt. Leslie smiled as widely as her lips would allow.

"Good Lord, you're having a great day," Leslie said.

"Yes. Where's Frank?"

"Well, this may top your day off. I called Frank to meet with us. I told him your idea of paying for the insurance and taxes with the sale of your baseball cards. He was ecstatic. He said waiting a year to sell, provided he didn't have to pay anything, might make more sense anyway. Something about his business troubles. I don't know, but it seemed to make sense to him."

"That's Frank," Timothy said.

"Yes, he said there was no reason to meet. Pay the bills, and we'll sell the house next year. He was thrilled he could catch an earlier flight and make it home today," Leslie said.

"Old Frank, huh?"

"Yes, brother Frank," Leslie said. "Do we need to go over anything else at this point?"

"None I can think of. I think I'm going to take off. I have someone I need to share some good news with," Timothy said.

"She deserves that, Tim."

"I know she does, thanks." He leaned over and gave his big sister a hug before leaving.

Timothy drove home and rushed into the house—his house—to immediately call Cheryl.

"Hey, I've got something to tell you," he said.

He shared his good news with her. Car. Father Schmitt. Frank.

Next, he owed Scoot a couple of beers, and they met at Junior's. Good sense prevailed, and they called it a night after two beers.

CHAPTER FORTY-TWO

TIMOTHY'S FIRST STOP for the day was the hospital. He needed to take of his mom's bills. He needed closure; loose ends haunted him. He went directly to the billing department.

"I would like to talk with someone about unpaid bills for my mother's hospital stay," Timothy said to the receptionist.

"Yes sir, that will be Miss Haynes. I will tell her you're here. What's the patient's name?" the receptionist asked. Within a couple of minutes, Miss Haynes came into the waiting area to meet him.

"Mr. O'Rourke, please come with me," Miss Haynes said. They walked to her cubicle. "Please have a seat. I understand you're here to discuss your mother's unpaid hospital bills."

"Yes, that's true."

"Okay, I have the file here based on the information you gave our receptionist. Your mother was in here for a breathing problem and again last week for a stroke. Is that correct?"

"Yes, it is." Timothy was impressed but saddened by how transactional and routine this sounded. *This feels like a government tax office. Maybe it is, since hospital bills are a tax on the living.* He smiled at his observation.

"I see your mother passed away last week. Please accept my condolences."

"Thank you."

"And you're an employee here?"

"Yes, part time. Right now, I work on Med-Surg," Timothy said.

"Okay, can you wait here a minute please?"

"Sure."

Miss Haynes left and returned a few minutes later. "I talked with our controller to get some clarity on our policy."

"Policy? What policy is that?"

"We have a debt-relief program here for employees, and I wanted to make sure it applies to part-time workers, too," Miss Haynes said.

"I don't understand. What is this program?"

"It's part of our bereavement policy. When an employee's next of kin expires in the hospital, we forgive that debt. To bill you for your loved one's death would be an extra burden, so we call it bereavement debt relief. Since you are unmarried and lived with your mother, you are considered next of kin, which means the debt is forgiven for both hospitalizations."

"I don't know what to say," Timothy said as he shook his head in disbelief.

"Just say yes, Mr. O'Rourke. It's our way of expressing our sympathy in your time of sorrow," said Miss Haynes.

"Thank you. I'm stunned."

"You've got a lot going on, I'm sure. We often hear that from other employees at this difficult time. We had to verify your employment with nursing, and they requested you stop by there before leaving," she said.

"Oh, yes. Sure. Again, thank you. This was going to be so hard—"

"We understand. Good luck, Timothy," she said.

He nodded and left the billing department. He went directly to the chapel to sit and think. Things happened so quickly his mind had difficulty keeping up. The car. The TA job. Temporary tuition deferment. Frank's decision not to battle him. And now, debt relief from the hospital that had been at the center of his stress universe. Once he collected his thoughts, he went to Nursing Service.

"Hello, Timothy. Please have a seat. Monica will be right with you," said the department secretary.

He sat for a few minutes considering his words for the director of nursing.

"Timothy, nice to see you. Come in, please." He noticed the change of tone from previous encounters.

"Again, we are sorry about your mother. I know loss is difficult. I lost my mother last year. It takes time."

"Thank you, Monica. I know it will be a while," Timothy said.

"I asked you to come by so I could explain our bereavement policy and see if you had any questions, and talk to you about your schedule."

"Sure. Miss Haynes explained it clearly to me. She said I owe nothing because it's the hospital's way of helping employees deal with loss."

"Yes, that's correct. We are in the healthcare business, and employee health, physical or psychological, is as important to us as our patients' health," Monica said as if reading from an employee handbook.

"Great. Thank you again. And what about my hours?" Timothy asked.

"I know we have you at two shifts a week now. How does that work for you?"

"It's okay. I'm making it."

"Would an extra shift make a difference?"

"Sure, it would help a lot. Could I do it on the Med-Surg unit and remain there?"

"Why yes, if that's what you want." Monica looked surprised.

"It is. That's where Mom passed, and I saw firsthand the importance of patient care. Sort of my way of giving back."

"That's a lovely thought. When you're ready to come back to work in a week or two, see the head nurse on the floor, and she will schedule however you want to work. We'll be flexible on evenings and nights or weekends."

"This is incredibly nice. I really appreciate it."

"When you run a business, which we do, people often mistake our focus on the business side as cold. We don't mean it that way. We're on your side, you know?" Monica said.

"Thank you again. This makes things a little easier."

"Good. I look forward to seeing you return to work."

"Me too."

Timothy left Monica's office trying to process everything he had experienced the past couple of days. Since he skipped breakfast, he decided to swing by the snack bar for a quick lunch before heading to Dez's place.

"Hi, Tim."

"Hey, Penny," Timothy said.

"Are you back at work already?" she asked.

"No, taking care of some family business here."

"Oh, yeah. I'm sorry about your mom. I know you were close. That was a nice service on Monday."

"Yes, it was."

"What can I get you?"

"How about a burger and fries."

"And a chocolate malt?"

"Sure, why not. For Mom," he smiled.

"For Mom," Penny said.

She returned in a few minutes with the malt. "The burger and fries will be right up. The malt's on the house," Penny said.

"Thanks, Penny. That was nice of you and Ginny to come to the funeral."

"Ginny was fond of your mom when she took care of her, and you know me—I'm fond of you."

Timothy smiled but had no interest or energy today for the banter. He held the malt up in a faux toast. Penny walked back to the kitchen to get the burger and fries.

"Here ya go," she said as she placed them in front of Timothy.

"Thanks, Penny. I appreciate it."

"Sure, and if I was inappropriate earlier, I'm sorry. You're a friend, and I don't like to see friends hurting."

"That's the way I took it." He smiled to let her off the hook.

Timothy finished his lunch, paid for the burger and fries, and left a generous tip. He said goodbye to Penny and thought about the next stop on his agenda for the day—Schoen's.

He dreaded this conversation but knew he must have it. On the one hand, Timothy wanted this over. On the other hand, he procrastinated because he wanted to hold out for the last minute in case he needed to change his mind. It was past time to face up to Dez and refuse his offer. Timothy strung him along for a while, which made this tougher than it should have been. He knew what he must do. He recalled what Hoffen said: "There's never a bad time to make a good decision." This felt like the right decision, regardless of the time.

Timothy pulled into Schoen's lot and parked his new old car toward the back. He didn't want to have to explain that transformation. Not that he was embarrassed, but he wanted to stay focused on his reason for being here. He walked around the side of the building.

"Hey, soldier boy. Where you been?"

"Hi, Kenny. Taking a few days off after the funeral," Timothy said.

"Yeah, sorry about that. Dez is inside. Think he's been waitin' for you. Come back out here before you leave," Kenny said.

"Okay, thanks," Timothy said.

Timothy walked into the shop and noticed mostly empty shelves. *Odd.*

"Well, well, well. Hey, Ed, look who just showed up. The gimp," Dez said.

Timothy smiled. "Dez, Ed."

Ed nodded and ashes fell off her cigarette onto the counter. She coughed and blew the ashes on the floor.

"So, did you make a decision?" Dez said.

"Yes, Dez, I did. What's with the empty shelves?" Timothy asked.

"Getting rid of stuff. Moving out. Setting up shop at the other place," Dez said.

"You're closing this store? Just like that?" Timothy asked.

"Just like that. What did you decide?" Dez pressed.

"I'm staying in school," Timothy said.

"Told you, Ed. This one ain't nearly as smart as he thinks he is. Like I said, boy, there's two kinds of people in this world—those that get it and those that don't."

"Get what?" Timothy said.

"Reality, that's what. I told ya. Life's mean and you gotta be meaner than life. You gotta take what ya can get when ya can get it. I gave ya a chance to take and ya didn't. You're gonna be the one that gets taken from. You'll be sorry for that, I guarantee. Right, Ed?" Dez said.

"Damn straight, Dez," Edna said.

"Dez, I'm pursuing my dream—an education," Timothy said.

"Won't matter," said Dez.

"It already matters. If I decided to stay here, you're moving. What would I have done? Gone to the other store?"

"Why not?" Dez countered.

"No, I made the right decision. I'm staying in school. I'll figure it out. My mind's made up."

"Your life, O'Rourke. Screw it up any way ya want to," Dez hacked.

"I will. Thanks for the work over the holidays. I needed the cash."

"Don't let the door slap ya on the ass on the way out, soldier boy," Dez said.

Edna laughed.

Timothy turned and stared at Dez and Ed. They looked older than a few days ago. *I guess cynicism ages people fast.* He left by the side door to say goodbye to Kenny.

"Hey, Kenny. Do you know what's going on in there?" Timothy asked.

"Yeah, the old bastard is closing down the shop. He's selling everything cheap so they can get outta here. Told me I could buy Parodis at his cost. That's a good deal. Better deal if I steal them, though." Kenny smiled and showed his rack.

"Are you going with him?" Timothy asked

"Nope. Got me another job."

"Where?"

"Down at the doughnut shop. Hoffen told me 'bout it. Went down there, and they told me I could get thirty-five hours a week makin' more than I'm making here. They don't sell no cigars, but I'll be able to eat all the doughnuts I want. That's a good deal 'cause I like doughnuts. Hours ain't bad either. Gotta be there by five in the morning, but I get off by noon. I get to screw off the rest of the day."

"I'm glad to hear you have something, Kenny. Hoffen told you about it, huh?" Timothy said.

"Yep. Told me on Monday when he came in to talk to Dez. Lots of yellin' goin' on in there. Couldn't understand it, but when Hoffen left, Dez said they was leavin' the place."

"That's odd," Timothy said.

"Oh yeah, Hoffen left this for ya. Told me you'd be by and I should give it to ya. Tell ya the truth, I was gonna open it for myself but figured since he helped me get that job at the doughnut place, I couldn't do that."

Kenny handed Timothy a rectangular package wrapped in grocery bag paper and tied with a piece of twine. Timothy held it for a moment and knew instantly it was a book.

"Hoffen said there's a card inside, and you'd know what to do with it."

"Okay, Kenny, and thanks. I enjoyed working with you," Timothy said.

"Even when I spit at ya?"

"Well, maybe not all the time."

Both grinned. Timothy extended his hand and Kenny shook it like a pump handle. Timothy turned to walk to his car.

"Come by and see me at the doughnut shop."

"I will, Kenny."

"And if the owner ain't there, I'll give ya some free doughnuts."

"Okay, Kenny, thanks."

"You was always nice to me, Tim. I'll never forget that. I'm sorry about your mom."

Timothy paused, turned, and smiled. A toned-down Kenny was a little out of character, but today was strange anyway. He made it to the car, sat, and stared at the package a few moments before opening it. He found a handwritten note.

Dear Tim

It has been a pleasure getting to know you and your family. Your world is a wonderful place. As we have often discussed, life is difficult but not impossible. At times, it overwhelms. You know this. You have lived this. You are also living on the possibilities side of life. The hope or despair people feel often result from the choices they make. There is never a bad time to make a good decision. I know you will make good decisions moving forward. You are standing at the gateway of your future. Behind you is everything that has made you the person you are. Before you lies everything that will make you the man you will become. The philosopher Mengzi wrote, "When Heaven is about to confer a great office upon you, it first exercises your mind with suffering and your sinews and bones with toil." When you pass through the gateway to your destiny and commit to its path, the same force that tested you will move in ways you never could have imagined and guide you with occurrences you never could have found on your own.

Please accept this book as a token of our friendship. It means a great deal to me. Take it immediately to Le Rive Gauche bookseller in Downtown Saint Louis. Ask for Louie, an old friend of mine. He knows what to do. And remember this: There is always hope in the shadows of war.

Your friend,
H.

This was the nicest goodbye Timothy had ever received. He opened the rest of the wrapping and saw a copy of *The Old Man and the Sea.* He thought, *I read this in high school.* He decided to drive to the bookstore, a place he knew well because it was close to school.

CHAPTER FORTY-THREE

TIMOTHY DROVE STRAIGHT to Le Rive Gauche. The building façade dripped with old-school architecture—brick, mortar, stone and an awning. The bookshop occupied the basement of an old apartment building. The name of the shop was hand-painted on the window in French script. Old volumes of books filled the store window. Passersby would recognize it as store for ancient, rare books without reading the sign.

An old-fashioned bell announced his arrival. The place smelled like old books—a blend of vanilla, almonds, and leather. New books smelled like chemicals. Creaky wooden floors counted every step he took and a couple of ceiling fans kept the air moving. A few wooden shelves housed current best-sellers, but this was a repository for old books. The cash register rang a sale for the only customer in the shop. Timothy heard a humming in the background and spotted a dehumidifier, a necessity to keep the air dry but cool. The customer smiled as he passed Timothy, clutching his purchase like it was a treasure, which it probably was. Timothy nodded.

Timothy approached the clerk. "Is Louie around?"

"I'm Louie, and who are you?"

"I'm Tim O'Rourke, and we apparently have a mutual friend."

"Oh yeah, who's that?"

"Hoffen."

"Ah yes, Hoffen. You're his new friend. You worked with him at the tree lot, right?"

"Yes. Did he tell you I would come by?" Timothy asked.

"He sure did. I know exactly why you're here."

"The book?"

"Yes, the book. I've wanted to get my hands on that book for a long time," Louie said.

"Why? What's special about that book?"

"Did you open it?"

"No, why?" Timothy said.

"Did Hoffen tell you anything about our friendship?"

"Not much. Just that you were old friends."

"Very old friends. We met in Paris in the twenties. We both hung around after the war and met while running in the same circles."

"Hoffen didn't tell me a whole lot about his past, but I knew he was in France."

"Yes, that's true. One of the guys we became friends with wrote for a newspaper and later became a novelist. There was a whole crowd of us. You may recognize some of the names."

Timothy looked at the book again.

"You can probably piece some things together here," Louie said.

"Whoa! You mean you guys knew Ernest Hemingway?"

"Yes, Hoffen more than I, but we all ran in this big circle. Hoffen became good friends with Ernest because of the war. They met in a hospital in Italy."

"I knew some of that," Timothy said.

"We palled around for a couple of years before we all moved around. I worked in a book shop on the Left Bank—"

"Le Rive Gauche? I get it," Timothy said.

"Yes, the Left Bank. I decided to move back to the States. I was following a girl I met who was a student in Paris. A beautiful woman. She stole my heart and my money, but that's another story. Anyway, I ended up here, and Hoffen eventually made his way back to the States, too. He got married and had a son whom he lost in the Second War. And we thought the first one would end all wars. Anyway, his wife grieved herself to death, and Hoffen kicked around for a while."

"What kind of work did he do?" Timothy asked.

"I don't know. Mostly labor, I think, which is strange because he was so well read. I never knew much about his past before the First War. I guess it didn't matter much back then. He and I remained in touch through letters. I still have a box of them in the back. I got a letter from him in '53 or '54. I don't remember exactly when it was. He asked if I saw Ernest's new book, *Old Man and the Sea*. He bragged he had a signed copy. I guess Ernest sent him one."

"This book?" Timothy said.

"Yes, that's the book. Have you read the inscription?"

"No, I didn't think to," Timothy said.

"Go ahead. Open it up."

Timothy opened the cover and read the inscription:

Hoffen,

Thanks for all the great memories and your friendship. Friends like you only come along once in a lifetime.

Your pal, Ernie

"Ernie? You're kidding, right?" Timothy said.

"Nope, Ernie. Hoffen was the only one I ever knew that called him Ernie. Or, should I say, he was the only one Hemingway allowed to call him Ernie."

"That's incredible!" Timothy said.

"That's the truth. That's why I want this book. It's the only book Hemingway ever signed *Ernie*. In my world, there has been a persistent rumor over the years this book exists, but it was shrouded in so much mystery that collectors began to doubt its existence," said Louie.

"The only one?"

"Yes, the only one," Louie said.

Timothy wore his surprise openly. "That means this thing is—"

"Worth a lot of money." Louie finished. "I know it's legitimate because Hoffen told me the story. Later, at a literary show, I ran into Ernest, and we had some drinks. I asked him if it was true. He told me it was."

"But how do you prove this to others?" Timothy asked.

"It doesn't matter. The words of two close friends are enough for me. I'm sure the experts will study the handwriting, but for me, seeing this is good enough."

"This is an amazing story. I can't believe Hoffen didn't tell me about it."

"Oh, he is, Timothy. He's using me to do it," Louie said.

"What should I do with it? I don't know if I feel safe hanging onto it. I mean, I don't want to lose it or worse," Timothy said.

"I know exactly what to do with it. Leave it here with me. I have a special safe to keep this in. It will be with good company, trust me. I collect these types of things. And for you, I have a check," Louie said.

"A check? How do you know I'll sell it?" Timothy said, protective of the book.

"Hoffen came to see me a few days ago. He told me what was happening in your life. He knew you needed some help. This is his way of helping you," Louie said.

"How much help are we talking about?"

"Five thousand dollars," Louie said.

"Five thousand dollars! For this book! You're kidding me, right?" Timothy stood incredulous.

"No, I'm serious. That's a lot of money, but that's how much it means to me. And know this, I have no plans to sell this book. It's here any time you want to come and see it or maybe reclaim it," Louie said.

Timothy smiled and laughed. "Five thousand dollars? I can't even get my head around that much money."

Louie smiled. "Hoffen knew it would open some doors for you that you thought were closed. Do yourself a favor. Take the check. Do me a favor. Let me hang onto this. We both get what we want. What do you say, Timothy?"

"I say yes. Absolutely. Hoffen set this up. He knew what he was doing. I trust him," Timothy said.

"Good. I have your check right here in the register." Louie opened the cash register and the bell rang again, like before. He lifted the cash drawer, removed the check. Timothy stared at it and shook his head.

"I don't know what to say. Yes, thank you. I keep hearing these words in my head, 'We must take the current when it serves or lose our ventures.' I think I understand that quote now."

"*Julius Caesar*," Louie said. "You're well read, too. How many psychology majors know Shakespeare?"

"Not many, I fear. How did you know I am a psychology major?"

"Hoffen," Louie said.

"Oh, of course."

"Perhaps someone with a thirst for literature should drink from that pond?" Louie said.

Timothy paused to consider Louie's words.

"How can I get hold of Hoffen? I need to thank him," Timothy said.

"He's gone. He left early this morning. I'm not sure where he's headed, but he'll write when he lands somewhere. He always does. He knew you would appreciate this. That's why he gave you this gift. Do you have plans for this money?"

"Oh yes, school, bills, living expense. But there is one thing I need to do right now—that is, after I deposit the check, I need to make a stop," Timothy said.

"Hoffen figured you would. What are you going to do next semester? Have you figured it out yet?"

"Yes, I have a TA position in the English department, and that will help me out a lot."

"Like I said, drink to satisfy your thirst."

Timothy stared at Louie. Even though this was the first time they met, he had a strangely familiar countenance about him. Timothy nodded.

"You're working at the hospital, right?" Louie asked.

"Yes."

"If you decide the hours don't work for you, I could use some help around here. I'm pretty flexible with scheduling, and the pay's not bad. That way you could see the book anytime you wanted."

"That's incredibly generous, Louie. Thank you. I may take you up on that offer. For now, I have to go see a man about something."

"You go, and good luck. We'll talk again," Louie said.

Timothy left the shop with the same ring of the bell that brought him in.

CHAPTER FORTY-FOUR

TIMOTHY LEFT LE Rive Gauche and drove to the bank to deposit his check. Louie banked at the same place as Timothy, which he thought a great coincidence. Timothy thought about the last few days and how quickly things had turned around for him. This much change unsettled him, even though it was good change. He discovered even good change could overwhelm. He parked in front of the bank and walked with purpose through the main entrance to the counter to write up a deposit slip and get in line.

"Good morning, sir," the teller said.

"It is, indeed," Timothy said. "How long will it take for this check to clear when I deposit it?"

"Since it's one of our commercial accounts, I will post it today, and it will show on your account in tomorrow's statement."

"Great. Just what I wanted to hear. Can I still do a partial cash withdrawal today on the deposit?"

"Sure, that's no problem."

He deposited the check and withheld one thousand in cash.

Timothy left the bank and drove to his next stop—Flagler's Jewelry Store. He and Cheryl visited this place earlier in the year for the most embarrassing window-shopping experience of his life. Cheryl put no pressure on him. Either she had low expectations or didn't want to add to his load. Today's excursion was different.

Flagler's was a small, family-owned jewelry store close to Cheryl's house. It had been in business for seventy-five years.

"Good morning, sir. How may I help you?" the clerk said.

The clerk had a Monet paint job on her face, the reddest hair Timothy had ever seen, and more jewelry on her hands than most people owned. She obviously spent a lot of time preparing for her workday. She fit the job perfectly. He choked on her perfume and heard Alvin and the Chipmunks singing Christmas music on the local radio station. The irony of his being here was not wasted on Timothy. A week ago he could not have imagined this.

"I'd like to see your engagement rings," he said.

"Excellent. Who's the lucky girl?" the clerk asked.

Timothy smiled at the routine question. *Who do you think it's for? My sister?* "My girlfriend and, hopefully, soon to be my fiancé."

"Wonderful. And what is the lucky girl's name?"

"Cheryl."

"Do you know what Cheryl likes?" the clerk asked.

"Yes, she's fond of a marquise setting."

"Okay, let's look at some marquises for Cheryl."

They moved to a display case that housed the engagement rings.

"Do you see anything Cheryl would like?" she asked.

It bothered Timothy that the clerk used Cheryl's name so casually.

"Yes, that one right there in the third row," he said, pointing to the ring.

"Oh, that's a beautiful selection."

"Yes, it is. We were in here a few months ago, and she liked this one. How do you work the sizing of rings?" Timothy asked.

"We have a few of these in common sizes. Do you have any idea?"

"Yes, I think she wears a six. The man who helped us when we were here took her measurement, as a matter of fact, and I seem to remember that," Timothy said.

"Yes, that's a common practice. We do that routinely so the man will know the lady's ring size. Most men remember it. But not to worry. If you need to have it resized, we can do that adjustment on the spot."

"How much?"

"The total weight is one carat, and in this setting, the price is nine hundred seventy-five. Do you plan to finance this or pay cash?" The clerk closed like a street vendor.

"I'll pay cash," Timothy said.

"In that case, I am prepared to give you a twenty-five-dollar discount if you buy today. It's our way of making sure the holidays are a little brighter for you and Cheryl."

"Good. What about a wedding band to go with this?" Timothy asked.

"I would wait on this, and let Cheryl pick out the one she wants. She may not want a band with the marquise setting. Many brides don't. Besides, you will have to select your band, and the bride customarily pays for that herself," the clerk said.

"Really?"

"Oh yes, there's a protocol to engagement rings. Have you talked to her father yet?" the clerk asked.

"Yes, we talked over a couple of beers last summer, and he said I had his blessing whenever I decided to pop the question. No pressure. I'm a student, and he knows my situation."

"That's wonderful. Have you picked out a spot to ask her?"

"Yes. I'm not waiting for Christmas. I'm going to take her to dinner tonight to ask her. It's a special place for us," Timothy said.

"That's sweet. Romantic. You know, women love that sort of thing," the clerk said.

"Yeah, I know. Guys don't mind it either," Timothy said.

"I'll write this up for you."

Timothy spent the next few minutes pacing the store, anticipating his plans for the evening. He and Cheryl already planned to go out, so she wouldn't suspect anything. He knew exactly what he wanted to say and where he wanted to say it. He hoped he knew what she would say.

"Okay, I need to get some personal information on you and Cheryl to finish the paperwork," the clerk said.

They spent the next few minutes filling in the blanks on the sales receipt and reviewing the documentation of authenticity.

"Remember, if Cheryl wants to bring this in for resizing, you guys can come in any time, and please ask for me. I can help with your wedding band, too. My name is Connie, and I would be thrilled to help you, and meet Cheryl."

Connie—of course.

Timothy smiled at the irony of a woman named Connie helping him buy a ring for Cheryl. He paid for the ring and left the store with a bag full of hope.

CHAPTER FORTY-FIVE

TIMOTHY ARRIVED A few minutes early at Cheryl's house for their date and eager to start the rest of his life. He rang the bell and Cheryl answered.

"For me?" she said as he handed her a dozen roses.

"For you."

"They're beautiful. Thank you."

Cheryl leaned forward and kissed Timothy.

"Boy, tonight keeps getting more special. Going to Mantia's twice in the same month and now flowers? A girl could get used to this. You're going to spoil me."

"This girl deserves some spoiling."

"You're sweet. I'm going to find something to put these in."

Cheryl left the living room, and Timothy looked around. Cheryl's father was reading his newspaper, and her mom was needlepointing.

"Evening," Timothy said.

"Good evening, Timothy. The flowers are beautiful," her mom said.

"Yes, it looks like you're trying to steal my little girl's heart," her father said with a smile.

"I'm trying," Timothy said.

"I understand you kids are going to Mantia's tonight?" her mother said.

"Yes, kind of our special place."

"That's nice, dear. You kids deserve a night like that." Her mom went back to needlepointing.

Cheryl's father took off his reading glasses and placed his paper on his lap. He looked at Timothy and flashed him a slight grin. Timothy responded with a grin and nod.

"Here, how do these look?" Cheryl said as she returned with the roses in a vase.

"They look perfect."

"They're lovely, dear," her mom said.

Her father grunted his approval.

"We're out of here, Mom, Dad," Cheryl said.

They walked arm in arm to the car. Timothy opened the door for Cheryl and went around to the driver's seat.

"This is so wonderful that Scoot fixed your car," Cheryl said. "He is such a good friend."

"That he is," Timothy said.

"Gosh, with the car and the TA position, do you feel things are beginning to turn for you?"

"For us," he corrected.

"Yes, for us," she smiled.

They drove in a few moments of silence. Cheryl noticed he did not take the usual route to Mantia's.

"Are we taking the long way to Mantia's?"

"Sure. There is more than one way to get there, you know."

Cheryl laughed. Timothy liked the sound of her laughter. He liked the sound of his own laughter. It sure beat the crying he'd heard lately. He stopped the car at the pavilion in Chambers Park. He shut off the engine and looked at Cheryl. She stared back at him, puzzled.

"Why are we stopping here?"

"You remember this place, don't you?"

"Yes. We met at the summer concert series here. Ebony was playing," she said.

"Yes, Ebony was playing that night. Let's walk up to the pavilion."

"Tim, what's going on?"

"Come with me. Trust me."

They held hands on their walk to the pavilion. The air felt cool and crisp but not stinging cold. Neither said anything. When they reached the pavilion, Timothy turned to Cheryl and took her hands in his.

"This is the exact spot where we met. This was the first time I looked into your eyes. This is the place where my life changed for the good. This is where I fell in love, the moment I met you. That's why this spot is special to me."

"Timothy." She hung onto her next words.

"Cheryl, you're the brightest star in my sky. You're my true north, my soul mate."

"Tim—" She stopped.

"When I think of my future, the only thing that seems certain is that you must be in it. There's no future in my life without you. There's nothing ahead of me more important than what's in front of me."

Her eyes welled.

"You've stayed with me when most people would walk away. I'm damaged goods, but you never made me feel that way. You made me want to believe I was worth something. You have always made me feel like my world was coming together, not breaking apart. I tried pushing you away, but you refused to leave. You knew you had to stay. I knew you had to stay. We're standing at the doorstep of destiny. I look forward and only see you. You have seen my past. You know where I am today. But when I look at you, all I see is my future, and that future is you."

Cheryl smiled, her tears of joy now spilling.

"Yes. Yes. Oh God, yes," she said, unable to contain the words.

"Will you marry me?" Timothy asked.

"Of course. We're supposed to be together. It has always been that way and will always be that way."

They kissed and embraced, holding onto each other and the moment. Timothy pulled back and looked into Cheryl's eyes. He saw the light in her soul. He showed her the light in his soul. Then, he took out the ring and asked for her hand.

"Please, give me your hand."

She extended her hand, he slipped on the engagement ring, and it fit as if it were made for her. She looked up, surprised.

"You remembered. How did you do this? How could you afford

to—" she said.

"Not now. We have a dinner table waiting for us. I have a lot to tell you, so I think we need to crack open a bottle of wine and drink to the future."

"To our future," Cheryl said.

"Yes, our future," he said.

CHAPTER FORTY-SIX

THE CHINESE CALLED 1978 the Year of the Horse—a year of energy, health, and easy disposition. For Timothy Patrick O'Rourke and his wife, Cheryl, 1978 was a very good year.

Much had happened to them in the past five years. He finished his graduate work in English, and they were expecting their first child. The memories of the war were finding a space to rest in his mind.

"Mail's here," Cheryl said.

"Anything for me?" Timothy asked.

"Yes. It looks like a letter from a publishing house—Cahners. It's a big envelope."

"That sounds promising. Let me see it. Yep, that's the one I've been waiting for."

Timothy stared at the envelope in a Zen-like trance, taking in every aspect of the experience. He ran his fingers along the outer edges and weighed it in his palms.

"Open it. Open it." Cheryl's excitement bubbled.

"It's heavier than all of the rejections I've gotten. It's kind of like getting the acceptance packet to graduate school. You know it's more than a thanks-anyway letter."

"C'mon, open it," she said.

He sliced open the envelope with a pencil he had been using. He carefully removed the contents, a packet of pages, and saw the word he hoped for. *Contract.*

"They want my manuscript!"

"Oh my God, that's wonderful, Timothy." Cheryl put her arms around him and held on. "What did they say?"

"They like it. It's exactly the kind of thing they publish, but it does need a little work."

"You expected that, right?"

"Sure, but the key word is a *little.*" He continued to read. "My God, they're offering me a five thousand dollar advance against royalties." At this, Timothy threw the papers in the air, and they floated around Timothy and Cheryl as they hugged and hollered.

"This calls for a celebration," she said.

"Absolutely," he said. "Mantia's, right?"

"Where else?"

"Get your jacket. Let's go. We have a stop to make on the way."

"Where?"

"Le Rive Gauche. I have to tell Louie."

"Can't you tell him when you go in to work tomorrow?"

"No, this can't wait."

"Let's go," said Cheryl.

They drove to the bookstore, joking, laughing, and enjoying the moment. They opened the door, and the bell announced their arrival. Louie looked up from the book he was studying with a magnifying glass, *The Battle of Adversus.* His vision had deteriorated over the past five years Timothy worked for him. He squinted at the couple.

"Timothy. Cheryl. It's good to see you. How's that baby doing?"

"Kicking, as usual. He's as impatient as his daddy," Cheryl said.

"Come on now," Timothy said. The smile on his face stretched from ear to ear.

"So what's the occasion? Why the visit? You don't work until tomorrow," Louie said.

"I got a letter today from Cahners Publishing. They want my book," Timothy beamed.

"Congratulations. I told you it would sell. It makes sense they would buy it. It's in their wheelhouse."

"You were right telling me to send a query to them," Timothy said.

"Well, I do know a little about this business."

"A lot. Don't sell yourself short. And, they offered me a generous advance. I'm hoping it's enough to buy something back from you," Timothy said.

Louis smiled. "You want the Hemingway book, right?"

"Yes," Timothy said.

"I'm not surprised. You look at it every month," Louie said.

"It reminds me of our friend, Hoffen."

"I understand. Why don't we do this? I will let you hang on to it as long as you safeguard it in somewhere special in your home. Protect it. Guard it. Treasure it. That's all I ask."

"I'm not sure what you're saying," Timothy said.

"I'm saying it's my gift to you and your lovely wife. You will need that advance for the baby. Besides, my eyesight is so bad these days I have trouble reading the signature anymore. I know you will treasure it as much as I do."

Timothy stood silent and then darted to Louie and gave him a hug.

"Let me go back and get this for you," Louie said. He turned and walked to the back room of the shop.

Timothy glanced at the book Louie had been reading and smiled. He remembered Hoffen talked about it once. Louie returned.

"Here you go. Enjoy."

"Thank you, Louie. I didn't expect this."

"I know. You're the only person other than me who values this book as much as I do. It's fitting you should have it. I don't need the money. Besides, if you develop a taste for these old, rare volumes, maybe you will get in on this side of the book business," Louie said.

"Uh, maybe. I guess. I don't know what to say."

"Say yes. Enjoy this. Enjoy your lives. Write good stuff. Entertain people. Make them think. Challenge them. And mostly, give them a little hope. The battle for hope never ends. The world needs more hope merchants. And that's you," Louie said.

Timothy clutched the book in one hand and Cheryl's hand in the other. They left through the door with the bell, and Louie went back to reading with his magnifying glass.

ACKNOWLEDGMENTS

As always, I must begin by thanking my partner and wife, Charlotte Reilly. She was there from the start, witnessing and participating in my journey home from Vietnam. She contributed significantly to this book with her patience, understanding, and editorial eye. Thanks to Linda Huizenga, who has read my writings for the past couple of decades and lent her expertise. Thanks to John Koehler at Koehler Publishing, who believed in and committed to this project. I especially want to thank Joe Coccaro and Hannah Woodlan for their editorial expertise. Additionally, I would like to thank Kellie Emery for her cover design which captures this story perfectly.

p52 thousand yard stare

119 — VN war scene

140 Catch 22

255 Things turned around fort.

p 3 People at the VA
can't help you.

p 4 Pain never slept —

p 7 Nobody wants to hire
a V N vet

p 3 2 boo Coo

3 3 Xin Joi M. F.
di di Mau

3 4 Summary of
Timothy's life

7 9 Hosp put him on
notice for talking to
union organizers —

CPSIA information can be obtained
at www.ICGtesting.com
Printed in the USA
FFHW02n0639081018
48704524-52773FF